# 天 方 夜 譚 一 百 段

# 100 EXCERPTS FROM THE ARABIAN NIGHTS

一百叢書㉔

英漢對照English–Chinese

張信威　高爲煇 編譯

# 天方夜譚一百段

# 100 EXCERPTS FROM THE ARABIAN NIGHTS

臺灣商務印書館發行

# 《一百叢書》總序

本館出版英漢（或漢英）對照《一百叢書》的目的，是希望憑藉着英、漢兩種語言的對譯，把中國和世界各類著名作品的精華部分介紹給中外讀者。

本叢書的涉及面很廣。題材包括了寓言、詩歌、散文、短篇小説、書信、演説、語錄、神話故事、聖經故事、成語故事、名著選段等等。

顧名思義，《一百叢書》中的每一種都由一百個單元組成。以一百為單位，主要是讓編譯者在浩瀚的名著的海洋中作挑選時有一個取捨的最低和最高限額。至於取捨的標準，則是見仁見智，各有心得。

由於各種書中被選用的篇章節段，都是以原文或已被認定的範本作藍本，而譯文又經專家學者們精雕細琢，千錘百煉，故本叢書除可作為各種題材的精選讀本外，也是研習英漢兩種語言對譯的理想參考書，部分更可用作朗誦教材。外國學者如要研習漢語，本書亦不失為理想工具。

商務印書館 (香港) 有限公司

編輯部

# 前　言

提起《天方夜譚》(*The Arabian Nights*)，許多讀者的腦海裏立刻就會浮現從孩提時代就熟悉的“阿拉丁神燈”、“阿里巴巴四十大盜”等奇妙故事中的形象：仙女、妖魔、神燈、飛毯、寶藏……把他們幼小的心靈帶進了一個光怪陸離的神話世界。可惜坊間所售大都是只有十多個故事的選本，難以充分反映書的宏偉全貌。而去通覽全集，對多數讀者來説，書既難覓，時間也不許可。為了滿足這種需要，本書特意從全集中精選出一百段一般選本不收的故事以饗讀者，使他們對全書有更多的了解。

《天方夜譚》原名《一千零一夜》(*The Thousand and One Nights*)，是一部阿拉伯民間故事集。全書共有二百多個故事，其中大故事一百多個，大故事中又包含若干小故事。這些故事以宰相的女兒給國王講故事為引子和框架。薩桑國國王薩力耶爾因王后不貞將其處死，並由此痛恨所有女子。他每天娶一少女過夜，次日即殺掉再娶，弄得全國未婚姑娘人人自危。為了拯救無辜受害的女子，宰相的女兒希拉莎德毅然挺身而出，自願嫁給國王；她每夜給他講一段故事，並設法在天亮時故事正好講到最精彩之處，使他為了知道結局而不得不暫時免她一死，讓她第二晚接着再講。這樣日復一日，故事一直講了一千零一夜，國王終於取消其惡毒計劃，宣佈永遠立她為后。這就是這部書原名的由來。

《天方夜譚》像一幅全方位地描繪中世紀阿拉伯帝國社會生活的歷史長卷。它題材廣闊，結構宏大，內容豐富多采，形象生動逼真，從各個不同的角度反映了阿拉伯各階層人民的喜怒哀樂、生活方式、風土人情、社會狀況，乃至建築藝術、精巧工藝、婚喪禮儀等，當中又蘊藏着深刻的人生哲理。書中的故事體裁多樣，有神話寓言、民間傳説、格言諺語、詩詞歌賦、名人軼事、歷史掌故、笑話趣聞以至戰爭、冒險、愛情故事等等，不一而足；書中的人物也是三教九流，應有盡有，上至帝王將相、公子王孫，下至漁農工商、販夫走卒。僧道醫卜，太監弄臣、乞丐奴隸、騙子盜賊等等，甚至還有神仙和妖魔鬼怪。其故事情節則離奇曲折，出人意表，有人妖鬥智、秘室尋寶、奪權篡位、貪贓枉法、征戰殺伐、謀財害命、男歡女愛等等，真是無奇不有，引人入勝。其語言生動自然，通俗易懂。中間不時穿插詩歌，借以抒情並刻劃人物心理。這些都體現了民間創作的語言特色。以上種種構成了《天方夜譚》獨特的藝術魅力，贏得了全世界讀者的喜愛。它不僅是阿拉伯藝術的瑰寶，也是世界文學寶庫中一顆光彩奪目的明珠。

當然，像《天方夜譚》這樣一部鉅著決非某個天才作家一人之力所能為。它是中世紀中近東阿拉伯地區廣大説唱藝人和文人學者經數百年共同收集、提煉、加工而成的。其最初的編者和確切的成書時間現在已不可考。多數學者認為其故事和手抄本早在八世紀中葉就已在中近東各國開始流傳，到十五世紀末或十六世紀才在埃及基本定型。

《天方夜譚》的故事有三個來源：一是一部名叫《赫左／扎爾・伊斯凡拿／艾夫薩乃》（即《一千個故事》）的古波斯故事集。據有些學者考證，這些故事可能源自印度。二是十至十一世紀在以巴格達為中心的伊拉克編的故事。三是十三至十五世紀在埃及流傳的故事。

《天方夜譚》經過數百年在印度、波斯、伊拉克、埃及等地的傳播，逐步形成各種手抄本。其故事大體相同，但內容常有出入，篇幅也不完全一樣。第一部阿拉伯文本在加爾各答發行（未完，僅二卷，1839 - 42；足本，四卷，1839-42）。1835年開羅發行了官方訂正的布拉克本，成為後來多數外文譯本的依據。十八世紀初，法國人加朗（Antoine Galland）根據敘利亞抄本首次把《天方夜譚》譯成法文出版，在歐洲引起轟動。隨之在歐洲出現多種文字的轉譯本和新譯本。十九世紀末葉出版了約翰・佩恩（John Payne, 1842 - 1916）和理查德・博登（Richard Burton, 1821 - 90）的英文全譯本。以後又出版了許多其他英譯者的全譯本和選譯本。在中國，《天方夜譚》的故事也早已流傳。1900年，周桂笙在《新庵諧譯》就有所介紹。1903

年出版的《海上述奇》和1904年出版的《俠女奴》(周作人譯)翻譯了“辛伯達”和“阿里巴巴”兩個故事，是中國最早的選譯本。1906年商務印書館出版奚若的四卷文言文選譯本包括五十個故事。以後又陸續出版過多種白話文譯本。五十年代人民文學出版社出版了納訓首次由阿拉伯原文譯出的全譯本，在讀者中影響最大。

本書的故事選自多種版本的英譯本，其譯文或古奧典雅或平易曉暢，可謂春蘭秋菊，各擅勝場。讀者可對照比較，以鑒賞不同的翻譯風格。對一些為現代讀者所不熟悉的舊詞義、舊文法現象以及古代阿拉伯地區的人名和地名則適當加註，幫助讀者排除閱讀上的困難。

張信威　高為輝

一九九七年三月於深圳

# PREFACE

To many readers, mention of *The Arabian Nights* will immediately call to mind fascinating images in such wonderful stories as "Aladdin and the Magic Lamp" and "Ali Baba and the Forty Thieves", which they have been familiar with since childhood: peris, genies, the magic lamp, the flying carpet, treasures and whatnot which took their young imagination into a bizarre mythical world. But the book they bought from the bookstore is often a selection of a mere dozen or so stories which can hardly do justice to the magnificence of the whole book. However, to most readers, a copy of the complete work is hard to come by and will take too much time to go through. Specially designed to meet their need, this book selects 100 exciting excerpts from the complete work, passages which are seldom included in the common selected editions, so as to give readers a better idea of the book.

*The Arabian Nights* was originally and is still otherwise called *The Thousand and One Nights*. It is a collection of over 200 stories, including 100 and more long ones and a number of shorter ones contained in them. The stories are introduced by and set within a frame story. King Shahriyar of Sasan kills his queen after discovering her infidelity and then, loathing all womankind, marries and kills a new wife each day, which throws all the unmarried girls in the country into great terror. To save other innocent girls, his vizier's daughter Shahrazad bravely offers herself to be married to the King. Each night she tells him a story, but devises to leave it incomplete at its most exciting point when dawn comes. As a result, the King eager to hear the end puts off her execution so that she may finish the story the following night. Thus, her story-telling goes on from day to day till the thousand and first night, when the King finally abandons his cruel plan and proclaims Shahrazad his wife forever. And that is the origin of the name of the book.

Like a long historical scroll, *The Arabian Nights* describes all aspects of the social life of the medieval Arabian Empire. With its wide range of subjects, grand structure, rich and colourful contents and vivid images, it reflects the emotions, life styles, customs and social conditions, architecture, craftsmanship and wedding and burial etiquette of the Arabian people. In all these lie profound and edifying philosophies of life. Its stories are varied in form, including fairy tales, parables, romances, legends, maxims, proverbs, poetry, songs, anecdotes, jokes as well as stories of war, love and adventure. It has a great variety of characters: kings, princes, viziers, eunuchs, jesters, priests, judges, doctors, teachers, merchants, fishermen, farmers, peddlers, soldiers, policemen, thieves, robbers, beggars, slaves, and even peris and genies. The plots of the stories are fascinating, complicated and unexpected: battles of wits between men and genies, treasure-hunting, struggles for power, bribery and injustice, bloody battles, robberies and murders, passionate love affairs, and whatnot. Its language is characteristic of folk literature: vivid, natural, figurative and easy to understand, spiced frequently with poetry and songs for emotional expression and psychological description. All these features are combined to form its unique artistic charm, which wins the love of readers all over the world. It is not only the treasure of Arabian literature but also a brilliant gem in world literature.

Naturally, a work of such dimensions is by no means the effort of one talented writer. It is a composite work consisting of popular stories originally transmitted orally and then collected and developed by numerous story-tellers, singers, writers and scholars in the medieval Middle and Near East over several centuries. While its first author and time of print are impossible to identify, most scholars believe that the stories and their hand-written copies began to circulate in countries of the Middle and Near East in the middle of the 8th century and their final versions began to take shape by the end of the 15th century or in the early 16th century.

The stories of *The Arabian Nights* come from three sources: one is an ancient Persian story book called *Hazar Isfana* (namely *A Thousand Tales*), which is believed to originate from India, another is stories compiled in Iraq with Baghdad as its centre during the 10th and 11th centuries, and the third is stories circulated in Egypt during the 13th-15th centuries.

Various hand-written copies of *The Arabian Nights* gradually took shape after several centuries of circulation in India, Persia, Iraq and Egypt. The stories in them are by and large similar, while discrepancies often exist and their lengths also vary. The first Arabic text was published at Calcutta (incomplete, 2 vols., 1814-18; in full, 4 vols., 1839-42). The source for most later translations was, however, an official recension published by Bulaq, Cairo, in 1835.

Early in the 18th century, a Frenchman called Antoine Galland made the first French translation of the book on the basis of a Syrian manuscript, which caused a sensation in Europe and was followed by various retranslations and new translations in other European languages. The end of the 19th century saw the publication of John Payne's and Richard Burton's full English translations, the latter being the most famous English version so far. In China, the stories of the *Nights* also became known quite early. In 1900, Zhou Guisheng wrote to introduce them in his *Xin An Xie Yi. Adventures on the Sea* (1903) and Zhou Zuoren's *A Brave Slave Girl* (1904) are Chinese versions of the stories of "Sinbad" and "Ali Baba", which are the earliest of its kind in China. In 1906, The Commercial Press published Xi Ruo's four-volumed version in classical Chinese, which contains fifty stories. Various versions in vernacular Chinese came out afterwards. In the 1950s, the People's Literature Publishing House published Na Xun's first full Chinese translation from Arabic, which has the greatest influence on the reading public.

The stories in this book are selected from various English versions whose styles of translation are different: some archaic and elegant, others easy and smooth. The reader may compare them in reading so as to appreciate the merits of each. Explanatory notes are provided for archaic words and grammatical usage an well as names of people and places in ancient Arabia.

*Zhang Xinwei, Gao Weihui*

*March, 1997*

# 目　錄
# CONTENTS

**Cops, Thieves and Frauds　警察、小偷、騙子**

**The Rich and the Poor　富人和窮人**

**The Commoners' Wisdom　平民的智慧**

**Allegories 動物寓言**



**Maxims and Philosophies 格言與哲理**

# How the Stories Came to Be Told
# 故事的由來

# 1 A New Wife Every Day

*— How the Stories Came to Be Told (1)*

It is well known that in former days the Sultans of the East[1] were great tyrants, and knew no law but their own will. Now one of them had a wife who did not obey him, and he was so angry that he had her put to death: and because he no longer had any faith in women, he caused it to be known that he meant to have a new wife every day, he would be married at night, and in the morning his wife was to have her head cut off. This threw all the women in the kingdom into a great fright, for the Sultan would have only a beautiful woman for his wife, and no one knew when her turn would come.

It was the duty of the Grand Vizier[2] to find a new wife for the Sultan each day, and you may be sure that he had to drag these poor girls to the palace, for no one wanted the honor of being the Sultan's wife for one night if she was to have her head cut off the next day.

---

1. the Sultans of the East：東方的蘇丹。sultan：蘇丹，伊斯蘭國家君主的稱謂。the East：指地中海以東亞洲西部各國。
2. the Grand Vizier： 宰相。vizier：伊斯蘭國家的大臣。

# 一　蘇丹天天換新娘

*—— 故事的由來（一）*

大家知道，從前東方的蘇丹都是暴君。他們無法無天，為所欲為。其中一位因妻子對他不忠，一怒之下，就將她處死了。由於他不再相信女人，他公開宣佈要每天娶一位新王后：晚上結婚，早晨就將她斬首。這一下可把全國的女子都嚇壞了。因為蘇丹只要漂亮女人做妻子，可誰都說不準甚麼時候會輪到自己頭上。

宰相的職責是每天給蘇丹找一個新娘。你可以相信，他得強拉這些可憐的姑娘到宮裏去，因為誰也不願意當一夜王后，第二天就給砍了頭。

## 2 Schehera-zade Begged to Be the Sultan's Wife

*— How the Stories Came to Be Told (2)*

What was the terror, then, of the Grand Vizier, when his own daughter, Schehera-zade, came forward and begged to be the Sultan's wife!

"Do you know, my daughter," he asked, "what that means? Though you are the daughter of the Grand Vizier, that will not save your life." Now Schehera-zade was as brave as she was beautiful, and she said: —

"I know it well, but I have thought of a plan by which I may put an end to this dreadful state of things. If you do not take me to the Sultan. I shall go by myself." So the Grand Vizier went to the Sultan and told him that his own daughter begged for the honor of being the Sultan's wife for one night. The Sultan was filled with wonder.

"Do not err," he said to the Grand Vizier. "Though she is your daughter, her head must be cut off in the morning."

"I know it well," said the Grand Vizier sadly; "but you know how it is with daughters[1]. It is hard to say 'no' to them."

---

1. how it is with daughters：女兒態，這裏指女兒在父親面前撒嬌的樣子。

## 二　宰相女毛遂自薦

*── 故事的由來（二）*

不料，一天他自己的女兒希拉莎德前來要求去當蘇丹的妻子，這一驚真非同小可！

宰相問道，“女兒，你明不明白這意味着甚麼？雖然你是宰相的女兒，那也救不了你的命。”可希拉莎德是個既美貌又有膽量的姑娘，她回答道：

“我很明白，但我想了條計策，可以結束這樁可怕的事情。你要是不帶我去見蘇丹，我就自己去。”宰相只好去見蘇丹，告訴他自己的女兒要求得到當一夜王后的榮幸。蘇丹奇怪極了。

他對宰相說，“別搞錯了，雖然她是你的女兒，早晨也得砍頭。”

宰相悲哀地說，“我很明白，但您知道女兒都是甚麼樣子。要對她們說個‘不’字，難哪！”

# 3 Grant Me One Favour

*— How the Stories Came to Be Told (3)*

Now when Schehera-zade was led into the presence of the Sultan, her veil was lifted, and the Sultan saw that she was very fair. But he saw also that there were tears in her eyes.

"Why do you weep?" said he.

"I weep," she said, "because of my sister. I have the honor to be the wife of the Sultan; but I love my sister, and I cannot bear the thought of saying good-by to her now. Grant me one favor. Let her pass this one night on a couch near me."

The Sultan had already been won by the beauty of Schehera-zade, and he found it easy to grant the favor. So the younger sister, Dinar-zade, was brought in.

# 三　新娘的請求

*—— 故事的由來（三）*

於是，希拉莎德被領到蘇丹面前，揭起了面紗。蘇丹發現她長得十分美麗，但又看到她眼裏含着淚水。

“你為甚麼流淚？”他問。

“因為我想妹妹，”她答道。“我有幸成為蘇丹的王后；但我愛妹妹，一想到不能向她告別就受不了。請答應我一個請求。讓她在我身邊的躺椅上過這一夜。”

蘇丹已經被希拉莎德的美貌所打動，很痛快地就答應了她的請求。於是，她的妹妹蒂娜莎德被領了進來。

## 4 Those Delightful Stories

*— How the Stories Came to Be Told (4)*

Now Schehera-zade had told her sister how she was to act, and about an hour before dawn Dinar-zade, who was wide awake, spoke and said:—

"Sister, if you are not asleep, I wish you would tell me one of those delightful stories you know so well. It will soon be light." Schehera-zade turned to the Sultan and said: —

"Will your Highness[1] suffer me to tell my sister a story?"

"Freely," said the Sultan, who liked stories himself; and Schehera-zade began to tell a story, and she told it in such a way that, when daylight came, she had reached the most interesting point. But at daylight the Sultan must needs[2] rise and go to his council.

"That is a most interesting story," said Dinar-zade, "but how does it end?"

"The end is more strange than the beginning," said her sister. "If Your Highness," she said, turning to the Sultan, "will let me live one more day, I can then finish the story."

---

1. Your Highness：殿下，對皇族的尊稱。
2. must needs：必須。這裏 needs 是副詞，只跟 must 連用。

## 四　新娘的計策

*—— 故事的由來（四）*

希拉莎德事先已經告訴她妹妹怎麼做，所以在天亮前半小時光景，根本沒有睡覺的蒂娜莎德開口説道："姐姐，要是你睡不着，給我講個好聽的故事好嗎？那些故事你記得最熟了。天快亮了。"希拉莎德轉身對蘇丹説：

"請殿下允許我給妹妹講個故事好嗎？"

"隨便吧，"蘇丹説，他自己也喜歡聽故事。這樣，希拉莎德就開始講了。她講故事的方法是：天亮時，故事正好講到最精彩之處。但是天一亮，蘇丹必須起身去上朝。

蒂娜莎德説，"故事真有意思，可結果呢？"

"結果要比開頭還要離奇，"姐姐説。她轉身又對蘇丹道，"如果殿下讓我再活一天的話，我就可以把故事講完。"

The Sultan wanted very much to hear the end, so he gave Schehera-zade one more day to live, meaning to have her head cut off after that. But when the next morning came, and Dinar-zade asked for the rest of the story, Schehera-zade told it in such a way that it carried her into the middle of another story; and daylight came, and that story was not done. The Sultan put off her death one day more.

...

Thus it went on and on; a story was never done, and for a thousand and one nights Schehera-zade told her stories to the Sultan. By that time, though she had not told nearly all her stories, the Sultan had grown so fond of her, and had come to have such faith in her, that he forgot the wife who once did not obey, and made it known throughout the kingdom that Schehera-zade was to be the one Sultaness[3] so long as he lived. The Grand Vizier and all the people had great joy at this; all the girls in the kingdom once more breathed freely, and Schehera-zade kept on telling her stories.

Now these are some of the tales of *The Thousand and One Nights*.

---

3. the one Sultaness：蘇丹的王后。sultaness：蘇丹的后妃，這裏大寫，前面還加上 one，意思就是“王后”。

蘇丹也很想知道結果，所以就同意讓希拉莎德多活一天，打算以後再把她砍頭。但是到了次日早晨，蒂娜莎德又要求聽完故事。希拉莎德總是正講到故事中間，天就亮了，而故事還沒有講完。蘇丹只好再讓她多活一天。

……

就這樣，故事一個接一個地講下去，總也講不完，講了一千零一夜。到那時，雖然希拉莎德還沒有把她的故事全部講完，蘇丹已經愛上了她，而且對她深信不疑，忘了對他不忠的前妻。他佈告天下：只要他在世就永遠立希拉莎德為王后。宰相和全國人民聞聽後大喜；全國的女孩子又可以自由自在地過日子了，而希拉莎德則繼續講她的故事。

下面就是《一千零一夜》故事的一部分。

# *Myths, Magic, Legends*

# 神話、魔法、傳奇

# 5 I Wish to Be the Emperor's Queen Consort

*— The Story of the Three Sisters (1)*

There was an Emperor of Persia who often walked in disguise through the city, attended by a trusty minister, and meeting with many adventures. Once when he was passing through a street in which dwelt only humble folk, he heard some people talking very loud within a certain house, and, looking in, saw three sisters sitting on a sofa.

"Since we have got upon wishes," said the eldest, "mine shall be to have the Sultan's baker for my husband, for then I should eat my fill of that excellent bread called the Sultan's."

"For my part," said the second sister, "I wish I were wife to the Sultan's chief cook, for bread must be common in the palace, and I should eat of the choicest dishes. You see that I have a better taste than you."

The youngest sister, who was very beautiful and has more charms and wit than the others, spoke in her turn: —

"For my part, since we are wishing. I wish to be the Emperor's queen consort, and the mother of a lovely prince, whose hair shall be gold on one side of his head and silver on the other; when he cries, the tears from his eyes shall be pearl; and when he smiles, his vermilion lips shall look like a rose-bud fresh blown."

# 五　願望成真

*——三姐妹的故事（一）*

從前波斯有個皇帝，他經常帶着一位可靠的大臣在城裏微服出巡，遇到不少奇事。有一次，他在平民區的 條街上走過時聽到有人在一座房子裏大聲説話。他往裏一看，看見沙發上坐着三姊妹。

大姐説，“説到願望，我希望我的丈夫是蘇丹的麵包師，那樣我就把為蘇丹做的上等麵包吃個夠。”

二姐説，“我的願望是做蘇丹的廚師長的妻子，因為麵包是宮裏的普通食物，我要吃的是山珍海錯。你看我的品味比你高吧。”

最小的妹妹十分美貌，也比兩位姐姐更有魅力，更聰明。最後輪到她説了：

“至於我的願望嘛，我但願成為皇后，生個可愛的王子。他的頭髮要一半是金色的，一半是銀色的；哭的時候，流的眼淚是珍珠；笑的時候，嘴唇紅得像剛開的玫瑰花蕾。”

# 6 The Older Sisters Made Plans to Revenge Themselves upon the Queen

*— The Story of the Three Sisters (2)*

Though the older sisters had got their wishes, they were far from being content, and made many plans to revenge themselves upon the Queen for having won a higher honor. Yet outwardly they showed nothing but love and respect.

When the Queen gave birth to a young prince, as bright as the day, the child was given into the sisters' care; but they wrapped it up in a basket, and floated it away on a canal that ran near the palace, and declared that the Queen had given birth to a little dog. This made the Emperor very angry.

In the meantime, the basket in which the little Prince was exposed was carried by the stream towards the garden of the palace. By chance the keeper of the Emperor's gardens, one of the chief officers of the kingdom, was walking by the side of this canal, and, noticing the basket, called a gardener who was not far off, to pull it to shore with the rake he had in his hand.

# 六　姐姐設計害皇后

*——三姐妹的故事（二）*

雖然兩個姐姐的願望也實現了，但她們卻極不滿足，妒忌皇后獲得崇高榮譽。她們千方百計要陷害皇后，可表面上還裝得若無其事，仍然相親相愛，畢恭畢敬。

皇后生了一個漂亮的王子，交給兩位姐姐撫養。但她們把孩子包起來，放進籃子，扔到皇宮附近的運河裏，同時宣稱皇后生了一隻小狗。皇帝聽了很生氣。

這時，裝着小王子的籃子隨着水流漂向御花園。碰巧王國的一位大臣御花園總監正在河邊散步，看到了籃子，就叫身邊的園丁用手裏的耙子把它拉上岸來。

When this was done, the keeper of the gardens was greatly surprised to see in the basket a child, newly born, but with very fine features. As he had no children of his own, he bore it with delight to his wife in their house at the entrance to the garden, and said: —

"God has sent us this child. Provide a nurse, and treat him as if he were our own son. From this moment, I hold him as such." The keeper's wife received the child with great joy.

...

When a princess was born the next year, the two sisters exposed it to the same fate as the Princes, her brothers[1], for they were bent upon seeing the Queen cast off, turned out, and humbled. But the Princess, like her brothers, was saved by the keeper of the gardens.

The Emperor was told this time that his child was a block of wood. He could no longer contain himself, but ordered a small shed to be built near the chief mosque, and the Queen to be confined in it, subject to the scorn of those who passed by. This cruelty she bore with such meekness that all who judged of things better than the vulgar[2] admired and pitied her.

---

1. 皇后在生公主之前生了兩位王子。第二位王子命運與第一位相似，這裏從略。

2. the vulgar：（書面語）普通人。

籃子上岸後，御花園總監驚奇地發現籃裏有個剛出生的嬰兒，五官長得十分端正。正好他自己沒有孩子，因此就高興地將嬰兒抱回他在花園入口處的家裏，交給妻子說：

“真主給我們送來了這個孩子。給他找個保姆，要像親生孩子那樣對待他。從現在起，我就這樣看待他。”總監的妻子非常高興地收養了這孩子。

……

次年皇后生了一位公主。兩個姐姐又使她遭到與兩位王子 —— 她的哥哥同樣的命運，因為她們一心要看到皇后被廢，趕出宮去並貶為庶人。但是公主也像她哥哥一樣被總監救起了。

她們告訴皇帝皇后這次生了塊木頭。皇帝再也控制不住自己了，命人在大清真寺旁搭了個小棚，把皇后關在裏面，讓過路人羞辱她。面對這種虐待，她只是逆來順受，使得凡是明理的人都欽佩她，同情她。

# 7 It Lacks but Three Things

*— The Story of the Three Sisters (3)*

One day when the two Princes were hunting and the Princess had remained at home, an old devout woman came to the gate at the hour for prayers, and asked leave to go in and say hers. The Princess ordered the servants to show her into the oratory, and when her prayers were done, the woman was brought before Perie-zadeh[1] in a great hall, more beautiful and rich than any other part of the house. When they had talked a little while, the Princess asked her what she thought of the house, and how she liked it.

"Madam," answered the devout woman, "if I may speak my mind freely, it lacks but three things to make it complete and beyond compare. The first of these is the speaking-bird, so strange a creature that it draws round it all the singing-birds near by, which come to accompany its song. The second is the singing-tree, the leaves of which are so many mouths, which form a harmonious concert of different voices, and never cease. The third is the yellow-water, of a gold color, a single drop of which being poured into a vessel properly prepared, increases so as to fill it at once, and rises up in the middle like a fountain, which always plays, and yet the basin never overflows."

# 七　老尼指點三件寶

*—— 三姐妹的故事（三）*

一天，兩位王子出門打獵，只有公主留在家裏。在祈禱的時間，一個老尼來到門外，要求進來祈禱。公主命僕人領她去祈禱室。老尼做完祈禱後，被帶到大廳見貝麗莎德公主。大廳比房子裏的其他地方更為富麗堂皇。談了一會兒後，公主問她覺得這房子怎麼樣，喜不喜歡。

老尼答道："小姐，恕我直言，這房子少了三件東西，不然就完美無比了。第一件是會説話的鳥。這鳥很稀奇，會吸引周圍所有的鳴禽來為它伴唱。第二件是會唱歌的樹。樹上的葉子都是嘴，會發出各種和諧動聽的聲音，而且永不停止。第三件是黃水。那水是金色的，只消在準備好的容器中倒入一滴，就會立刻漲滿整個容器，並像噴泉似地從中間往上連續不斷地冒升，而容器裏的水卻永遠不會溢出。"

---

1. Perie-zadeh：貝麗莎德的公主身份此時尚未為人所知。

# 8 I Will Go for Them Myself

*— The Story of the Three Sisters (4)*

"Sister," replied Prince Bahman, "it is enough that you wish these rarities; I will go for them myself, and set out tomorrow. You, brother, shall stay at home with our sister. I commend her to your care. Yet, as I may fail, all I can do is to leave you this knife. If, when you pull it out of the sheath, it is clean as it is now, it will be a sign that I am alive; but if you find it stained with blood, then you may believe me to be dead."

Then he bade adieu to her and Prince Perviz for the last time, and rode away.

From the time Prince Bahman left home the Princess Perie-zadeh always wore the knife and sheath in her girdle, and pulled it out several times a day, to know whether her brother were yet alive. She found that he was in perfect health, and talked of him often with Prince Perviz.

On the twentieth day, as they were talking thus, the Prince asked his sister to pull out the knife to know how their brother did. When she saw the blood run down the point, she was seized with horror and threw it down.

# 八　王子尋寶

*—— 三姐妹的故事（四）*

巴曼王子回答説，“妹妹，只要你想要這些奇物，我就親自去找，明天就出發。弟弟，你和妹妹留在家裏。我拜託你照看她。但是，我也可能失敗，我能做的就是給你們留下這把刀。當你把刀拔出鞘時，如果刀像現在這麼亮，説明我活着；如果刀上染了血，那麼你們可以相信我已經死了。”

然後他最後一次向她和伯維茲王子告別，就騎馬走了。

巴曼王子離家後，貝麗莎德公主時刻把刀佩在腰帶上，每天拔出來好幾次，看看哥哥是否還活着。她發現他平安無事，又常常跟伯維茲王子談起他。

在第二十天，他們又像往常一樣談起他，伯維茲要求妹妹拔出刀來看看哥哥怎麼樣了。她看到血順着刀尖流下來時，不禁大驚失色，將刀扔在地上。

Prince Perviz was as much distressed as the Princess at their brother's death, but he knew how greatly she still desired to possess the speaking-bird, the singing-tree, and the golden-water, and resolved to set out on the morrow to obtain them. Before he went, he left her a string of a hundred pearls, telling her that if they would not run when she should count them upon the string, but remain fixed, that would be a certain sign that he had met the fate of their brother, but that, he hoped, would never be.

Day after day the Princess Perie-zadeh had counted her pearls, and on the twentieth, instead of moving as they had done, all at once they became firmly fixed, and the token told her surely that the Prince her brother was dead. She had made up her mind what to do if this should happen, and set about the carrying out of her plan at once. She disguised herself in her brother's robes, told her servants that she would return in two or three days, and, well armed and equipped, mounted her horse the next morning, and took the same road as her brothers.

伯維茲王子像妹妹一樣對哥哥的死非常難過，但知道她非常想得到能言鳥、唱歌樹和黃金水，於是決心第二天就動身去尋找。臨行前，他給她留下一串有一百顆珍珠的鏈子，告訴她如果數珍珠時，珍珠在鏈上不能移動，那就說明他已經遭到與哥哥同樣的命運，但是他希望事情不至於那樣。

貝麗莎德公主每天數珍珠，到了第二十天，珍珠突然一反常態紋絲不動了。這個跡象明確地告訴她哥哥已經死了。她早就想好，萬一發生這種情況，自己該怎麼辦。於是，她就立即開始把計劃付諸實施。她穿上哥哥的袍子假扮男人，告訴僕人她兩、三天後回來。第二天，她就全副武裝並帶上旅行裝備，騎馬走上了她兩位哥哥的道路。

## 9 "Bird, I Have You."

*— The Story of the Three Sisters (5)*

On the twentieth day she met the Dervis[1], who urged her, as strongly as he had urged her brothers, to turn back, and told her of the dangers in store for her.

"By what I understand," she said to him when he had finished speaking, "the two difficulties are, first, to reach the cage without being frightened at the terrible din of voices I shall hear; and, second, not to look behind me. For this last caution, I hope I shall be mistress enough of myself[2] to heed it. As for the first, if it is permitted, I will stop my ears with cotton, that the voices, however loud and terrible, may not cause me to lose the use of my reason."

The Dervis did not object to this plan, and the Princess, throwing down the bowl he gave her, followed it to the foot of the mountain.

---

1. the Dervis：土耳其文為乞丐，這裏指為尋寶者指路的山下老人。
2. mistress enough of myself：mistress 為 master 之陰性名詞，而 master of myself 指自我主宰、自我控制。

## 九　公主得寶

*—— 三姐妹的故事（五）*

在第二十天，她遇到了一個老乞丐。他像勸她的哥哥那樣竭力勸她回去，告訴她將要遇到的種種危險。

他說完後，她對他說，“據我理解，那兩個困難是：第一，在拿到鳥籠前不要被聽到的可怕的吵聲嚇倒；第二，不要回頭看。對於後者，我完全有把握做到。對於前者，如果允許的話，我會用棉花塞住耳朵；這樣，不管聲音多大，多可怕，也無法使我喪失理智。”

老乞丐不反對這個辦法。公主就扔下他給她的碗，跟着它到了山腳下。

Here she alighted, and stopped her ears with cotton. After she had looked well at the path leading to the summit, she began at a moderate pace, and walked on without fear. She heard the voices, and perceived the great service the cotton was to her. The higher she went, the louder and more numerous the voices seemed, but they could make no impression upon her. At the insulting speeches which she did hear, she only laughed. At last she saw the cage and the bird, and at the same moment the clamor and thunders of the voices greatly increased.

The Princess, rejoicing to see the object of her search, doubled her speed, and soon gained the summit of the mountain, where the ground was level. Then, running directly to the cage, and clapping her hand upon it, she cried: "Bird, I have you, and you shall not escape me." At this moment the voices ceased.

While Perie-zadeh was pulling the cotton out of her ears, the bird said to her: "Heroic Princess, since I am destined to be a slave, I would rather be yours than any other person's, since you have obtained me so bravely."

"Bird," said Perie-zadeh, "I have been told that there is not far off a golden-water, which is very wonderful. Before all things, I ask you to tell me where it is."

The bird showed her the place, which was just by, and she went and filled a little silver flagon which she had brought with her. Then she returned to the bird and said:—

在這裏，她下了馬，用棉花塞住耳朵。她看好通往山頂的路綫後，開始以正常的速度上山，毫無懼色地走着。她聽到了聲音，感到棉花幫了她很大的忙。她爬得越高，聲音好像也越大、越多，但它們對她起不了作用。對那些辱罵，她只是一笑置之。最後她看到了籠子和鳥；同時像吵鬧和雷鳴似的聲音也大大地提高了。

為看到她尋找的目的物而興高彩烈，公主加快了腳步，很快到達了平坦的山頂。然後，她徑直向籠子跑去，一手抓住籠子，大叫："鳥兒，我可得到你了，你跑不了啦。"這時，所有的聲音都停止了。

貝麗莎德從耳中取出棉花。鳥兒對她說："勇敢的公主啊，既然我注定要當奴隸，我就寧願當您的奴隸，而不願當別人的奴隸，因為您如此勇敢才得到我。"

貝麗莎德說："鳥兒，我聽說附近有神奇的金水。首先，我要你告訴我它在哪裏。"

鳥兒把地方指給她看，它就在旁邊。她走過去用帶來的小銀瓶裝滿了一瓶。然後又回到鳥兒旁邊，說：

"Bird, this is not enough; I want also the singing-tree. Tell me where it is."

"Turn about," said the bird, "and you will see behind you a wood, where you will find this tree. Break off a branch, and plant it in your garden; it will take root as soon as it is put into the earth, and in a little time will grow to a fine tree."

The Princess went into the wood, and by the sweet concert she heard soon found the singing-tree. When she had taken one of its branches, she returned again to the bird and said: —

"Bird, this is not yet enough. My two brothers, in search of thee, have been changed into black stones on the side of the mountain. Tell me how I may restore them to life."

... The bird bade her sprinkle every stone on her way down the mountain with a little water from the golden fountain. As she did this, each stone became a man on a horse, fully equipped. Among these men were her brothers, Bahman and Perviz, who exchanged with her the most loving embraces.

“鳥兒，這還不夠。我還要會唱歌的樹。告訴我它在哪兒。”

鳥兒說：“轉過身去，你可以看到身後有一個樹林，在那兒可以找到這棵樹。折下一枝樹枝，栽在你的花園裏；它一入土就會紮根，不久就會長成一棵大樹。”

公主走進樹林，循着她聽到的美妙的音樂，很快就找到了唱歌樹。她折了一根樹枝後又回到了鳥兒旁邊，說：“這還不夠。為了找你，我兩個哥哥都在山腰上變成了黑石頭。告訴我怎樣才能使他們復活。”

……鳥兒囑咐她下山時一路在每塊石頭上灑一點金泉的水。她照辦後，每塊石頭都變成了一個裝備完善的騎馬人。這些人中就有她兩個哥哥巴曼和伯維茲，他們跟她極其親切地互相擁抱。

# 10 Tomorrow I Will Bring the Queen Your Mother

*— The Story of the Three Sisters (6)*

The report of these wonders soon spread abroad, and many persons came to see and admire them. The two Princes soon took up their old way of living, and one day, when they were hunting two or three leagues from the house, they chanced to meet with the Emperor of Persia.

...

The Princes returned home and told their sister of the favor with which they had been received, and of the visit that was to be paid them in the morning.

"Then we must think," said the Princess, "of preparing a repast fit for his majesty. Let us consult the speaking-bird, he will tell us, perhaps, what meats the Emperor likes best."

When the bird was asked this question, his answer was:—

"Good mistress, you have excellent cooks; let them do the best they can; but, above all things, let them prepare a dish of cucumbers stuffed full of pearls, which must be set before the Emperor in the first course before all the other dishes."

She and her brothers had agreed that the bird's advice must be closely followed. The cook was as much amazed at

# 十　沉冤昭雪慶團圓

*——三姐妹的故事（六）*

這些奇事很快傳開了，許多人前來探訪他們，且讚嘆不已。兩位王子很快恢復了原來的生活方式。一天，他們在離家十多里的地方打獵時，偶然遇到了波斯皇帝。

……

王子回家告訴妹妹他們受到的恩典以及皇帝第二天上午臨幸的消息。

公主說：“那我們得考慮準備一席迎駕的宴會了。讓我們問問能言鳥，也許它能告訴我們皇上最喜歡吃甚麼。”

當她向鳥兒提出這個問題時，它回答道：“女主人，你們有出色的廚師，讓他們都拿出自己的拿手好菜來；不過，最重要的是，叫他們做一盤塞滿珍珠的黃瓜，這道菜必須在上別的菜之前作為第一道菜擺在皇上面前。”

她和兩位哥哥都同意照鳥兒的意見辦。廚師像公主一

his order as the Princess had been, but took the pearls, and in the morning everything was ready for the Emperor's coming.

The Emperor entered the hall; and, as the bird continued singing, the Princess raised her voice, and said: "My slave, here is the Emperor; pay your compliments to him."

The bird left off singing that instant, when all the other birds ceased also; then it said: "God save the Emperor. May he long live!" The repast was served at the sofa near the window where the bird was placed, and the Emperor replied, as he was taking his seat: "Bird, I thank you, and am rejoiced to find in you the sultan and king of birds."

As soon as the Emperor saw the dish of cucumbers before him, he reached out his hand, and took one; but when he had cut it he was in extreme surprise to find it stuffed with pearls.

"What novelty is this?" he said; "and why were these cucumbers stuffed thus with pearls, since pearls are not to be eaten?"

He looked at the two Princes and Princess to ask them the meaning, when the bird, breaking in, said:

"Can your majesty be so greatly surprised at cucumbers stuffed with pearls, which you see with your own eyes, and yet so easily believe that the Queen your wife was the mother of a dog, a cat, and a piece of wood?"

樣對點這道菜感到十分驚奇，但還是拿了珍珠。第二天上午，接駕的一切準備工作都做好了。

皇上進了大廳；在鳥兒不斷歡叫聲中，公主高聲說：“鳥奴，皇上駕到，致頌辭。”

鳥兒立即停止了唱歌，所有別的鳥兒的叫聲也停了下來；然後它說：“天佑皇上。皇上萬歲！”掛着鳥籠的窗戶旁邊的沙發前面擺上了食物。皇帝一面就座一面答道：“鳥兒，謝謝你，朕封你為鳥中之王。”

皇帝一看到面前的那盤黃瓜，就伸手拿了一根；但切開一看，發現裏面塞滿了珍珠，不禁大為驚訝。

他說：“這是甚麼新玩意兒？這些黃瓜為甚麼要塞滿珍珠？珍珠又不能吃！”

他望着兩位王子和公主，問他們是甚麼意思，這時鳥兒插嘴說：

“陛下親眼看到黃瓜裏塞滿珍珠就如此驚奇，但對您的皇后生了小狗、小貓和一塊木頭這樣的怪事卻輕易地相信了？”

"I believed these things," replied the Emperor, "because the nurses assured me of the facts."

"Those nurses, sire," replied the bird, "were the Queen's two sisters, envious of the honors you bestowed upon her, and burning for revenge. If you examine them, they will confess their crime. The two brothers and the sister whom you see before you are your own children, exposed by them, and saved by the keeper of your gardens, who adopted and brought up the children as his own."

"Bird," cried the Emperor, "I believe the truth which you reveal to me. The feeling which drew me to them told me plainly that they must be my own kin. Come, then, my sons, come, my daughter, let me embrace you, and give you the first marks of a father's tender love."

Weeping tears of joy they embraced one another. The Emperor finished his meal in haste, and said: "My children, tomorrow I will bring the Queen your mother; therefore make ready to receive her."

皇帝回答道：“朕相信這些事是因為奶媽向朕保證那是事實。”

鳥兒答道：“那些奶媽是皇后的姐姐，她們嫉妒陛下賜給皇后的榮耀，急於復讎。陛下一審，她們就會招供。陛下面前的兄弟倆和妹妹是被她們拋棄的陛下的親生兒女。他們獲御花園總監搭救、收留並像親生兒女一樣撫養成人”。

皇帝喊道：“鳥兒，朕相信你揭露的事實。朕情不自禁地親近他們的感覺就清楚地說明他們一定是朕的親骨肉。來，兒子，來，女兒，讓朕擁抱你們，讓你們第一次感受到父親的慈愛。”

他們流着高興的眼淚互相擁抱。皇帝很快吃完了飯，說：“孩子們，明天朕要把皇后你們的母親帶來，你們要準備好迎接她。”

## 11 A Copper Jar

*— The Fisherman and the Genie (1)*

There was once an old Fisherman who was very poor. He could hardly keep himself, his wife, and his three children from starving. Every morning he went out early to fish, but he had made it a rule[1] never to cast his net more than four times a day.

...

It was now dawn, and he stopped to say his prayers, for in the East pious men say their prayers five times a day. And after he had said his prayers he cast his net for the fourth and last time. When he had waited long enough, he drew the net in, and saw that it was very heavy.

There was not a fish in the net. Instead, the Fisherman drew out a copper jar. He set it up, and the mouth of the jar was covered with a lid which was sealed with lead. He shook the jar, but could hear nothing.

---

1. made it a rule：慣於，養成……的習慣。

## 十一　奇怪的銅瓶

*— 漁夫和妖怪（一）*

從前有個貧窮的老漁夫，家裏有妻子和三個孩子，收入僅能勉強養家糊口。他每天一早就出去打魚，但總是一天最多只撒四次網。

……

天亮了，他停下來去做禱告，因為在東方虔誠的教徒一天要做五次禱告。禱告後，他第四次也是最後一次下了網。他等了很長時間才起網，發現網很重。

網裏一條魚也沒有，卻撈出了一個銅瓶。漁夫將它豎了起來，發現瓶口有個鉛封的蓋子。他搖了搖瓶子，但沒聽到甚麼聲音。

"At any rate," he said to himself, "I can sell this to a coppersmith and get some money for it." But first, though it seemed empty, he thought he would open it. So he took his knife and cut away the lead. Then he took the lid off. But he could see nothing inside. He turned the jar upside down, and tapped it on the bottom, but nothing came out. He set the jar upright again, and sat and looked at it.

他自言自語道：“不管怎樣，我可以把它賣給銅匠，換幾個錢。”但是，雖然瓶子好像是空的，他還是想先打開看看。他拿出小刀，割開鉛封，打開蓋子。但是裏面甚麼也看不見。他將瓶子倒過來，拍了拍瓶底，也沒有東西倒出來。他又將瓶子立着放，坐在那裏看着它。

## 12 A Great Giant of a Genie

*— The Fisherman and the Genie (2)*

Soon he saw a light smoke come slowly forth. The smoke grew heavier, and thicker, so that he had to step back a few paces. It rose and spread till it shut everything out, like a great fog. At last it had wholly left the jar and had risen into the sky. Then it gathered itself together into a solid mass, and there, before the Fisherman, stood a great giant of a Genie[1].

...

"Get down on your knees," said the Genie to the Fisherman, "for I am going to kill you."

"And why do you kill me? Did I not set you free from the jar?"

"That is the very reason I mean to kill you; but I will grant you one favor."

"And what is that?" asked the Fisherman.

---

1. a great giant of a Genie：巨人般的妖怪。這裏 of 表示相似，如：a palace of a house 一幢宮殿般的房子；that fool of a man 那個傻瓜。

## 十二　巨妖現形

*—— 漁夫和妖怪（二）*

不久，他看見一股輕煙慢慢地冒出來。煙越來越濃，他不由得倒退了幾步。煙不斷上升並漫延開來，像一大團濃霧遮住了一切。最後，它離開了瓶子，升入天空，然後凝集成一個實體。啊呀，在漁夫面前站着一個巨人般的妖怪。

……

妖怪對漁夫說，“跪下，我要殺你。”

“不是我把你從瓶子裏放出來的嗎？為甚麼還要殺我？”

“正因為這個緣故，我才要殺你；不過我可以答應幫你一個忙。”

“幫我甚麼忙？”漁夫問。

"I will let you choose the manner of your death. Listen, and I will tell you my story. I was one of the spirits of heaven. The great and wise Solomon[2] bade me obey his laws. I was angry and would not. So, to punish me, he shut me up in a copper jar and sealed it with lead. Then he gave the jar to a Genie who obeyed him, and bade him cast it into the sea."

---

2. Solomon：所羅門，古代以色列國王，以智慧著稱。事載於基督教聖經舊約全書。

“我讓你選擇怎麼死。聽着，我還要告訴你我的來歷。我本是個天神。偉大而賢明的所羅門要我遵守他的法律。我很生氣，拒不服從。所以，為了懲罰我，他把我裝入銅瓶並用鉛封住口。然後他把瓶子交給一個聽他話的妖怪，吩咐他將瓶子扔進海裏。”

# 13 A Great Oath

*— The Fisherman and the Genie (3)*

"During the first hundred years that I lay on the floor of the sea, I made a promise that if any one set me free I would make him very rich. But no one came to set me free. During the second hundred years, I made a promise that if any one set me free I would show him all the treasures of the earth. But no one came to set me free. During the third hundred years, I made a promise that if any one came to set me free I would make him king over all the earth, and grant him every day any three things he might ask.

"Still no one came. Then I became very angry, and as hundreds of years went by, and I still lay in the jar at the bottom of the sea, I swore a great oath that now if any one should set me free I would at once kill him, and that the only favor I would grant him would be to let him choose his manner of death. So now you have come and have set me free. You must die, but I will let you say how you shall die."

The Fisherman was in great grief. He did not care so much for himself, for he was old and poor, but he thought of his wife and children, who would be left to starve.

# 十三　恩將讎報

*——漁夫和妖怪（三）*

“在海裏最初一百年期間，我許願：如果誰救我出來，我就使他成為富豪。但是沒有人來救我。到了第二個一百年，我又許願：如果誰救我出來，我就把世界上所有的寶藏指點給他。但是還沒有人來救我。到了第三個一百年，我再許願：如果誰來救我，我就讓他做全世界的王，並答應每天給他任何三樣他要求的東西。

“還是沒人來救我。於是，我憤怒極了。就這樣，幾百年過去了，而我仍然關在海底的瓶子裏。我發誓：如果現在誰救我出來，我就立刻殺了他，並且只准許他選擇怎樣死法。現在你來救了我。你就必須死，但我讓你說你要怎麼死。”

漁夫很傷心。他自己倒無所謂，因為他又老又窮，但是他惦念妻子孩子，她們可要挨餓了。

"Alas!" he cried. "Have pity on me. If it had not been for me you would not be free."

"Make haste!" said the Genie. "Tell me how you wish to die."

他大聲呼喊：“可憐可憐我吧！要不是我，你是不會得救的。”

妖怪說，“快點！告訴我你想怎麼死。”

## 14 In Such Great Peril His Wits Fly Fast

*— The Fisherman and the Genie (4)*

When one is in such great peril his wits fly fast, and sometimes they fly into safety. The Fisherman said: —

"Since I must die, I must. But before I die answer me one question."

"Ask what you will, but make haste."

"Dare you, then, swear that you really were in the jar? It is so small, and you are so vast, that the great toe of one of your feet could not be held in it."

"Verily I was in the jar. I swear it. Do you not believe it?"

"No, not until I see you in the jar."

At that the Genie, to prove it, changed again into smoke. The great cloud hung over the earth, and one end of it entered the jar. Slowly the cloud descended until the sky was clear, and the last tip of the cloud was in the jar. As soon as this was done[1], the Fisherman clapped the lid on again, and the Genie was shut up inside.

---

1. this was done：= the last tip of the cloud was in the jar。

# 十四　情急智生

*— 漁夫和妖怪（四）*

人在危險的時候，往往能情急智生，轉危為安。漁夫說：

“既然我非死不可，那就只好死啦。不過，死前你要回答我一個問題。”

“那就隨便問吧，不過要快。”

“那麼，你敢不敢發誓；你原來真的在瓶子裏？瓶子那麼小，你卻那麼大，瓶子連你的一個腳指頭也裝不下。”

“我發誓，我原來的確在瓶子裏。你不信嗎？”

“我不信，除非我親眼看見你在瓶子裏。”

聽了這話，為了證明是真的，妖怪又變成了煙。地面上籠罩着大團煙霧，它的一頭鑽進瓶中。煙慢慢地往下降，天空又漸漸變得明朗了。最後，煙完全進了瓶子。漁夫急忙蓋上蓋子，妖怪又被關在裏面了。

# 15 The Tale of the Old Man and the Hind

The hind, whom you, Lord Genie, see here, is my wife. I married her when she was twelve years old, and we lived together thirty years, without having any children. At the end of that time I adopted into my family a son, whom a slave had born. This act of mine excited against the mother and her child the hatred and jealousy of my wife. She availed herself, during my absence on a journey, of her knowledge of magic, to change the slave and my adopted son into a cow and a calf, and sent them to my farm to be fed and taken care of by the steward.

Immediately, on my return, I inquired after my child and his mother. "Your slave is dead," said she, "and it is now more than two months since I have beheld your son; nor do I know what is become of him." I was sensibly affected at the death of the slave; but as my son had only disappeared, I flattered myself that he would soon be found. Eight months, however, passed, and he did not return; nor could I learn any tidings of him. In order to celebrate the festival of the great

## 十五　老人與雌鹿的故事

魔王啊，你看到的這雌鹿是我的妻子。她十二歲時，我跟她結了婚。我們一起生活了三十年，但是沒有孩子。最後，我要了個養子，他是一個奴隸生的。我這個行動引起我妻子對這母子倆的忌恨。她乘我出門的機會用巫術把那奴隸和我的養子變成了母牛和牛犢，然後把牠們送到農莊，交給管家餵養和照料。

我一到家就問起我兒子和他母親的情況。我妻子說：“你的奴隸死了。你的兒子不見有兩個月了，我也不知道他現在怎麼樣。”聽說奴隸死了，我很難過；但既然我兒子只是失蹤，我自以為很快就會找到的。誰知八個月過去了，他還沒有回來，我聽不到他的一點消息。為了慶祝即

Bairam[1], which was approaching, I ordered my bailiff to bring me the fattest cow I possessed, for a sacrifice. He obeyed my commands. Having bound the cow, I was about to make the sacrifice, when at the very instant she lowed most sorrowfully, and the tears even fell from her eyes. This seemed to me so extraordinary, that I could not but feel compassion for her, and was unable to give the fatal blow. I therefore ordered her to be taken away, and another brought.

My wife, who was present, seemed very angry at my compassion, and opposed my order.

I then said to my steward, "Make the sacrifice yourself; the lamentations and tears of the animal have overcome me."

The steward was less compassionate, and sacrificed her. On taking off the skin we found hardly anything but bones, though she appeared very fat. "Take her away," said I to the steward, truly chagrined, "and if you have another very fat calf, bring it in her place." He returned with a remarkably fine calf, who, as soon as he perceived me, made so great an effort to come to me, that he broke his cord. He lay down at

1. Bairam：土耳其字，意為“節日”或“假日”。該節從 Ramadan（回教徒的齋戒期）結束時開始，是日要殺牛宰羊，先將一部分肉施捨給窮人，然後與朋友共食其餘。

將來臨的白拉姆節，我吩咐管家給我牽來一頭最肥的牛作為祭品。他照我的吩咐辦了。把牛綁上以後，我正要下刀，那牛突然悲鳴起來，眼裏也流出了淚水。我覺得十分奇怪，不由得發了慈悲之心，不忍下手。因此，我吩咐把牠帶走，另換一隻來。

我的妻子當時也在場，對我的慈悲很生氣，反對我的命令。

我於是對管家説："你自己動手吧，這畜牲的哀嚎和眼淚使我受不了。"

管家的心腸比我硬，就把她殺了。剝皮的時候，我們發現這牛雖然看起來肥，其實是皮包骨頭。我實在很失望，對管家説："快拿走。要是還有肥牛的話，就換一隻來。"他回來時牽了一隻特別漂亮的牛犢。那牛犢一看到我就奮力向我跑來，把韁繩都掙斷了。牠躺倒在我腳下，

my feet, with his head on the ground, as if he endeavored to excite my compassion, and to entreat me not to have the cruelty to take away his life.

...

"Wife," answered I, "I will not sacrifice this calf, I wish to favor him: do not you, therefore, oppose it." She, however, did not agree to my proposal; and continued to demand his sacrifice so obstinately, that I was compelled to yield. I bound the calf, and took the fatal knife to bury it in his throat, when he turned his eyes, filled with tears, so persuasively upon me, that I had no power to execute my intention. The knife fell from my hand, and I told my wife I was determined to have another calf. She tried every means to induce me to alter my mind; I continued firm, however, in my resolution, in spite of all she could say; promising, for the sake of appeasing her, to sacrifice this calf at the feast of Bairam on the following year.

The next morning my steward desired to speak with me in private. He informed me that his daughter, who had some knowledge of magic, wished to speak with me. On being admitted to my presence, she informed me that, during my absence, my wife had turned the slave and my son into a cow and calf, that I had already sacrificed the cow, but that she could restore my son to life, if I would give him to her

腦袋觸地，好像想竭力引起我的憐憫，並懇求我不要殘酷地奪走牠的生命似的。

……

我回答道：“老婆，我不想殺這牛犢了，想留它一命。你就不要反對了。”但是她不同意，堅持要求殺牠，我只好讓步了。我綁住牛犢，操起殺牛刀，正要插入牠的喉嚨時，牠雙眼滿含淚水，哀求似地看着我，弄得我實在下不了手。我扔下刀，對妻子説我決定換一隻牛犢。她想盡辦法誘使我改變主意，但我不管她説甚麼，堅持自己的意見；不過，為了安撫她，我答應下一年白拉姆節時宰這頭牛犢來獻祭。

第二天早晨，管家要求跟我私下談話。他告訴我他女兒會點兒巫術，想要跟我談談。她來到我面前對我説，我不在家時我妻了把那奴隸和我兒子變成了母牛和牛犢，我已經殺了母牛，但她能使我兒子恢復人形，如果我讓他做

for her husband, and allow her to visit my wife with the punishment her cruclty had deserved. To these proposals I gave my consent.

The damsel then took a vessel full of water, and pronouncing over it some words I did not understand, she threw the water over the calf, and he instantly regained his own form.

"My son! my son!" I exclaimed, and embraced him with transport; "this damsel has destroyed the horrible charm with which you were surrounded. I am sure your gratitude will induce you to marry her, as I have already promised for you." He joyfully consented; but before they were united the damsel changed my wife into this hind, which you see here.

她的丈夫，並答應她給我妻子以應得的懲罰。我同意了她的要求。

姑娘於是拿起一滿碗水，對着水說了些我不懂的話，然後把水潑在牛犢身上。牛犢立刻恢復了人形。

“我的兒子！我的兒子！”我大喊起來，滿懷喜悅地擁抱了他。“這姑娘把加在你身上的可怕咒語破掉了。我相信你會感恩圖報，娶她為妻的，我也已經替你答應她了。”他高興地同意了；但是在他們完婚前，姑娘把我妻子變成了您面前的這隻雌鹿。

# 16 The Tale of the Old Man and the Two Black Dogs

Great Prince of the genies, you must know that these two black dogs, which you see here, and myself are three brothers. Our father, when he died, left us one thousand sequins[1] each. With this sum we all embarked in business as merchants. My two brothers determined to travel, that they might trade in foreign parts. They were both unfortunate, and returned at the end of two years in a state of abject poverty, having lost their all. I had in the meanwhile prospered, and I gladly received them, and gave them one thousand sequins each, and again set them up as merchants. My brothers frequently proposed to me that I should make a voyage with them for the purpose of traffic. Knowing their former want of success, I refused to join them, until at the end of five years I at length yielded to their repeated solicitations. On consulting on the merchandise to be bought for the voyage, I discovered that nothing remained of the thousand sequins I had given to each. I did not reproach them;

1. sequins：西昆（意大利、土耳其和馬耳他的古金幣）。

## 十六　老人和兩隻黑狗的故事

魔王啊，您要知道我和您面前的這兩隻黑狗本是三兄弟。我父親死的時候給我們每個人留下一千金幣。用這筆錢，我們開始做生意。我的兩個兄弟決定出門到外國做買賣。他倆運氣都不好，兩年後把老本蝕光，兩手空空地回來了；而我卻發了財。我高興地接待了他們，給他們每人一千金幣，讓他們又當上了商人。我的兄弟時常建議我跟他們一起出海去經商。但我知道他們過去的失敗，就一直沒有答應，直到五年以後，我才終於在他們的反覆請求下讓了步。在商量買甚麼貨物出海時，我發現我給他們每人的那一千金幣都花得一乾二淨了。我沒有責備他們；相

on the contrary, as my capital was increased to six thousand sequins, I gave them each one thousand sequins, and kept a like sum myself, and concealed the other three thousand in a corner of my house, in order that if our voyage proved unsuccessful, we might be able to console ourselves and begin our former profession. We purchased our goods, embarked in a vessel, which we ourselves freighted, and set sail with a favorable wind. After sailing about a month, we arrived, without any accident, at a port, where we landed, and had a most advantageous sale for our merchandise. I, in particular, sold mine so well, that I gained ten for one.

About the time that we were ready to embark on our return, I accidentally met on the seashore a female of great beauty, but very poorly dressed. She accosted me by kissing my hand and entreated me most earnestly to permit her to be my wife. I stated many difficulties to such a plan; but at length she said so much to persuade me that I ought not to regard her poverty, and that I should be well satisfied with her conduct, I was quite overcome. I directly procured proper dresses for her, and after marrying her in due form, she embarked with me, and we set sail.

During our voyage, I found my wife possessed of so many good qualities, that I loved her every day more and more. In the meantime my two brothers, who had not traded so advantageously as myself, and who were jealous of my

反，因為我的本錢已增加到六千金幣，我又給了他們每人一千金幣，給我自己也留下一筆數目相同的錢，然後把其餘的三千金幣藏在房子的角落裏，以備萬一出海經商失敗時還可回來幹老行當。我們採購了貨物，自己裝上了船，乘着順風就揚帆啟航了。大約航行了一個月後，我們平安地到了一個港口，在那裏上了岸，把貨賣了個好價錢。特別是我，我的貨賣得更好，賺了十倍。

我們正準備上船返航時，我偶然在海邊遇到一位衣着差勁的絕色美女。她上來吻我的手與我搭訕，並竭力懇求我娶她為妻。我提了許多難處，但最後，在她反覆勸說我不應考慮她的貧窮，而應喜歡她的品行之後，我終於被說服了。我立刻給她買了體面的衣服。在以適當的儀式舉行了婚禮後，她跟我上了船，我們就揚帆啟航了。

在航行中，我發現我妻子有許多優良品性，使我對她的愛與日俱增。同時，我那兩個兄弟因為生意上運氣沒我

prosperity, began to feel exceedingly envious. They even went so far as to conspire against my life; for one night, while my wife and I were asleep, they threw us into the sea. I had hardly, however, fallen into the water, before my wife took me up and transported me to an island. As soon as it was day she thus addressed me: "You must know that I am a fairy, and being upon the shore when you were about to sail, I wished to try the goodness of your heart, and for this purpose I presented myself before you in the disguise you saw. You acted most generously, and I am therefore delighted in finding an occasion of showing my gratitude, and I trust, my husband, that in saving your life, I have not ill rewarded the good you have done me, but I am enraged against your brothers, nor shall I be satisfied till I have taken their lives."

I listened with astonishment to the discourse of the fairy, and thanked her, as well as I was able, for the great obligation she had conferred on me. "But, madam," said I to her, "I must entreat you to pardon my brothers." I related to her what I had done for each of them, but my account only increased her anger. "I must instantly fly after these ungrateful wretches," cried she, "and bring them to a just punishment; I will sink their vessel, and precipitate them to the bottom of the sea." "No, beautiful lady," replied I, "for heaven's sake, moderate your indignation, and do not execute so dreadful an intention; remember they are still my brothers, and that

好，就開始妒忌我的發達。他們甚至打算謀財害命。一天夜裏，他們乘我和妻子睡熟的時候，把我們扔進了海裏。但是，我剛掉進水裏，我妻子就把我撈了出來，送到了一個島上。天一亮，她就對我說："你要知道我是個仙女，你快要開船時，我正好在岸邊；我想試試你的心腸好不好，所以就以化身出現在你面前。你表現很慷慨，因此我很高興有機會來表達我的感激之情。丈夫，我相信我救了你的命也就足以報答你對我的恩情了，但我對你的兩個兄弟非常生氣，我非取了他們的性命不可。"

聽了仙女的話，我十分驚訝，對她的救命之恩竭力稱謝。我對她說；"但是，仙姑，我必須求您饒了我的兩個兄弟。"我對她講了我為他們每人做的事情，但我的話越發激怒了她。她大叫道："我必須馬上飛去追趕那兩個忘恩負義的壞蛋，給他們應得的懲罰；我要弄翻他們的船，叫他們葬身海底。"我回答道："不，美麗的姑娘，看在老天爺份上，你消消氣，千萬別那麼辦，別忘了他們畢竟

we are bound to return good for evil."

No sooner had I pronounced these words, than I was transported in an instant from the island, where we were, to the top of my own house. I descended, opened the doors, and dug up the three thousand sequins which I had hidden. I afterward repaired to my shop, opened it, and received the congratulations of the merchants in the neighborhood on my arrival. When I returned home, I perceived these two black dogs, which came toward me with a submissive air. I could not imagine what this meant, but the fairy, who soon appeared, satisfied my curiosity. "My dear husband," said she, "be not surprised at seeing these two dogs in your house; they are your brothers." My blood ran cold on hearing this, and I inquired by what power they had been transformed into that state. "It is I," replied the fairy, "who have done it, and I have sunk their ship; for the loss of the merchandise it contained, I shall recompense you. As to your brothers, I have condemned them to remain under this form for ten years, as a punishment for their perfidy." Then informing me where I might hear of her, she disappeared.

The ten years are now completed, and I am traveling in search of her. "This, O Lord Genie, is my history; does it not appear to you of a most extraordinary nature?"

是我的兄弟呀，而且我們也應該以德報怨。”

我的話剛說完，就立刻被送到了我自己家的房頂上了。我從房頂下來，開了門，把藏起來的三千金幣挖了出來。後來，我到我的鋪子去，開了門，接受附近的商人們對我平安歸來的祝賀。我回到家後，看到這兩隻黑狗俯首貼耳地向我跑來。我想不出這是怎麼回事兒，那仙女不久就出現在我面前，滿足了我的好奇心。她說：“親愛的丈夫，不要為在家裏看到這兩隻狗而感到奇怪；那是你的兄弟。”聽到這話，我的心都寒起來了。我問是甚麼力量把他們變成這個樣子的。仙女回答道：“是我幹的。把他們的船弄沉的也是我。船上貨物的損失，我會償還你的。至於你的兄弟，我已經罰他們變狗十年，作為不忠不義的懲罰。”然後，她告訴我在哪裏可以打聽到她的消息。說完，她就不見了。

現在，十年已經到了。我正在到處尋找她。“魔王啊，這就是我的經歷，難道你不覺得稀奇嗎？”

# 17 We Must Find Some Way

*— The Story of Prince Ahmed (1)*

There was a Sultan of India who, after a long reign, had reached a good old age. He had three sons: the eldest was named Houssain, the second Ali, the youngest Ahmed. He had also a beautiful niece who had grown up with his sons.

Now, when his niece was old enough to marry, the Sultan sought for a husband among the princes of the country. But no sooner did he make this known than he found that each of his sons was in love with the girl. This made him most unhappy, for he saw that if one married her the others would quarrel with him. He called his three sons to him and said:—

"My sons, I see that it will go hard with you. Your cousin loves each of you, but she can marry one only. We must find some way by which you can agree. Let each go on a journey to a separate country, and return here twelve months from today. I will give you each a large sum of money, that you may travel as befits your rank. Then let each bring back some rare gift, and he who brings the rarest shall have the Princess, my niece."

# 十七　國王的難題

*—— 阿默德王子的故事（一）*

從前，印度有個國王，長期在位，已經年老。他有三個兒子，老大叫胡賽因，老二叫阿里，最小的叫阿默德。他還有一個跟他們一起長大的美麗的外甥女。

外甥女到了結婚的年齡，國王想在各個親王中給她找個丈夫。但是他剛一宣佈就發現他的三個兒子都愛上了這女孩。這使他很不高興，因為他明白，如果他讓她跟其中的一個結了婚，那兩個就會跟他吵鬧。他把三個兒子叫來，對他們說：

“我的孩子，我知道這是件令你們痛苦的事。你們的表妹愛你們每個人，但她只能跟一個人結婚。我們必須找到一個你們都能同意的辦法。我想讓你們各自到一個不同的國家去旅行，從今天算起十二個月以後回到這裏。我會給你們每個人一筆巨款，供你們以適合的身份旅行。然後，各人帶回一件稀罕的禮物，誰的禮物最稀罕，誰就得到公主，我的外甥女。”

# 18 The Carpet, the Ivory Tube and the Apple

*— The Story of Prince Ahmed (2)*

Prince Houssain went to the seacoast, to a town where merchants came together from all parts of the world. Here he saw shops filled with wonderful goods.... As he rested, a man passed by with a carpet about six feet square, and cried with a loud voice that its price was forty purses[1]. The Prince called him to him, and looked at the carpet.

"This is a good carpet," said he, "but why should it cost so much? I see nothing wonderful about it."

"It is true," said the crier, "you can see nothing wonderful, and yet this carpet is well worth forty purses; for if you own the carpet and sit on it, you will be carried to any place you wish in the twinkle of an eye."... They sat on the carpet, and at once were in the room where the Prince lodged. The Prince gladly gave forty purses for the carpet, and it was now his.

---

1. purses：土耳其貨幣名。

## 十八　飛毯、象牙管和蘋果

*—— 阿默德王子的故事（二）*

胡賽因王子去了海邊，到了一個各國商人雲集的城市。在這裏，他看到商店裏的商品琳琅滿目。……在他休息時，有個人拿了一塊六英尺見方的毯子走過，大聲叫喊毯子要價四十土幣。王子叫他過來，看看毯子。

他說："這毯子不錯，但為甚麼這麼貴呢？我看不出有甚麼稀奇的地方。"

叫賣者說；"的確，你看它不稀奇，但它完全值四十土幣；因為如果你有了這毯子，坐在上面，轉瞬間它就可帶你到你想去的任何地方。"……他們坐上毯子，立刻就到了王子下榻的房間。王子高興地給了他四十土幣，買下了這塊毯子。

Prince Ali, the second brother, made his way to Persia. When he reached the capital, he walked about the streets and heard the criers calling out their goods. There was one who had in his hand an ivory tube about a foot long and an inch thick. He cried out that he would sell this to any one for forty purses.

"This is a very simple tube," said the Prince. "Why do you ask such a high price for it? I see nothing wonderful about it."

"It is true," said the crier, "you can see nothing wonderful, and yet this tube is well worth forty purses; for if you own the tube you have but to look through it and you can see whatever you wish to see. Indeed, you may now try it, and see if I am not right."

... He gladly paid his forty purses, for he was sure there could be no greater gift.

Now Prince Ahmed, the youngest, made his way to Arabia, and as he walked through a bazaar he heard a crier, with an apple in his hand, calling out that he would sell it for forty purses.

"Forty purses!" he said. "An apple for forty purses? Why do you ask such a high price for it? I see nothing wonderful about it."

老二阿里王子去了波斯。他到了京城後，在街上閒逛，聽叫賣人叫賣貨物。其中一個手裏拿着一支大約一英尺長、一英吋粗的象牙管。他叫喊這管要賣四十土幣。

王子說：“這是個很普通的管子。你為甚麼要這麼高的價錢？我看它沒甚麼特別。”

叫賣人說：“不錯，你看不出它有甚麼特別，但它完全值四十土幣；因為如果你有了這管子，你只要用它就可以看到你想看的一切。真的，你現在就可以試試，看看我說的對不對。”

……他高興地付了四十土幣，因為他相信不可能有比這管子更好的禮物了。

小王子阿默德去了阿拉伯。當他走過集市時，聽到一個人在叫賣。他手裏拿着一個蘋果，叫喊要賣四十土幣。

王子說：“四十十幣！一個蘋果要四十土幣？你為甚麼要這麼高價？我看不出它有甚麼奇妙的地方。”

"It is true," said the crier, "you can see nothing wonderful, and yet this apple is well worth the price I ask. For it will cure any sick person, even if he is at the point of death. He has but to smell of it, and he will be made well at once."

"If that be so," said Prince Ahmed, "the apple is well worth the price. But how can I know if it really works this great cure?"

"Every one here knows it to be true," said the crier; and one after another came up and said he knew the apple would thus cure the sick. One man said he had a friend who lay very ill, and he was very sure the apple would make him well. Prince Ahmed made haste to buy the apple, for he was sure there could be no greater gift.

叫賣人說：“是啊，你覺得它毫不出奇，可是這蘋果完全值我要的價，因為它能治好任何病人，即使他快要死了。他只要聞一聞蘋果，就能馬上起死回生。”

阿默德王子說：“要是這樣，這蘋果完全值這個價錢。但是我怎麼能知道它真有這麼大的療效呢？”

叫賣人說：“這裏每個人都知道這是真的。”隨後，人們一個接着一個走上前來說他們知道這蘋果確有此療效。一個人說他有個朋友患了重病，臥牀不起，但他確信這蘋果能把他朋友治好。阿默德王子趕快買下了蘋果，因為他相信沒有比它再好的禮物了。

# 19 Each Was Sure He Had the Greatest Gift

*— The Story of Prince Ahmed (3)*

When the year drew near its end, Prince Houssain got on his carpet, and wished himself back at the inn where he was to meet his brothers and in the twinkle of an eye he was there. Not long afterward Prince Ali came, and last of all Prince Ahmed. They met one another joyfully, for each was sure he had the greatest gift. The eldest brother said "Let us at once show what we have brought. Do you see this plain carpet? Yet I paid forty purses for it, and it is worth it, for I came here from the seacoast on it in a moment of time. What can you show equal to this?"

Prince Ali said: —

"Your carpet is truly wonderful. Yet see this simple tube. I paid forty purses for it. Look through it. You can see whatever you wish. Tell me if it is not worth more than your carpet." Prince Houssain took the tube and turned it toward the palace of the Sultan, and looked through it. At once he turned pale.

"Alas, my brothers!" he said. "Of what avail is it that we should bring our gifts? I see the Princess lying on her bed, with all her maids about her, and she is about to die."

# 十九　寶物救公主

*—— 阿默德王子的故事（三）*

年底將至，胡賽因王子坐上毯子，默念回到客棧，好與他的兄弟會合；轉瞬間就到了那裏。不久阿里王子也來了，阿默德王子最後到達。他們相遇都很開心，因為每人都確信自己的禮物是最好的。大哥說："快讓我們看看都帶了甚麼東西。你們看見這塊不起眼的毯子嗎？我可花了四十土幣才買下來的；它值這個價，因為我坐上它不一會兒就從海邊飛到這裏。你們有甚麼能與這相比的？"

阿里王子說："你的毯子確實神奇。不過看看這普通的管子。我也是花了四十土幣買的。你用它想看甚麼就可以看到甚麼。難道它不比你的毯子更值錢？"胡賽因王子接過管子朝着蘇丹王宮的方向看去。突然，他臉色蒼白。

"糟糕，弟弟！"他說。"我看到公主躺在牀上，牀邊圍着她所有的侍女，她像是要死了。我們帶的禮物還有甚麼用呢？"

"Say you so?" said Prince Ahmed, and he looked through the tube also. "If we can but reach her in time I can save her by this apple. See! it looks like a common apple. Yet I paid forty purses for it, and it is well worth the price; for if one smells of it, no matter how sick one is, there will be an instant cure."

"Then let us get at once on my carpet," said Prince Houssain. "There is room for us all three, and we will wish ourselves in the Princess's room." This they did, and no sooner were they there amongst the weeping maids than Prince Ahmed held the apple to the face of the Princess. With her last breath she drew in the odor of the apple. She opened her eyes and looked about her.

"Why do I lie here?" She asked, "and why are you weeping? I am perfectly well."

“真的？”阿默德王子說，拿過管子也看起來。“如果我們能及時趕到她身邊，我就能用這蘋果救她。瞧！它看起來像一隻普通蘋果。但我是花四十土幣買的。它完全值這些錢，因為不管一個人病多麼重，只要一聞蘋果，病馬上就好。”

“那麼我們就快坐上我的毯子吧，”胡賽因王子說。“我們三個人都能坐下，大家要默念去公主的房裏。”果然，轉瞬間他們就已經置身於正在哭泣的侍女中間了。阿默德王子立刻把蘋果拿到公主的鼻子下面。在最後一口呼吸時，她吸進了蘋果的香味。她睜開眼睛看看周圍。

“我怎麼躺在這兒？”她問。“你們為甚麼哭？我不是好好的嗎？”

## 20 He Who Shot His Arrow the Farthest Should Have the Princess

*— The Story of Prince Ahmed (4)*

The three Princes now left the room and came to the Sultan, their father. He was overjoyed to see them once more, and they told their tales, and gave their gifts, and bade him say which of them should have the Princess. He took long to think it over, and then said: —

"It is not possible to say with perfect justice. It is true, Ahmed, that you cured the Princess with your apple. But you could not have known she was sick if she had not been seen through Ali's tube; and you could not have reached her in time if you had not ridden on Houssain's carpet. It is true, Ali, that your tube showed you the Princess [was] sick; but that would have done no good if you had not Houssain's carpet to ride on, and Ahmed's apple for her to smell of. It is true, Houssain, that your carpet brought all three here in time, but you would not have come at once before the Princess died if you had not seen her through Ali's tube; and if you had come, it would have done no good if Ahmed had not brought his apple. No. You have all brought wonderful gifts, but it would not be right to give the Princess to one more than to another. We must try another way."

# 二十　射箭定親

*——阿默德王子的故事（四）*

三位王子離開公主的房間去見父王。蘇丹見兒子回來心中大喜。他們報告了各自的經歷，獻上了禮物並請他決定誰該得到公主。他仔細考慮了很久，然後說：

“要作出完全公正的決定是不可能的。不錯，阿默德，是你用蘋果治好了公主。但是，如果沒有阿里的管子，你就不可能知道她病了；而且如果沒有胡賽因的毯子，你也無法及時趕到她身邊。不錯，阿里，是你的管子讓大家看到公主病了。但是，如果沒有胡賽因的飛毯和阿默德的蘋果，那也沒用。不錯，胡賽因，是你的飛毯把三個人都及時帶到了這裏。但是，如果你們沒有用阿里的管子看到公主病了，就不會馬上來到她身邊；而且如果沒有阿默德的蘋果，那也沒用。是啊，你們都帶來了稀罕的禮物，但是將公主嫁給這一個而不嫁給那一個都是不公平的。我們得試試別的辦法。”

So he bade them go out to the plain, each with a bow and an arrow; he who shot his arrow the farthest should have the Princess. They were followed by the Sultan and all the people, and the three brothers shot in turn. Houssain drew his bow and shot his arrow a great distance. Then Ali, seeing where that arrow had flown, pulled his bow with all his might, and his arrow flew still farther. Last came Ahmed, who drew his bow. Away sped the arrow, far, far, away. They looked for it, but could not find it. And so, in spite of all Ahmed could say, the Sultan gave the Princess to Ali, and there was a great wedding.

因此，他吩咐他們每人拿一張弓和一支箭到外面空地上去；誰把箭射得最遠，誰就得到公主。後面跟着蘇丹和所有的百姓。三兄弟就輪流射箭。胡賽因拉弓把箭射出很遠。隨後，阿里看着箭落之處，用盡全力開弓，他的箭飛得更遠。最後輪到阿默德了。他拉開弓一箭射去。箭一直向前飛去，越飛越遠。他們去找，卻找不到。就這樣，不管阿默德說甚麼，蘇丹把公主許配給了阿里，並且舉行了盛大的婚禮。

## 21 I Am a Peri

*— The Story of Prince Ahmed (5)*

Prince Ahmed, who was very curious to know what had become of his arrow, went in search of it. He went to the spot where he had shot his arrow, and then walked on and on; he looked on one side and the other, but he did not see it, but still went on. At last he came to a steep pile of rocks, and there, at the foot of the rocks, was the arrow. He was amazed. He knew he could not have shot so far, that no man could; but there it was.

As he stood in front of the rock he saw an iron door. He pushed it and it opened. With his arrow in his hand he pressed in. At first he stood in a dark cave. Then it became very bright, and he found himself in a great palace, and before him stood a lady with the air of a queen. She came forward and said: —

"Welcome, Prince Ahmed. I have been waiting for you. I am a Peri, the daughter of one of the mightiest of the genies. I know all about you and your brothers, and the Princess whom you did not marry. It was I who caused the carpet to be made, and the tube, and the apple. I also caused your arrow to fly out of sight, for I wished to draw you to this place. If

## 二十一　仙緣

*——阿默德王子的故事（五）*

阿默德王子很想知道箭的下落，就去尋找。他來到射箭的地點，然後一直向前一邊走一邊左右張望，但是看不見箭的蹤影。他繼續往前走，最後來到一堆巉巖前面。他的箭就在那兒，在巉巖腳下。他奇怪極了。他知道自己不可能射得那麼遠，沒人能射得那麼遠的，但是箭確實是在那兒。

當他站在巖石前面時，他發現一道鐵門。他一推，門就開了。他拿着箭擠了進去。開頭是一個黑暗的山洞、然後就漸漸亮了。他發現自己在一個很大的宮殿裏，面前站着具有王后風度的女士。她走上前來說：

“歡迎，阿默德王子。我一直在等你，我是個仙女，是一位偉大神靈的女兒。你和你哥哥的事以及你沒能與公主成婚的事，我都知道。是我造了飛毯、象牙管和蘋果。也是我使你的箭飛得無影無蹤，因為我要把你引到這裏

you will live with me and be my husband, I will make you happy as long as you live."

Prince Ahmed let himself be led through the palace. He saw all the wonders of the place. He saw the fairies and genies who lived there, and he sat down at a great feast. Every day the Peri planned some surprise, some new and strange thing, and for six months Prince Ahmed lived happily with her.

來。如果你願意和我一起生活，做我的丈夫，我會讓你一生快活。”

阿默德王子被領着走過宮殿，看了這裏所有的奇物美景。他看到了住在這裏的仙女和神靈。他參加了盛大的宴會。仙女每天都為他安排了令他大開眼界的事情，一些新鮮而又稀奇的東西。阿默德王子和她一起快樂地生活了六個月。

# 22 He Caused Zeyn to Be Educated with the Greatest Care

*— The Ninth Statue (1)*

There was a Sultan of Bussorah, prosperous and beloved. He had only one source of sorrow, that he was childless. He therefore gave large alms to the dervishes in his dominions, that they might pray for the birth of a son. Their prayers were granted, and a son was born to him and his Queen; the child was named Zeyn Alasnam, which means "Ornament of the Statues."

All the astrologers of the kingdom were called together to foretell the infant's future. They found by their calculations that he would live long, and be very brave; but that all his courage would be little enough to carry him through the misfortunes that threatened him. The Sultan was not alarmed, but said: "My son is not to be pitied, since he will be brave; it is fit that princes should have a taste of misfortunes, for thus is their virtue tried, and they are the better prepared to reign."

He rewarded the wise men and dismissed them, and caused Zeyn to be educated with the greatest care. But while the Prince was still young, the good Sultan fell sick of an illness which all the skill of his physicians could not cure. Knowing that he must die, he sent for his son, and advised

## 二十二　蘇丹的教子之道

*—— 第九尊神像（一）*

從前布索拉有個蘇丹。他富有而且受人敬愛。唯一的愁事就是沒有兒女。因此，他向國內的苦行僧大量布施，以求他們為他祈禱求子。他們的禱告應驗了。王后生了一個兒子，取名為澤恩·阿拉斯南，意思是“神像的裝飾”。

國內所有的占星家都應邀前來給王子算命。他們算出他會長命，而且會很勇敢；但是他的勇敢不足以幫助他度過危險的難關。蘇丹沒有害怕，反而說：“既然我的兒子勇敢，他就不需要憐憫。王子應當嚐嚐艱辛的滋味，因為這正好能考驗他的品德，使他將來能更好地治理國家。”

他給了這些賢人賞錢，打發他們走了。他命人在教育王子時要十分用心。但是，王子還小時，蘇丹就得了不治之症。他知道要死了，就把兒子叫來，告誡他要讓人愛

him to try to be loved rather than to be feared, to avoid flatterers, and to be as slow in rewarding as in punishing.

After his father's death, Prince Zeyn soon began to show that he was unfit to govern a kingdom. He gave way to all kinds of dissipation, conferred upon his young but evil mates the chief offices of the land, lost all the respect of his people, and emptied his treasury.

The Queen, his mother, discreet and wise, tried to correct his conduct, and warned him that he would lose his crown and life if he did not mend his ways.

戴，而不要讓人懼怕；要遠離阿諛奉承的人；刑賞都要慎重。

父親死後不久，澤恩王子就開始表現出他不宜治理國家。他荒淫無度，縱情聲色，把國家的要職授給他那幫年輕的酒肉朋友，以至失去了百姓的尊敬，國庫也被他揮霍一空。

他的母后穩重而聰慧，力圖糾正他的行為，警告他如不改過必將亡國喪命。

# 23 In a Dream a Venerable Old Man Came towards Him

*— The Ninth Statue (2)*

One night in a dream a venerable old man came towards him, and said, with a smiling face, "Know, Zeyn, there is no sorrow that is not followed by mirth, no misfortune that does not bring at last some happiness. If you desire to see the end of your affliction, set out for Grand Cairo, where great prosperity awaits you."

After much trouble and fatigue he arrived at that famous city. He alighted at the gate of a mosque, where, being spent with weariness, he lay down. No sooner [had] he fallen asleep than he saw the same old man, who said to him: "I am pleased with you, my son; you have believed me. Now, know I have sent you on this long journey only to try you; I find you have courage and resolution. You deserve that I should make you the richest and happiest prince in the world. Return to Bussorah, and you shall find immense wealth in your palace. No king ever possessed so rich a treasure." Prince Zeyn was not pleased with this dream. But the very night after he returned to his palace, the old man came to him for the third time in a dream, and said:—

# 二十三　老人託夢

*——第九尊神像（二）*

一天夜裏，他夢見一位可敬的老人向他走來並笑着對他說：“澤恩，你要明白：禍兮福所依，福兮禍所伏。如果你想結束你的痛苦，就動身到開羅去吧，財富在那裏等着你。”

經過許多艱難和勞累之後，他來到了這座名城。他在一座清真寺門前下了馬。這時他已精疲力盡，便在那兒躺了下來。他剛進入夢鄉，就又見到那位老人。老人對他說：“我喜歡你，孩子。你信了我的話。要知道，我讓你長途跋涉只是為了考驗你；我發現你有勇氣和決心，值得我讓你成為世上最富有、最快樂的王子。回布索拉去吧，你會在你的宮中找到巨大的財富。沒有哪個國王有過這麼大的財富。”這夢並沒有使王子高興。但他回到宮中的當天夜裏，老人第三次在夢中出現，對他說：

"The time of your prosperity is come, brave Zeyn; tomorrow morning, as soon as you are up, take a little pickaxe, and dig in the former Sultan's closet; you will find there a rich treasure."

“勇敢的澤恩，你的福氣來了。明天早上，起牀後，拿一把小鶴嘴鋤，到你父王的密室去挖掘，你就會在那裏找到寶藏。”

# 24 He Went Alone into His Father's Closet

*— The Ninth Statue (3)*

Then he left the Queen, caused a pickaxe to be brought to him, and went alone into his father's closet. He began at once to break up the ground, and took up more than half the square stones with which it was paved, but yet saw no sign of what he sought. Resting for a moment, he thought within himself, "I am much afraid my mother had cause enough to laugh at me." But he took heart, and went on with his labor. On a sudden he discovered a white slab, which he lifted up, and under it he found a staircase of white marble. He lighted a lamp at once, and went down the stairs into a room, the floor of which was laid with tiles of chinaware, and the roof and the walls were of crystal. The room contained four golden tables, on each of which were ten urns of beautiful stone. He went up to one of these urns, took off the cover, and, with no less joy than surprise, found it full of pieces of gold. He looked into all the forty, one after another, and found them full of the same coin, and taking out a handful, he carried it to the Queen.

...

## 二十四　密室尋寶

*——第九尊神像（三）*

然後他離開母后，叫人給他拿來一把鶴嘴鋤，一個人走進父親的密室。他馬上動手挖開地面，搬開鋪在上面的過半的方石，但並未看到他尋找的東西。他休息一會兒，心想：“這一回恐怕母后真要笑話我了。”但他鼓起勇氣，繼續幹了起來。突然，他發現一塊白色的石板。抬起石板後，他看到下面有一白大理石的階梯。他立刻點上燈，走下階梯，進了一個房間，房裏地上鋪了瓷磚，房頂和牆壁都是水晶做的。房裏有四張金桌子，每張上面放着十個漂亮的石甕。他走到一個石甕前面，打開蓋子，發現裏面裝滿金幣，不禁又驚又喜。他逐個查看了這四十個石甕，個個都裝滿了金幣。他抓了一把，拿去給母后看。

……

Zeyn led her to the closet, down the marble stairs, and into the chamber where the urns were. She looked curiously at everything, and in a corner spied a little urn of the same sort of stone as the others. The Prince had not noticed it before, but opening it found within a golden key.

"My son," said the Queen, "this key certainly belongs to some other treasure; let us search well; perhaps we may discover its purpose."

They examined the chamber with the greatest care, and at length found a keyhole in one of the panels of the wall. Here the key readily opened a door which led into a chamber, in the midst of which were nine pedestals of massy gold. On eight of them stood as many statues, each of them made of a single diamond, and from them darted such a brightness that the whole room was perfectly light.

澤因領着母后來到密室，走下雲石階梯，進入有石甕的房間。她好奇地查看每件東西，在角落裏發現一個同款石造的小甕。這是王子先前沒有發現的。他打開一看，裏面有一把金鑰匙。

太后說“孩子，這把鑰匙肯定是另一個寶庫用的。我們好好找找，也許能找到。”

他們十分仔細的查看房間，最後在一塊牆板中找到一個鑰匙孔。在這裏插進鑰匙立刻就打開一道通向另一房間的門，裏面有九個巨大的黃金基座。其中八個基座上站着八尊神像，每個神像都是用整塊鑽石雕刻成的。它們閃閃發光，把整個房間照得通亮。

# 25 The Ninth Alone Is Worth a Thousand Such as These

*— The Ninth Statue (4)*

The ninth pedestal surprised him most of all, for it was covered with a piece of white satin, on which were written these words:—

"Dear son, it cost me much toil to procure these eight statues; but though they are wonderfully beautiful, you must know that there is a ninth in the world, which surpasses them all; that alone is worth more than a thousand such as these. If you desire to be master of it, go to the city of Cairo in Egypt. One of my old slaves, whose name is Mobarec[1], lives there; you will easily find him. Visit him, and tell him all that has befallen you. He will conduct you to the place where that wonderful statue is, and you will obtain it in safety."

...

When King Zeyn had spoken the words taught him by Mobarec, the Sultan of the Genii, smiling, answered:—

---

1. Mobarec：此人年輕時窮困潦倒，得到澤恩的父親的救助，發迹後感恩圖報。澤恩找到他後，他陪澤恩去求諸神之王指點，並教了他一套說話。

# 二十五　第九尊神像的秘密

*——第九尊神像（四）*

最使他們詫異的是第九個基座，因為它上面蓋着一塊白綢，上面寫着這些話：

“親愛的孩子，我花了很大力氣才得到這八尊神像。雖然它們都很美，但是你要知道世上還有勝過它們的第九尊，這一尊的價值等於上千個這樣的神像。如果你想成為它的主人，就到埃及開羅城去吧。那裏住着一個我從前的奴隸，名叫莫巴萊克；找他很容易。你去拜訪他，並告訴他你的遭遇。他會領你去那尊奇妙的神像所在的地方，你就可以安全地得到它了。”

……

當澤恩國王說完莫巴萊克教給他的話後，諸神之王笑着答道：

"I know what brought you hither, and on certain conditions you shall obtain what you desire. You must return with Mobarec, and you must swear to come again to me, and to bring with you a young maiden who has reached her fifteenth year, and has never wished to be married. She must be perfectly beautiful, and you so much master of yourself as not even to wish to marry her as you are bringing her hither. I will give you a looking-glass, which will clearly reflect no other image than that of the young maiden you seek."

At this time there lived at Bagdad an imam named Boubekir Muezin, famous for his charity. On hearing the purpose of his visit to Bagdad, he told him of a young maiden, the daughter of a former vizier of the Sultan of Bagdad, of whom he felt sure that she would fulfill the required terms. He offered to ask her from her father as the wife of the Prince, if he would go with him to her father's mansion. As soon as the Vizier learned the Prince's birth and purpose, he called his daughter, and made her take off her veil. Never had the young Sultan of Bussorah beheld such a perfect and striking beauty. He stood amazed and taking out his glass at once, found that it remained bright and clear.

“我知道你此行的目的；在一定的條件下，你可以得到你想要的東西。你必須跟莫巴萊克回去，而且你必須發誓再來我這兒，帶着一位從未想過結婚的十五歲少女。她必須美艷絕倫，而你能在帶她來這兒的路上克制自己不想跟她結婚。我給你一面鏡子，它照不出別人，只能清楚地照出你尋找的那個少女。”

那時候，在巴格達住着一位以慈善著稱的伊斯蘭教長，名叫波伯克·繆曾。他聽了王子此行的目的後，說他相信巴格達蘇丹的前大臣的女兒能滿足所要求的條件。如果王子願意跟他一起去她父親的公館，他願意向她父親提出把她嫁給王子為妻。大臣一聽王子的門第和此行的目的，就把女兒叫來，吩咐她摘下面紗。巴索拉小蘇丹從來沒見過這樣的絕色美女。他驚訝得目瞪口呆，馬上拿出鏡子一照，鏡子裏的影像果然明亮清晰。

# 26 The Ninth Statue — a Most Beautiful Maiden

*— The Ninth Statue (5)*

The young Sultan and his mother, both impatient to see the wonderful statue, went down into the room; but how great was their surprise, when, instead of a statue of diamonds, they beheld in the ninth statue a most beautiful maiden, whom the Prince knew to be the one he had conducted into the island of the Genii!

"Prince," said the young maid, "you are surprised to see me here. You expected to find something more precious, and I doubt not that you now repent having taken so much trouble. You expected a better reward."

"Madam," answered Zeyn, "Heaven is my witness that more than once I nearly broke my word with the Sultan of the Genii to keep you to myself. Whatever be the value of a diamond statue, is it worth as much as your being mine? I love you above all the diamonds and wealth in the world."

Zeyn, enchanted with the young lady, caused her that very day to be proclaimed Queen of Bussorah, over which they reigned together in happiness for many years.

## 二十六　竟然是位絕色美女

*——第九尊神像（五）*

年輕的蘇丹和他母后都急於看到那座奇妙的神像，就來到王宮下面的那個房間。但是他沒有看見鑽石的雕像，卻發現站在第九個基座上的竟是一位絕色美女。這一驚真非同小可！王子知道這位佳人就是他帶到神島去的姑娘！

姑娘說：“王子，你在這兒見到我一定很驚訝。你本來要找的是更珍貴的東西，我相信你現在一定後悔白費了那麼多功夫。你本來指望得到更好的回報的。”

澤恩說：“老天爺作證，姑娘，我不只一次差點違背對諸神之王的諾言，想把你留給自己。不管鑽石雕像有多麼貴重，難道會比得上你做我的妻子？我愛你勝過世上所有的鑽石和財富。”

澤恩迷上了姑娘，當天就宣佈她為布索拉王后。他們一起快樂地治理國家許多年。

# 27 The City of Lebtait

There was once a city in the land of the Franks, called the City of Lebtait[1]. It was a royal city and in it stood a tower which was always shut. Whenever a King died and another King of the Franks took the Kingship after him, he set a new and strong lock on the tower, till there were four-and-twenty locks upon the gate. After this time, there came to the throne a man who was not of the old royal house, and he had a mind to open the locks, that he might see what was within the tower. The grandees of his kingdom forbade him from this and were instant with him to desist, offering him all that their hands possessed of riches and things of price, if he would but forego his desire; but he would not be baulked and said, "Needs must[2] I open this tower." So he did off the locks and entering, found within figures of Arabs on their horses and camels, covered with turbans with hanging ends, girt with swords and bearing long lances in their hands. He found there also a scroll with these words written therein: "Whenas[3] this door is opened, a people of the Arabs, after the likeness of the

1. Lebtait：現名托萊多(Toledo)，西班牙中部城市。

2. Needs must：= must needs，must。

## 二十七　列泰城

從前在法蘭克國土上有一個城市叫列泰城。這是一座王都。城裏有一座塔，這座塔總是關閉着。每當一個國王去世，另一個國王繼承王位時都要在塔上加一把堅固的新鎖，直到門上有了二十四把鎖。後來有一個不是出身古老王族的人當上了國王，他有心想打開這些鎖，看看塔裏究竟有些甚麼。貴族們都禁止他這樣做，甚至要求他克制，表示只要他放棄這個念頭他們願意獻出他們所有的財寶。但是他不為所動，說：“我一定要打開這座塔。”於是他真的開了鎖，進了塔，發現塔裏有很多阿拉伯人雕像，騎在馬和駱駝上，披着帶穗的頭巾，佩着劍，手持長矛。又看見一個卷軸，上面寫道：“當這扇門打開時，有一個阿

3. Whenas：= When。

figures here depictured, will conquer this country; wherefore beware, beware of opening it."

Now this city was in Spain, and that very year Tarik ibn Ziyad conquered it, slaying this King after the sorriest fashion and sacking the city and making prisoners of the women and boys therein. Moreover, he found there immense treasures; amongst the rest more than a hundred and seventy crowns of pearls and rubies and other gems, and a saloon, in which horsemen might tilt with spears, full of vessels of gold and silver, such as no description can comprise. Moreover, he found there also the table of food of the prophet of God, Solomon, son of David; it is told that it was of green emerald, with vessels of gold and platters of chrysolite; likewise, the Psalms written in the [ancient] Greek character, on leaves of gold set with jewels, together with a book setting forth the properties of stones and herbs and minerals, as well as the use of charms and talismans and the canons of the art of alchemy, and another that treated of the art of cutting and setting rubies and other [precious] stones and of the preparation of poisons and antidotes. There found he also a representation of the configuration of the earth and the seas and the different towns and countries and villages of the world

拉伯民族，就像這兒的這些人像，將會征服這個國家，萬勿開門，切記，切記。”

這個城市在西班牙，就在那一年塔立克・齊葉德征服了它，用最殘酷的手段殺死這位國王，洗劫了城市，擄走了婦孺。另外，他還在裏面發現了巨大的財富；其中有一百七十多頂用珍珠、紅寶石和其他寶石造的皇冠，還有一個大廳，大得騎士們可以持矛衝刺，內有滿罐的金銀，多得無法形容。另外他還發現了真主的先知，大衛王的兒子所羅門的餐桌，據說是用綠寶石造的，上面擺着金碗玉碟，還有〔古〕希臘文的讚美詩寫在鑲有珠寶的金葉上。還有一本書說明石頭、草藥及礦物的性能，以及咒語、辟邪符的用法和煉金術的方法。另有一本書寫着紅寶石和其它寶石的切割鑲嵌工藝以及毒藥和解毒藥的製法。他還找到了地形、海洋、世界各國城市和鄉村的繪圖，還有一個

and a great hall full of hermetic powder, one drachm[4] of which would turn a thousand drachms of silver into fine gold; likewise a marvellous great round mirror of mixed metals, made for Solomon, son of David, wherein whoso looked might see the very image and presentment of the seven divisions of the world, and a chamber full of carbuncles, such as no words can suffice to set forth, many camel-loads. So he despatched all these things to Welid ben Abdulmelik[5], and the Arabs spread all over the cities of Spain, which is one of the finest of lands. This is the end of the story of the City of Lebtait.

---

4. drachm：= dram，得藍（常衡和藥衡單位）。
5. Welid ben Abdulmelik：奧麥德（Ommiade）王朝的第六位國王（公元 705-716)。

大廳裝滿了煉金用的粉末，一得藍這種粉末就能把一千得藍的銀子變成金子；還有一面奇妙巨大的合金鏡，是為大衛王的兒子所羅門製造的，不論誰去照這面鏡子，都能看見世界上七大部分的景象。還有一個小房間，裏面裝滿了紅玉，美不勝收，要很多匹駱駝才能搬走。於是他立刻把這些東西給魏立德·阿卜杜默列克國王送去，從此阿拉伯人就遍布這個世上最美好的國土之一的西班牙的各個城市。列泰城的故事也就完了。

## 28 The Moor's Story of the Roc

There was once a man of the people of Morocco, called Abdurrehman the Moor, and he was known, to boot[1], as the Chinaman, for his long sojourn in Cathay[2]. He had journeyed far and wide and traversed many seas and deserts and was wont to[3] relate wondrous tales of his travels. He was once cast upon an island, where he abode a long while and returning thence to his native country, brought with him the quill of the wing-feather of a young roc, whilst yet unhatched and in the egg; and this quill was big enough to hold a skinful of water, for it is said that the length of the young roc's wing, when it comes forth of the egg, is a thousand fathoms. Abdurrehman related to them the following adventure.

He was on a voyage in the China seas, with a company of merchants, when they sighted a great island: so they steered for it and casting anchor before it, saw that it was large and spacious. The ship's people went ashore to get wood and water, taking with them skins and ropes and axes, and presently espied a great white gleaming dome, a hundred

---

1. to boot：（古）= besides。
2. Cathay：（古）中國。

## 二十八　大鵬鳥的故事

從前有一個摩洛哥人，叫阿卜杜勒曼・摩爾。由於他曾長期住在中國，人們叫他中國人。他曾到各處旅行，穿越過無數的海洋和沙漠，而且慣常講述旅行中的奇遇。有一次，他來到一個島上，在那裏住了很長時間，回來時帶了一根幼鵬翅膀的羽毛管。雖然這隻幼鵬在蛋內尚未孵出，但這根羽毛管卻大得可以裝下一皮囊水。據說孵出後的幼鵬的翅膀有一千噚長。阿卜杜勒曼講了以下一段經歷。

他和一羣商人在中國海上航行。他們看見一個大島，就向島駛去，並在島前下了錨。這個島很大很空曠。船員們上岸砍柴取水，並帶着皮囊、繩索和斧頭。不久他們看到一個巨大的又白又亮的拱形物，有一百肘尺高。走近後

3. was wont to：was used to。

cubits[4] high. So they made towards it and drawing near, found that it was a roc's egg and fell on it with axes and stones and sticks, till they uncovered the young bird and found it as it were a firm-set mountain. They went about to pluck out one of its wing-feathers, but could not win to do so, for all the feathers were not full grown; after which they took what they could carry of the young bird's flesh and cutting the quill away from the feather-part, returned to the ship. Then they spread the canvas and putting out to sea, sailed with a fair wind all that night, till the sun rose, when they saw the old roc come flying after them, as he were a vast cloud, with a rock in his talons, like a great mountain, bigger than the ship. As soon as he came over the vessel, he let fall the rock upon it; but the ship, having great way on her, forewent the rock, which fell into the sea with a terrible crash. So God decreed them safety and delivered them from destruction; and they cooked the young bird's flesh and ate it. Now there were amongst them old grey-bearded men; and when they awoke on the morrow, they found that their beards had turned black, nor did any who had eaten of the young roc ever grow grey. Some held the cause of the return of youth to them and the ceasing of hoariness from them to be that it came of eating the young roc's flesh; and this is indeed a wonder of wonders.

---

4. cubits：肘尺（古代的長度單位，約 45-56 公分長，為手腕至手肘的長度）。

才發現是一個大鵬蛋，他們用斧頭、石頭、棍子砸開蛋殼，看見了幼鳥，它簡直像座堅硬牢固的山。他們想拔下它翅膀上的一根羽毛，卻做不到，因為所有的羽毛都還未長成。後來他們帶了一些幼鵬肉，又從羽毛上切下一截羽毛管，便回到船上。然後揚帆出海，一夜順風而下。當早晨太陽升起時，看見一隻年老的大鵬鳥趕着他們飛來，像一大片烏雲。它爪子裏抓着一塊大石頭，那石頭就像一座大山，比船還要大。鵬鳥飛過船的上空時，扔下石頭，但因船速很快，石頭落到船後的海裏，發出可怕的撞擊聲。真主保佑使他們免受滅頂之災。他們把幼鵬肉煮熟吃了。他們中年紀較大的人鬍鬚已白，但第二天起來時鬍鬚都變黑了。而且吃過幼鵬肉的人，再也沒有長白鬍鬚的了。有人說他們返老還童的原因就是因為吃了幼鵬的肉。這真是奇中之奇。

# 29 The Angel of Death and the Rich King

A certain king had heaped up treasure beyond count and gathered store of all [precious] things, that God the Most High hath[1] created, that he might take his pleasure thereof, against such time as he should have leisure to enjoy all this abounding wealth that he had collected. Moreover, he builded him a wide and lofty palace, such as beseemeth[2] kings, and set thereto strong doors of cunning fashion and appointed for its service and guard servants and soldiers and door-keepers. One day, he bade the cooks dress him somewhat of the goodliest of food and assembled his household and retainers and lords and servants to eat with him and partake of his bounty. Then he sat down upon the throne of his kingship and the chair of his state and leaning back upon his cushion, bespoke himself, saying, "O soul, behold, thou[3] hast[4] gathered together all the riches of the world; so now take thy[5] leisure therein and eat of this good at thine[6] ease, in long life and abounding prosperity!"

---

1. hath：（古）= has，have 的第三人稱單數現在式。
2. beseemeth：（古）= befits（-eth 為動詞後綴，構成陳述語氣第三人稱單數現在式）。

## 二十九　死神和國王

有一個國王聚斂了無數的財富，他把真主創造出的所有珍貴物都收藏在一起，供自己消閒享用。此外，他還造了一座寬敞高大的王宮足以匹配國王，裝上牢固而巧妙的門，並派了僕人，守衛士兵及守門人來幹雜役和守衛。一天，他吩咐廚師做了最好的食物，召集他的家族和侍從還有貴族和僕人和他一起吃飯，分享他的慷慨。他坐在御座上，背靠墊子說："看吧！你們已聚集了全世界的全部財富。現在就慢慢地享用，隨意地吃吧！祝大家長命百歲，榮華富貴！"

---

3. thou：（古）＝ you。
4. hast：（古）= have，用於第人二人稱單數現在式，與 thou 連用。
5. thy：（古）= your。
6. thine：（古）= your，用在母音字母或 h 開始的詞前面。

Hardly had he made an end of speaking, when there came so terrible a knock at the gate that the whole palace shook and the king's throne trembled. The servants were affrighted and ran to the door, where they saw a man clad in tattered raiment, with a cadger's wallet hanging at his neck, as he were one who came to beg food. When they saw him, they cried out at him, saying, "Out on thee[7]! What unmannerly fashion is this? Wait till the king eateth and [after] we will give thee of what is left." Quoth[8] he, "Tell your lord to come out and speak with me, for I have a pressing errand to him and a weighty matter." "Away, fool!" replied they. "Who art thou[9] that we should bid our lord come out to thee?" But he said, "Tell him of this." So they went in and told the king, who said, "Did ye[10] not rebuke him and draw upon him and chide him!" But, as he spoke, behold, there came another knock at the gate, louder than the first, whereupon the servants ran at the stranger with staves and weapons, to fall upon him; but he cried out at them, saying, "Abide in your places, for I am the Angel of Death." When they heard this, their hearts quaked and their wits forsook them; their understandings were dazed and their nerves trembled for fear and their limbs lost

---

7. thee：（古）= you 的受格。
8. Quoth：（古）= said，用於第一人稱和第三人稱陳述語氣過去式。
9. art thou：（古）= are you。

他的話還沒説完，大門上傳來猛烈的敲門聲，整個宮殿都震動了，御座也搖晃了。僕人們很害怕，跑到門口見到一個人破衣爛衫，頸上掛一個乞丐用的錢袋，好像是來討飯的。僕人見他這副樣子，對他吼道：“滾出去，太不成體統了。等國王吃完後，我們才能給你殘羹剩飯。”他説：“叫你們國王出來跟我説話，我有要緊的事找他，很重要的事。”“滾，笨蛋！”他們答道，“你是甚麼東西，怎麼能叫國王出來見你？”他説，“把我剛才説的話告訴他。”他們進去告訴國王，國王説，“你們怎麼不訓斥他責罵他呢？” 但他止説着，門上又是重重一擊，比第一次還響，僕人們拿着棍棒武器跑去，要打這陌生人。但他叫道，“站住別動，我是死神。”他們聽了膽顫心寒，失去理智，茫然不知所措，，一個個嚇得發抖，手腳

10. ye：（古）= you，作為第二人稱複數代詞。

the power of motion. Then said the King to them, "Bid him take a substitute in my stead." But the Angel answered, saying, "I will take no substitute, and I come not but on thine account, to make severance between thee and the good thou hast gathered together and the riches thou hast heaped up and treasured." When the King heard this, he wept and groaned, saying, "May God curse the treasure that has deluded and undone me and diverted me from the service of my Lord! I deemed it would profit me, but to-day it is a regret for me and an affliction unto me, and behold, I [must] go forth, empty-handed of it, and leave it to mine enemies."

Therewith God caused the treasure to speak and it said, "Why dost[11] thou curse me? Curse thyself, for God created both me and thee of the dust and appointed me to be in thine hand, that thou mightest[12] provide thee with me for the next world and give alms with me to the poor and sick and needy and endow mosques and hospices and build bridges and aqueducts, so might I be a succour unto[13] thee in the life to come. But thou didst garner me and hoard me up and bestowedst me on thine own lusts, neither gavest thanks for

11. dost：（古）= do（-st 或 -est 為動詞後綴，用於第二人稱單數）。
12. mightest：（古）= might。

都不能動彈了。後來國王對他們說，“告訴他另找個人替我好了。”但死神說，“我不要替代的人，我是專為你來的，我要把你和聚斂起來的財富分開。”國王聽後，哭了起來，呻吟着說：“願主咒詛這些財富，它引誘了我，毀了我，使我不能侍奉我主。我原以為它會給我帶來好處，但今天它卻給我帶來了悔恨和苦惱。我馬上就要空着手離開人世，而把它留給我的敵人了。”

這時，主讓財富說話了，它說，“你為甚麼詛咒我？詛咒你自己吧！主用泥土創造了你和我，把我交在你手中是讓你能用我為來世造福，施捨窮人、病人和有需要的人，贊助寺廟和福利事業，以及造橋修渠，這樣來世我才能解救你。但你卻為了私慾將我積聚起來據為己有，不但

---

13. unto：（古）= to。

me, as was due, but wast[14] ungrateful; and now thou must leave me to thine enemies and abidest in thy regret and thy repentance. But what is my fault, that thou shouldest revile me?" Then the Angel of Death took the soul of the King, before he ate of the food, and he fell from his throne, dead.

14. wast：（古）be 的第二人稱單數過去式（與 thou 連用）。

不感謝我，而且忘恩負義。現在你必須把我留給你的敵人，而你自己將生活在悔恨之中。可我有甚麼錯你要罵我？”於是國王還沒吃東西，死神就取走了他的靈魂，他從御座上跌下來，一命嗚呼了。

# Cops, Thieves and Frauds
# 警察、小偷、騙子

# 30 Story of the Chief of the Old Cairo Police

I once had ten thieves hanged, each on his own gibbet, and set guards to watch them and hinder the folk from taking them down. Next morning, when I came to look at them, I found two bodies hanging from one gibbet and said to the guards, "Who did this, and where is the tenth gibbet?" But they denied all knowledge of it, and I was about to beat them, when they said, "Know, O Amir[1], that we fell asleep last night, and when we awoke, we found one of the bodies gone, gibbet and all, whereat we were alarmed fearing thy wrath. But, presently, up came a peasant, jogging along on his ass; so we laid hands on him and killing him, hung his body upon this gibbet, in the stead of the missing thief."

When I heard this, I marvelled and said to them, "Had he aught[2] with him?" "He had a pair of saddle-bags on the ass," answered they. "What was in them?" asked I; and they

---

1. Amir：= Emir，埃米爾，（亞非地區）穆斯林酋長（王子或長官）。
2. aught：古語，此處 = anything。

## 三十　老開羅城警察局長的故事

有一次我將十個賊處了絞刑，一個人掛一個絞架，並且派了衛兵守衛以免有人把屍體從絞架上取下來。第二天我去看時，有一個絞架上吊了兩具屍體，我對衛兵說，“這是誰幹的？那第十個絞架呢？”但他們都說不知道。我正要打他們，他們說，“長官，我們昨晚睡着了，醒來後發現少了一具屍體，連絞架也不見了。我們很恐慌，怕你發怒。正好來了一個農民，騎着驢子慢騰騰地走來，我們就抓了他，把他殺了吊在這個絞架上頂替那不見了的賊。”

我聽見後大吃一驚，問道，“他帶甚麼東西了嗎？”“他的驢子上有一對鞍袋，”他們答道。“裏面有甚

said, "We know not." Quoth I, "Bring them hither." So they brought them to me and I bade open them, when, behold, therein was the body of a murdered man, cut in pieces. When I saw this, I marvelled and said in myself, "Glory be to God! The cause of the hanging of this peasant was no other but his crime against this murdered man; and the Lord is no unjust dealer with [His] servants."[3]

---

3. 引自《古蘭經》第 四十六 章。

麼？”我問。他們說，“不知道。”我說，“把袋子拿來。”於是他們把袋子拿到我面前。我命人把袋子打開，天哪！裏面竟是一個被謀殺的人，身體被砍成數塊。我見此情景，非常驚異，暗想，“聖明的主啊！絞死這農民正是事出有因，原來他犯了殺人罪！主對〔他的〕僕人真是公正啊！”

# 31 Story of the Chief of the Police of New Cairo

There were once, in this city, two men apt to bear witness in matters of blood and wounds; but they were both given to wine and women and debauchery; nor, do what I would, could I succeed in bringing them to account.

One night, a man came to me and said, "O my lord, know that the two witnesses are in such a house in such a street, engaged in sore wickedness." So I disguised myself and went out, accompanied by none but my page, to the street in question. When I came to the house, I knocked at the door, whereupon a slave-girl came out and opened to me, saying, "Who art thou?" I made her no answer, but entered and saw the two witnesses and the master of the house sitting, and lewd women with them, and great plenty of wine before them. When they saw me, they rose to receive me, without showing the least alarm, and made much of me, seating me in the place of honour and saying to me, "Welcome for an illustrious guest and a pleasant cup-companion!"

# 三十一　新開羅城警察局長的故事

從前在這個城裏有兩個人常為兇殺案做證人，但他倆自己都是貪杯好色之徒。我儘管努力也無法將他們二人繩之以法。

有天晚上，有個人跑來對我說，“長官，那兩個證人正在某條街某棟房子裏幹壞事呢！”我立即喬裝打扮，只帶了一個小聽差就到那條街去了。到了那座房子門前，我敲敲門，一個女奴出來開門，問我，“你是誰？”我沒回答就進了屋子，看見那兩個人和房主正坐在那裏，有一些放蕩下流的女人陪着，面前擺了很多酒。他們看見我，就站起來歡迎我，絲毫沒有露出驚慌的樣子。他們恭敬地給我上座，對我說，“歡迎尊貴的客人和好酒友！”

Presently, the master of the house went out and returning after a while with three hundred dinars, said to me, without the least fear, "O my lord, it is, we know, in thy power both to disgrace and punish us; but this will bring thee nothing but weariness. So thou wouldst[1] do better to rake this money and protect us; for God the Most High is named the Protector and loveth those of His servants who protect each other; and thou shalt[2] have thy reward in the world to come." The money tempted me and I said in myself, "I will take the money and protect them this once; but, if ever again I have them in my power, I will take my wreak of them."

So I took the money and went away; but, next day, one of the Cadi's serjeants[3] came to me and cited me before the court. I accompanied him thither, knowing not the meaning of the summons; and when I came into the Cadi's presence, I saw the two witnesses and the master of the house sitting by

---

1. wouldst：（古）= would。
2. shalt：（古）= shall。
3. Cadi's serjeants：法警。Cadi 為根據伊斯蘭教教法進行宗教審判的法官。serjeants 亦拼寫成 sergeants。

不久，房主出去了，過了一會兒帶了三百第納爾回來，毫無懼色地對我說，“長官，我們知道你有權讓我們丟臉並懲罰我們，但那樣做你除了勞累一場甚麼也得不到。不如你收下這筆錢保護我們，因為至高無上的主就叫保護神，他愛護他那些相互保護的僕人們；你在來世也會得到報答的。”我受金錢的誘惑，心想，“我收下錢，就保護他們這一次；但是以後一旦他們再落入我手中，我絕不饒他們。”

於是我拿了錢就走了。第二天，法警就找上門來，傳我到庭。我跟他去了，不知道為甚麼召我出庭。我到了法官面前，看見那兩個證人和房主人坐在法官旁邊。房主人

him. The latter rose and sued me for three hundred dinars, nor was it in my power to deny the debt; for the two others testified against me that I owed the amount. Their evidence satisfied the Cadi and he ordered me to pay the money; nor did I leave the Court till they had of me the three hundred dinars. So I went away, in the utmost wrath and confusion, vowing vengeance against them and repenting that I had not punished them.

站起來控告我欠他三百第納爾。我無法賴賬，因為那兩個人也證明我欠了這筆錢。他們的證詞法官認為可以成立，就命令我付錢。我給了他們三百第納爾後才得以脱身。我離開時極端憤怒及慌亂，發誓一定要報復，真後悔當時沒有懲罰他們。

# 32 The Chief of the Cous Police and the Sharper

It is related that Alaeddin, chief of the Police of Cous[1], was sitting one night in his house, when a man of comely aspect and dignified port, followed by a servant bearing a chest upon his head, came to the door and said to one of the young men, "Go in and tell the Amir that I would speak with him privily." So the servant went in and told his master, who bade admit the visitor. When he entered, the Amir saw him to be a man of good appearance and carriage; so he received him with honour, seating him beside himself, and said to him, "What is thy business?" "I am a highwayman," replied the stranger, "and am minded to repent at thy hands and turn to God the Most High; but I would have thee help me to this, for that I am in thy district and under thine eye. I have here a chest, wherein is that which is worth nigh[2] forty thousand dinars; and none hath so good a right to it as thou; so do thou

1. Cous：上埃及的一個城鎮。

2. nigh：= near。

# 三十二　庫斯城警察局長和騙子

傳說庫斯城警察局長阿拉丁有一天晚上正坐在家裏，這時 個相貌俊美，儀態高貴的人領着一個頭頂木箱的僕人來到他門前並對一名看門的年青人說："請進去報告長官，我要跟他私下談話。"僕人進去報告了主人，主人吩咐請客人進來。客人進來後，長官一看客人相貌堂堂，儀表出眾，就很客氣地接待他，讓他坐在自己身邊，對他說："你有甚麼事？"來人答道：我是一個攔路搶劫的強盜，我想向你悔過自新，皈依至高無上的真主，請大人幫助我實現這一願望，因為我在您的轄區受您的監督。我帶來一個箱子，裏面裝的東西總值約四萬第納爾，這些財物

take it and give me in exchange a thousand dinars of thy money, lawfully gotten, that I may have a little capital, to aid me in my repentance, and not be forced to resort to sin for subsistence; and with God the Most High be thy reward!" So saying he opened the chest and showed the Amir that it was full of trinkets and jewels and bullion and pearls, whereat he was amazed and rejoiced greatly. Then he cried out to his treasurer, to bring him a purse of a thousand dinars, and gave it to the highwayman, who thanked him and went his way, under cover of the night.

On the morrow, the Amir sent for the chief of the goldsmiths and showed him the chest and what was therein; but the goldsmith found it nothing but pewter and brass and the jewels and pearls all of glass; at which Alaeddin was sore chagrined and sent in quest of the highwayman; but none could come at him.

只有您最有權享用；請大人務必收下。你只要換給我一千第納爾，我好拿這合法得來的錢作本錢做個小生意，使我在悔改中可以糊口度日，免得再做壞事。求真主保佑您！”説完，他打開箱子，讓長官看箱子裏裝的首飾、珠寶、金銀和珍珠。看到這些局長驚喜萬分。於是，他把司庫叫來，吩咐他拿一個裝有一千第納爾的錢袋給這強盜。強盜謝過他就連夜走了。

第二天局長請來金匠總管，讓他看箱子裏的東西；但金匠發現裏面只有銅錫製品，玻璃首飾和珠子，阿拉丁火冒三丈，派人去抓強盜，但誰也沒有找到他。

# 33 The Thief of Alexandria and the Chief of Police

Once upon a time there was a chief of police in Alexandria called Husam al-Din, the sharp Scimitar of the Faith. Now one night, as he was sitting at his desk, a trooper came running into his office and said, "My lord, I entered your city this very night, and soon after I went to sleep at a certain khan[1], I awoke to find my saddlebags sliced open and a purse with a thousand gold pieces missing!"

No sooner had he finished speaking than the chief summoned all his officers and ordered them to seize all the people in the khan and throw them into jail. The next morning, he had rods and whips brought to his office, and after sending for the prisoners, he intended to have them flogged until someone confessed to the theft in the presence of the owner. Just then, however, a man broke through the crowd of people at his office and went straight to the chief.

"Stop!" he cried out. "Let these people go! They've been falsely accused. It was I who robbed this trooper. Look, here's the purse I stole from his saddlebags."

---

1. khan：土耳其或中東的小客棧，商旅客店。

## 三十三　亞歷山德里亞竊賊和警察局長

從前，亞歷山德里亞有個警察局長，名叫胡薩姆·阿爾丁，號稱信仰之劍。一天晚上，他正坐着辦公，一名士兵跑進他的辦公室，說："大人，我今晚剛到這個城市，在客棧裏睡下後不久，醒來發現我的鞍囊被人用刀劃開，一個裝着一千金幣的錢包不見了。"

他剛說完，局長就召集全體警察，命令他們把客棧裏所有的人都抓起來，投入監獄。第二天早晨，他吩咐在他的辦公室裏備好棍棒和鞭子，打算把囚犯帶上來痛打一頓，直到有人當着失主的面承認盜竊為止。但是，正在這時，一個人穿過辦公室裏的人羣，一直向局長走來。

他喊道："住手！放了這些人！他們是無辜的。是我偷這個兵的錢包的。瞧，這就是我從他的鞍囊裏偷來的錢包。"

Upon saying this, he pulled out the purse from his sleeve and laid it before Husam al-Din, who said to the soldier, "Take your money, and put it away. You no longer have any grounds to lodge a complaint against these people of the khan."

Thereupon, the people of the khan and all those present began praising the thief and blessing him. However he said, "Please stop. It doesn't take much skill to bring the purse to the chief in person. But it does take a great deal of skill to take it a second time from this trooper."

"And how did you manage to do that?" asked the chief.

And the robber replied, "My lord, I was standing in the money changer's shop at Cairo, when I saw this soldier receive the gold in change and put it into this purse. So I followed him from street to street but did not find the right opportunity to steal it. Then he left Cairo, and I followed from town to town, plotting along the way to rob him without avail, until I entered this city, where I dogged him to the khan. There I took my lodgings next to him and waited until he fell asleep. Then I went up to him quietly, and I slit open his saddlebags with this knife and took the purse just as I am taking it now."

說完，他就從袖筒裏掏出錢包，放在胡薩姆·阿爾丁面前。局長對士兵說：“把錢拿去放好吧。你現在沒有理由再控告客棧裏的人了。”

這時，客棧裏的人和所有在場的人都開口稱讚竊賊並為他祝福。但是，他說：“請別這樣。把錢包親自送來給局長算不了甚麼本事。但是，把它又一次從士兵身上拿走倒真要點本事呢。”

局長問：“那你是怎麼辦到的呢？”

竊賊答道：“大人，我在開羅一家外幣兌換店裏看到這個士兵收下換來的金幣，放在這個錢包裏。所以我就從一條街到另一條街老跟着他，但是找不到機會下手。後來，他離開了開羅，我又跟着他，從一個城市到另一個城市，一路上都在算計如何偷他，但還是不行，直至進了這個城裏，我跟他到了那家客棧。我在他隔壁住了下來，等他睡着了。於是，我悄悄地走到他身邊，用這把刀割開他的鞍囊，拿了這個錢包，就像我現在這樣拿法。”

No sooner had he spoken those words than he stretched out his hand and grabbed the purse from the trooper in front of the chief, and everyone thought that he was merely demonstrating how he had committed the theft. But, all at once, he broke into a run and sprang into a nearby river. The chief of police shouted to his officers, "Stop that thief!" And his men ran after him. But before they could doff their clothes and descend the steps of the river, he had made it to the other side. Of course, they continued searching for him, but there was no way they could find him, for he was able to escape through the back streets and lanes of Alexandria.

So the officers returned without the purse, and the chief of police said to the trooper, "I can't do anything for you now. The people are innocent, and your money was returned to you. But you weren't wise enough to protect it from the thief."

Consequently, the trooper was compelled to leave without his money, while the pople were delivered from his hands and those of the chief of police. And all this had the blessing of Almighty Allah[2].

---

2. Allah：真主，阿拉，伊斯蘭教的主神。

他話音剛落，就當着局長的面伸手從士兵身上搶走了錢包。所有的人都以為他是在演示當時偷竊的樣子。但是，突然，他奔跑起來，跳進附近的一條河裏。

局長向警察們大喊：“抓住他！”他的手下就在後面追。但是在他們脱掉衣服，走下河邊的台階以前，竊賊已經游到了對岸。當然，他們繼續搜捕，但根本無法找到他，因為他已經穿過亞歷山德里亞的後街小巷逃之夭夭了。

警察們就這樣兩手空空地回來了。局長對士兵説“現在我幫不了你甚麼忙了。那些人是無辜的，你的錢也曾經歸還給你了。但你不能把錢保護好，又讓小偷偷去了。”

結果，士兵只好丟了錢走了，而老百姓卻得救了。他們沒有吃他和警察局長的苦頭。這一切都是萬能的真主的恩典啊。

## 34 A Merchant and Two Thieves

In a city called Sindah there was once a very wealthy merchant who loaded his camels with goods and set out for a certain city with the purpose of selling his merchandise there. Now he was followed by two thieves, who had made bales out of whatever goods they could find, and pretending to be merchants themselves, they managed to join the merchant along the way. Beforehand they had agreed to trick the merchant at the first resting place they reached and to take all that he had. At the same time, each of the thieves had secretly planned to trick the other and thought that if he could cheat his comrade, he could have all the goods to himself, and everything would go well for him.

So, after planning their scheme, one of them took food and put poison in it and brought it to his comrade. Meanwhile the other had done the same, and they both ate poisoned food and died. Now, right before this they had been sitting with the merchant, and he began wondering why they were staying away so long. So he went in search of them and found the two lying dead. As a result, he knew the two were thieves who had plotted against him, but their rotten scheme had backfired. So the merchant was saved and took what they had.

# 三十四　商人和兩個小偷

從前，在一個名叫新達的城裏有個富商。一天，他用駱駝馱着貨物，動身去一個城市賣貨。他受到兩個小偷的跟蹤。他們把能找到的貨品綑成貨包，假裝自己也是商人，一路上跟那位商人作伴。他們事先已經商量好在到達第一個息腳處時就把商人的全部貨物騙走。同時，每個騙子又各自心懷鬼胎，謀劃騙對方，好獨吞全部贓物。

因此，在打定主意後，其中一人就在食物中下了毒，拿去給同夥吃。不料，另一個也依法炮製，結果兩人都吃了有毒的食物死了。剛才商人還跟他們坐在一起，他開始奇怪他們怎麼離開這麼長時間還不回來。所以他就去找他們，發現兩個人都躺在那兒死了。他這才恍然大悟，原來他們是賊，想要謀財害命，結果害人不成反害了自己。商人平安無事，還得到了小偷的東西。

## 35 Stolen Goods

There was once a man who had a monkey, and this man was a thief who never entered any of the market streets of the city without walking off with some great profit. Now, it so happened that one day he saw a man offering worn clothes for sale in the market, but nobody desired to buy from him. Soon the thief who had the monkey saw the man with the old clothes place them in a wrapper and sit down to rest out of exhaustion. So the thief made the monkey play around in front of him to catch his eye, and while the man was busy gazing at the animal, he stole the parcel from him. Then he took the monkey and went off to a private place, where he opened the wrapper, took out the old clothes, and folded them neatly in a piece of costly stuff. Then he carried this bundle to another bazaar and offered the costly stuff and its contents for sale but only on the condition that the parcel not be opened at the market. Indeed, he tempted prospective buyers by setting a low price on the bundle. Some man was attracted by the beautiful wrapper and bought it under the condition set by the thief. When he took it home, he was certain that he had a bargain with him, and his wife asked him what he had bought.

## 三十五　賊贓

從前有人養了一隻猴子。這人是個小偷，每次進城趕集，總要順手牽羊撈一大把。一天，他看到一個人在集市上賣舊衣服，但沒人去買。不久，養猴子的小偷看見賣舊衣的把衣服包了起來，累得坐下來休息。小偷就讓猴子在他面前耍把戲，來吸引他的注意；趁他聚精會神地看猴的當兒，小偷就把那包衣服偷走了。然後他牽着猴子走到一個沒人的地方，打開包袱，拿出舊衣服，疊得整整齊齊，再用一塊貴重的包裹布包好。然後他帶着這包東西來到另一個市場叫賣，但有個條件：包袱不許當場打開。真的，為了引誘買主，他要價很低。終於有個人被那塊漂亮的包裹布所吸引，按小偷的條件買了下來。拿回家後，他滿以為撿了個便宜。妻子問他買了甚麼。

"It's valuable stuff that I bought at an extremely low price, and I intend to sell it again and make a big profit," he boasted.

"You fool," she said, "would this stuff have been sold at such a low price unless it had been stolen? Don't you know that whoever buys something without examining it is bound to make a mistake?"

...

"Not every wise man is saved by his wisdom," responded her husband, "nor is every fool lost by his folly. I have seen a skillful snake charmer bitten to death by the fangs of a snake, and I have watched others who know nothing whatsoever about serpents manage to tame them."

So he did not listen to his wife and continued to buy stolen goods below their value until he came under suspicion by the authorities and was sentenced to death.

他洋洋得意地說：“我以極低的價錢買了一包值錢的東西。我打算再賣了它，大賺一筆。”

妻子說：“你這笨蛋，不是賊贓會這麼便宜就賣給你嗎？你難道不知道買東西不查清楚肯定要上當嗎？”

……

他回答道：“聰明人不一定因為聰明就保險，傻瓜也不一定因為傻就吃虧。我就見過一個耍蛇能手給蛇咬死，也看到過對蛇一竅不通的人把蛇擺弄得服服貼貼。”

就這樣，他不聽妻子的勸告，繼續以低價收買賊贓，最後引起當局的懷疑，把他處了死刑。

# 36 The Thief and the Money-changer

A money-changer, bearing a bag of money, once passed by a company of thieves, and one of the latter said to the others, "I know how to steal yonder bag of money." "How wilt[1] thou do it?" asked they. "Look," answered he and followed the money-changer, till he entered his house, when he threw the bag on a shelf and went into the draught-house, to do an occasion, calling to the slave-girl to bring him an ewer of water. So she took the jug and followed him to the draught-house, leaving the door open, whereupon the thief entered and taking the bag of money, made off with it to his companions, to whom he related what had passed. "By Allah," said they, "this was a clever trick! It is not every one could do it: but, presently, the money-changer will come out of the draught-house and missing the bag of money, will beat the slave-girl and torture her grievously. Meseems[2] thou hast at present done nothing worthy of praise; but, if thou be indeed a sharper, thou wilt return and save the girl from being beaten." "If it be the will of God," answered the thief, "I will save both the girl and the purse."

---

1. wilt：will 的第二人稱單數的古體。

# 三十六　小偷與錢商

從前，一位錢商揹着一袋錢在一幫小偷面前走過，一個小偷對夥伴說："我有辦法把那袋錢偷來。"後者問："你有甚麼辦法？""你們看吧！"他答道，隨即跟着錢商，一直跟他進了家門。錢商把袋子扔在架子上就進茅房解手，吩咐女奴給他拿一缸水來。她拿着水缸跟他走進茅房，卻沒有關門。小偷就乘機進來，偷走錢袋，回到他同夥那裏，向他們講了事情的經過。他們說："真主作證，這計策可真高明，不是隨便哪個人都能辦到的。不過，錢商很快就會從茅房出來，發現錢袋沒了，就會把女奴打得死去活來。看來，你現在做的事還不值得稱讚，要是你的騙術確實高明，你就回去，想法讓女奴不挨打。"小偷答道："如果天意如此，我可以救那女奴又拿了錢。"

---

2. Meseems：（古）= It seems to me that。

Then he went back to the money-changer's house and found him beating the girl, because of the bag of money; so he knocked at the door and the man said, "Who is there?" Quoth the thief, "I am the servant of thy neighbour in the bazaar." So he came out to him and said, "What is thy business?" "My master salutes thee," replied the thief, "and says to thee, 'Surely, thou art mad to cast the like of this bag of money down at the door of thy shop and go away and leave it! Had a stranger chanced on it, he had made off with it.' And except my master had seen it and taken care of it, it had been lost to thee." So saying, he pulled out the purse and showed it to the money-changer, who said, "That is indeed my purse," and put out his hand to take it; but the thief said, "By Allah, I will not give it thee, till thou write me a receipt; for I fear my master will not believe that thou hast duly received the purse, except I bring him a writing to that effect, under thy hand and seal." So the money-changer went in to write the receipt; but, in the meantime, the thief made off with the bag of money, having [thus] saved the slave-girl her beating.

於是他回到了錢商的家，發現他正為了那袋錢打女奴。他敲了敲門，那人問：“誰？”小偷說：“我是您在市場的鄰攤的傭人。”錢商就出來對他說：“甚麼事？”小偷答道：“我東家向您問好，並要我轉告：‘你把這一大袋錢丟在舖子門口就走開，不是真的發神經病了！要是給陌生人發現的話，他會把它偷走的。’要不是給我東家看到了，收起來的話，這錢就非丟不可。”說着，他掏出錢包給錢商看。錢商說：“這的確是我的錢包。”同時伸出手去接，但小偷說：“真主作證，您得親筆寫個收條，並蓋上印章，我才能給你，因為我怕我東家不相信您已收妥了錢包。”錢商就進去寫收條；就在這時，小偷帶着那袋錢溜走了，也使女奴逃過一頓打。

# 37 Donkey Transformed into a Human Being

*— The Donkey (1)*

It is related that a pair of tricksters once saw a simpleton leading a donkey by its halter along a deserted road. "I will steal that beast," said one of them to his companion, "and make an ass of[1] its master. Follow me and you shall see."

He went up behind the simpleton without a sound, and, deftly loosing the halter from the donkey, placed it round his own neck. He then jogged along as though nothing had happened.

When his friend had safely made off with the beast, the thief abruptly halted and would not yield to the repeated jerks of the rope. Looking over his shoulder, the simpleton was utterly confounded to see his donkey transformed into a human being.

"Who in heaven's name are you?" he cried.

---

1. make an ass of：愚弄，耍弄。ass 本意是"驢"，又作"笨人"解，這裏一語雙關。

## 三十七　驢變人

*—— 驢子的故事（一）*

傳說從前有兩個騙子看到一個傻子用韁繩牽着一頭驢在一條荒僻的路上走。一個騙子對他的同夥說，“我要偷那頭驢，還要把它的主人耍弄一頓。跟我來，瞧我的本事。”

他悄悄地走到傻子身後，靈巧地解開驢子的韁繩，把它纏到自己的脖子上，然後若無其事地慢慢向前走。

等同夥安全地偷走驢子之後，騙子突然停住腳步，任憑傻子怎麼拉韁繩也不肯往前走了。傻子回頭一看，發現自己的驢子變成了人，感到莫名其妙。

“天哪，你是誰？”他叫了起來。

"Sir," replied the thief, "I am your donkey; but my story is marvellously strange. It all happened one day when I returned home very drunk, as was my custom. My pious old mother received me with an indignant rebuke and pleaded with me against my evil ways. But I took up my staff and beat her. Whereupon she invoked Allah's vengeance and I was instantly transformed into the donkey which has faithfully served you all these years. Today the old woman must have taken pity on me and prayed to Allah to change me back into human shape."

驢子答道，“先生，我是你的驢；但我的經歷卻非同尋常。事情是這樣的：有一天，我像往常一樣酒醉回家。我那虔誠的老母親氣得把我罵了一頓，懇求我不要學壞。我卻拾起棒子打了她。因此，她祈求真主懲罰我，把我變成了驢，我這條驢就一直忠心耿耿地為您服務了這麼多年。今天，一定是老人太可憐我，祈求真主將我變回了人形。”

## 38 I Will Not Buy You a Second Time!

*— The Donkey (2)*

"There is no strength or help save[1] in Allah!" cried the simpleton. "I beg you to pardon the treatment you have received at my hands and all the hardships you have endured in my service."

He set the robber free, and returned home in a pitiful state of bewilderment and dejection.

"What has happened to you, and where is your donkey?" asked his wife.

When he had related to her the strange story, the woman began to wring her hands, crying: "The wrath of Allah will be upon us now for having used a human being so brutally." And she fell down penitently on her knees, reciting verses from the Koran[2].

For several days afterwards the simpleton stayed idle at home. At length his wife counselled him to go and buy another donkey in order that he might resume his work. So he went off to the market-place, and, as he was inspecting

---

1. save：介詞，作“除了”解。
2. the Koran：《可蘭經》或《古蘭經》，伊斯蘭教經典。

## 三十八　人又變驢

——*驢子的故事（二）*

“除了真主，誰也沒有力量來幫助你！”傻子叫道。“我求你原諒我對你的虐待和你為我幹活時所受到的痛苦。”

他把盜驢人放了，帶着迷茫和沮喪的神情回到家裏。

“你這是怎麼了？你的驢呢？”他妻子問道。

他向妻子講了這個離奇的故事之後，妻子扭着雙手哭道：“我們這樣殘暴地將一個人當驢使，真主會降怒於我們的。”然後，她懺悔地跪了下來，開始背誦《可蘭經》。

以後幾天，傻子閒居無事。最後，妻子勸他再去買一頭驢，好繼續幹活。於是，他來到集市上。就在他察看待

the animals put up for sale, he was astounded to see his own donkey amongst them. Having identified the beast beyond all doubt, the simpleton whispered in its ear:

"The Devil take you for an incorrigible wretch! Have you been drinking and beating you mother again? By Allah, I will not buy you a second time!"

出售的牲口時，他猛然發現自己的驢就在其中。在確認無疑之後，傻子對驢子附耳低聲説：

“讓魔鬼把你抓了去，你這不可救藥的壞蛋！，你是不是又酗酒並打你母親了？真主作證，我不會再買你了！”

# The Rich and the Poor
# 富人和窮人

# 39 The Fashions of the Magnanimous

Jaafer ben Mousa el Hadi[1] once had a slave-girl, a lute[2]-player, called El Bedr el Kebir, than whom there was not in her time a fairer of face nor a better-shaped nor a more elegant of manners nor a more accomplished in singing and smiting the strings; she was indeed perfect in beauty and charm. Mohammed el Amin[3] heard of her and was instant with Jaafer to sell her to him; but he replied, "Thou knowest it beseems not one of my rank to sell slave-girls nor traffic in concubines; but, were it not that she was reared in my house, I would send her to thee, as a gift, nor grudge her to thee."

Some days after this, El Amin went to Jaafer's house, to make merry; and the latter set before him that which it behoves to set before friends and bade El Bedr sing to him and gladden him. So she tuned the lute and sang right ravishingly; whilst El Amin fell to drinking and making merry and bade the cupbearers ply Jaafer with wine, till he became

---

1. Jaafer ben Mousa el Hadi：當時知名的語法學家和守舊主義者，後來成為邁蒙國王手下柯拉桑地方的總督。
2. lute：魯特琴: 十四至十七世紀西方流行的撥弦樂器。
3. Mohammed el Amin：雷希德宮中的總管。

## 三十九　富豪的派頭

從前，賈凡爾·莫薩·何迪有一個女奴，會彈弦琴，名叫愛貝德。她容貌美麗，身段窈窕，舉止文雅，能彈善唱，無人能比，真是個絕代佳人。穆罕默德·艾敏聽說了她，就要賈凡爾把她賣給他；但賈凡爾說"閣下知道，出賣女奴或拿侍妾作交易，對我的身份地位來說都是不適宜的。要不是她是在我家撫養長大的，我就會毫不吝嗇地把她當禮物送給你。"

過了幾天，艾敏去賈凡爾家玩，賈凡爾像對好朋友一樣款待他而且吩咐愛貝德唱歌助興。她調好弦，唱了起來，歌聲令人陶醉。艾敏開懷暢飲，老催斟酒者給賈凡爾

drunken, when he took the damsel and carried her to his own house, but laid not a finger on her. On the morrow, he sent to invite Jaafer; and when he came, he set wine before him and bade the girl sing to him, from behind the curtain. Jaafer knew her voice and was angered at this, but, of the nobleness of his nature and the greatness of his mind, he dissembled his vexation and let no change appear in his demeanour.

When the carousal was at an end, El Amin commanded one of his servants to fill the boat, in which Jaafer had come, with dirhems[1] and dinars and all manner[2] jewels and jacinths and rich clothes and other treasures of price till the boatmen cried out for quarter, saying, "The boat cannot hold any more;" whereupon he bade them carry all this to Jaafer's palace. Such are the fashions of the magnanimous.

---

1. dirhem(s)：亦作 dirham(s)，迪拉姆（一些阿拉伯國家的貨幣單位）。

2. all manner：= all manner of，各式各樣的。

上酒，直到把他灌得酩酊大醉，他就帶姑娘回到自己家裏，但沒敢碰她一個手指頭。第二天，他派人去邀請賈凡爾。賈凡爾來了以後，他設酒款待，並吩咐愛貝德在幕後彈唱。賈凡爾聽出是她的聲音，十分生氣。但是，由於他生性高貴，襟懷豁達，所以壓住了心中的不快，絲毫不動聲色。

席罷，艾敏吩咐僕人用金、銀、珠寶、綾羅綢緞以及其他值錢的東西裝滿賈凡爾來時所乘的船，直到船夫叫着："船不能再裝了"；然後艾敏吩咐他們把所有這些金銀珠寶都運到賈凡爾的宮中。這就是慷慨大度的富豪們的派頭。

# 40 The Khalif El Hakim and the Merchant

The Khalif[1] El Hakim bi Amrillah was riding out in state[2] one day, when he came to a garden, in which he saw a man, surrounded by slaves and servants. He asked him for a draught of water, and the man gave him to drink, saying, "Peradventure[3], the Commander of the Faithful will honour me by alighting in this my garden." So the Khalif dismounted and entered the garden with his suite; whereupon the man brought out to them a hundred carpets and a hundred leather mats and a hundred cushions and set before them a hundred dishes of fruits, a hundred saucers of sweetmeats and a hundred bowls full of sherbets of sugar; whereat the Khalif marvelled and said to his host, "O man, this thy case is a strange one. Didst thou know of our coming and make this preparation for us?" "No, by Allah, O Commander of the Faithful," answered the other, "I knew not of thy coming and am but a merchant of the rest of thy subjects. But I have a

---

1. Khalif：又作 Khaliph, Calif, Khalifat；伊斯蘭教統治者或教主。
2. in state：隆重地。
3. peradventure：（古）= perhaps.

# 四十　國王與商人

一天，哈金阿姆利拉國王帶着全副儀仗騎馬出遊。他來到一座花園時，看到一個人身邊圍繞着一大羣奴僕。國王向他要一口水喝，那人就給了他水，説：“不知陛下肯否賞光駕幸草民的花園？”於是，國王就下馬並在隨從的陪同下進了花園。那人給他們拿來一百條毯子、一百張皮蓆、一百個坐墊，並在他們面前擺上一百盤水果、一百碟甜食和一百碗果汁。國工大為驚奇，對主人説：“奇怪，你難道事先知我來而作了這些準備？”那人答道：“不，陛下，真主作證，我不知道您要來，我只不過是個商人，

hundred concubines; so, when the Commander of the Faithful honoured me by alighting with me, I sent to each of them, bidding her send me the morning-meal here. So they sent me each of her furniture and of the excess of her meat and drink: and every day each sends me a dish of meat and another of marinades, also a plate of fruits and a saucer of sweetmeats and a bowl of sherbet. This is my every-day noon-meal, nor have I added aught thereto for thee."

The Khalif prostrated himself in thanksgiving to God the Most High and said, "Praised be God, who hath been so bountiful to one of our subjects, that he entertaineth[4] the Khalif and his suite, without making ready for them, but of the surplus of his day's victual!" Then he sent for all the dirhems in the treasury, that had been struck that year, — and they were in number three thousand and seven hundred thousand; — nor did he mount, till the money came, when he gave it to the merchant, saying, "Use this for the maintenance of thy state; and thy desert[5] is more than this." Then he mounted and rode away.

---

4. entertaineth：（古）= entertain（-eth 是動詞後綴，用於第三人稱單數現在式）。

5. desert：應得的。

像您的其他子民一樣。但我有一百個侍妾，所以當陛下賞光隨我下馬時，我派人向她們每人傳話，吩咐把早餐給我送到這裏來。所以她們每人就給我送來了自己的用具和吃喝；每天她們每人給我送來一盤肉和一碟鹵汁，還有一盆水果和一碟甜食和一碗果汁。這就是我每天的午餐，我並沒有特意為您多準備甚麼。”

國王跪下來感謝上蒼，說：“讚美真主祂對我的這一個子民如此慷慨，使他可以用他每天多餘的食物來款待國王及其隨從，而無需作準備。”隨後，他吩咐把國庫裏當年鑄造的三百七十萬個銅幣都拿來給了商人，說：“就用這錢來維持你的氣派吧。你應該得到更多。”說完，他就上馬走了。

# 41 The Niggard and the Loaves of Bread

There was once a merchant, who was niggardly in his eating and drinking. One day, he went on a journey to a certain town and as he walked in the market streets, he came upon an old woman with two cakes of bread. He asked her if they were for sale, and she said, "Yes." So he chaffered with her and bought them at a low price and took them home to his lodging, where he ate them that day. On the morrow, he returned to the same place and finding the old woman there with other two cakes, bought these also; and thus he did twenty days' space, at the end of which time the old woman disappeared. He made enquiry for her, but could hear nothing of her, till, one day, as he was walking about the streets, he chanced upon her; so he accosted her and asked why she had ceased to attend the market and bring him the two cakes of bread. At first, she evaded giving him a reply; but he conjured her to tell him; so she said, "Know, O my lord, that I was attending upon a certain man, who had an ulcer on his spine, and his doctor used to knead flour with butter into a plaster and lay it on the place of the pain, where it abode all night. In the morning, I used to take the flour and make it into two cakes, which I sold to thee or another; but presently the man

# 四十一　吝嗇鬼和麵包

從前有個商人，吃喝都極吝嗇。有一天他出門到一市鎮，在市場上碰見一個老婦人，拿着兩塊麵包。他問她這麵包賣不賣，她回答，“賣。”於是他向她討價還價，最後花很少的錢買到了麵包，把麵包拿回家，當天就吃掉了。第二天他又到老地方，看到那位老婦人又拿着兩塊麵包在賣。他又買了這兩塊麵包。就這樣他一連買了二十天。後來這老婦人就不見了。他到處打聽她，都沒有她的消息。後來有一天他正在街上逛，突然碰見了她，便問她為甚麼不來市場上賣麵包給他。起初，老婦人不肯回答，但他一再要求告訴他原因，她說“好吧，先生！我原先一直在照顧一個病人，他脊背上長了一個惡瘡。醫生用麵粉加一點黃油和成膏藥貼在他疼痛的地方，敷上一夜。第二天我就用這塊麵粉做成兩塊麵包賣出去。不久這人死了，

died and I was cut off from making the cakes." When the merchant heard this, he repented, whenas repentance availed nothing. And he repeated the saying of the Most High, "Whatsoever betideth thee of good, it is from God and whatsoever betideth thee of ill, it is from thyself."

我也不能做麵包了。”商人聽見此話，十分後悔，但已於事無補了。他反覆引述真主的話：“好事由天賜，惡果皆自尋。”

# 42 Shacabac Caught the Spirit of the Barmecide's Jest

*— The Barmecide Feast (1)*

Now, I will tell the story of my sixth brother, called Shacabac. After beginning his life in comfort, a reverse of fortune brought him to beg his bread. One day as he passed a great house, with many servants standing within its spacious court, he went to one of them, and asked him to whom the house belonged.

"Good man," replied the servant, "whence do you come that you ask me such a question? Does not all that you see tell you that it is the palace of a Barmecide[1]?"

My brother, knowing well how generous all the Barmecides were, prayed one of the gate-keepers at once to give him an alms. "Go in," said the man; "nobody hinders you, and speak to the master of the house; he will send you back satisfied."

---

1. a Barmecide：一位波斯王子，假意請乞丐飲宴，但不給食物，僅以想像，畫餅充飢。故一種虛偽的殷勤、好意，或口惠而實不至的慷慨就稱為“a Barmecide feast”。

# 四十二　拿窮人開心

*——巴氏宴（一）*

現在，我開始講我六弟夏克巴的故事。他早年生活優裕，後來運氣逆轉，淪落到以乞討為生。一天，他經過一幢大廈，看到寬敞的院子裏站着許多僕人。他走到一個僕人面前，問大廈的主人是誰。

僕人答道：“先生，你是哪兒來的，居然連這都不知道？你看這個排場，難道還看不出這是巴米賽德的宮殿嗎？”

我弟弟知道巴米賽德一家人都樂善好施，就馬上求一個門房給他一點施捨。那人說：“進去吧，沒人會攔住你的。你直接去對老爺說，他會讓你滿意的。”

My brother, who expected no such politeness, thanked the porter, and entered the palace. He went on till he came to a richly furnished hall, at the upper end of which he saw an old man, with a long, white beard, sitting on a sofa. He thought it must be the master of the house, and indeed it was the Barmecide himself, who said to my brother, in a very civil manner, that he was welcome, and asked him what he wanted.

"My lord," answered my brother, "I am a poor man who needs help. I swear to you I have not eaten one bit to-day."

"Is it true," demanded the Barmecide, "that you are fasting till now? Alas, the poor man is ready to die for hunger! Ho, boy!" cried he, with a loud voice, "bring a basin and water at once, that we may wash our hands."

Though no boy appeared, and my brother saw neither water nor basin, the Barmecide fell to rubbing his hands as if one had poured water upon them, and bade my brother come and wash with him. Shacabac caught the spirit of the Barmecide's jest, and knowing that the poor must please the rich, if they would have anything from them, came forward and did as he was bidden.

"Come on," said the Barmecide, "bring us something to eat, and do not let us wait." Then, though nothing appeared, he began to eat, as if something had been brought him upon a plate, and putting his hand to his mouth, began to eat; and said to my brother:—

我弟弟沒想到會對他這麼客氣，就謝過門房，進了宮裏。他一直走到一間陳設富麗堂皇的大廳，看到大廳上首的一張沙發上坐着一位有長長的白鬍子的老者。他想那一定是這裏的主人，實際上那正是巴米賽德本人。他很客氣地對我弟弟說，他歡迎他來，並問他要甚麼。

我弟弟回答：“老爺，我是個窮人，來求你救濟。我向你發誓我今天還沒吃過一點東西。”

巴米賽德問：“你真的到現在還沒吃東西嗎？唉呀，這可憐的人快餓死了！來人哪！”他高聲叫道：“馬上端盆水來讓我們洗手。”

雖然並沒人前來，我弟弟也沒見甚麼水和盆，但巴米賽德開始搓着雙手，就好像有人在給他倒水似的，還叫我弟弟來跟他一起洗。夏克巴對巴米賽德的玩笑心領神會，明白窮人如果有求於富人就必須討他們的歡心，所以就走過來照他的吩咐做。

巴米賽德說：“來啊，快給我們拿點吃的來，別讓我們等着。”然後，儘管甚麼也沒拿來，他開始吃起來，就像已經給他端來了一盤食物。他一面裝着把食物送向嘴裏，一面對我弟弟說：

"Come, friend, eat as freely as if you were at home; you said you were almost dying of hunger, but you eat as if you had no appetite."

"Pardon me, my lord," said Shacabac, who perfectly imitated what he did. "You see I lose no time, and that I play my part[2] well enough."

"How like you this bread?" said the Barmecide. "Do not you find it very good?"

"O my lord," replied my brother, who saw neither bread nor meat, "I have never eaten anything so white and so fine."

"Eat your fill," said the Barmecide. "I assure you that it cost me five hundred pieces of gold to purchase the woman who bakes me this good bread."

Soon the Barmecide called for another dish, and my brother went on eating, only in idea[3]. There was never better mutton and barley broth, the Barmecide said, and my brother assented....

"You honor me by eating so heartily," said the Barmecide. "Ho, boy, bring us more meat."

"No, my lord, if it please you," replied my brother, "for indeed I can eat no more."

---

2. I play my part：原義是“我扮演我的角色”但也理解為“我吃我的一部分”，一語雙關。

3. in idea：在想像中。

“請，朋友，隨便吃吧，就像在自己家裏一樣。你剛才說你都快餓死了，但你吃東西的樣子卻像沒胃口似的。”

“對不起，老爺，”夏克巴說，完全模仿着主人的樣子。“您瞧我這不是一刻不停地在吃着嗎？”

巴米賽德問：“你覺得這麵包怎麼樣？你不覺得很好吃嗎？”

我弟弟既沒看到麵包也沒看到肉，但還是回答：“老爺，我從來沒吃過這麼白這麼好吃的麵包。”

“那就吃個夠，”巴米賽德說。“我告訴你，買烤這麵包的女人花了我五百金幣呢。”

不一會兒，巴米賽德叫上另一道菜，我弟弟也就繼續裝模作樣地吃。巴米賽德說大麥羊肉湯再好沒有了，我弟弟就連忙表示同意。……

巴米賽德說：“你吃得這麼開心，我很榮幸。來人哪，再上點肉。”

“不了，老爺，如果你不介意的話，”我弟弟答道。“我實在不能再吃了。”

"Come, then," said the Barmecide, "and bring the fruit." When he had waited long enough for the servants to appear again, he said to my brother: "Taste these almonds. They are good and fresh gathered. Look, here are all sorts of fruits, cakes, and sweetmeats. Take what you like."

"My lord," replied Shacabac, whose jaws ached with moving and having nothing to eat, "I assure you I am so full that I cannot eat one bit more."

“那麼就來點兒水果吧。”他假裝等了一會兒，讓僕人端來水果以後，對我弟弟說：“嚐嚐這杏子。這是剛從樹上摘下來的。瞧，還有各種別的水果、糕點和甜食。隨便吃吧。”

“老爺，我實在飽得一點也吃不下了，”夏克巴說，他的牙關因未吃東西卻上下嚼動而疼痛起來。

## 43 He Gave the Barmecide Such a Box on the Ear

*— The Barmecide Feast (2)*

"Well then, friend," the Barmecide went on, "we must drink some wine now, after we have eaten so well."

"I see you will have nothing wanting," said Shacabac, "to make your treat complete; but since I am not used to drinking wine, I am afraid I may not act with the respect that is due to you[1]. Therefore let me be content with water."

"No, no!" said the Barmecide; "you shall drink wine;" and at the same time he commanded some to be brought, as the meat and fruit had been served before. He made as if he poured out for both, and said, "Drink my health[2], and let us know if you think this wine good."

My brother pretended to take the glass, and looked to see if the color was good, and put it to his nose, to try the flavor. He then made a low bow to the Barmecide, to show that he took the liberty to drink his health; and then drank with all the signs of a man that drinks with pleasure.

---

1. with the respect that is due to you：給你應得的，或適合你的身份的一份尊敬。

2. Drink my health：亦作 Drink to my health。

# 四十三　還以顏色

*——巴氏宴（二）*

“那好吧，朋友，”巴米賽德接着說：“既然吃好了，現在我們得喝點酒了。”

夏克巴說：“我明白您是非要把這頓飯吃得樣樣齊全、一無所缺不可。但是我不習慣喝酒，我怕自己會酒後失態。所以我還是喝水吧。”

“不行，不行，”巴米賽德說。“你一定要喝酒。”說完，他就命人拿酒來，就像剛才命人上菜上水果一樣。他假裝給兩個人都倒了酒，說：“為我的健康乾杯，你看看這酒好不好。”

我弟弟假裝拿起酒杯，看看酒的顏色好不好，又放在鼻子下面聞聞香味。然後他向巴米賽德深深鞠了一躬，表示他冒昧為他的健康乾杯，然後煞有介事地開懷暢飲。

"My lord," said he, "this is very excellent wine, but I think it is not strong enough."

"If you would have stronger," answered the Barmecide, "you need only speak, for I have several sorts in my cellar. Try how you like this."

Then he made as if he poured out another glass for himself and one for my brother, and did this so often that Shacabac, feigning that the wine had gone to his head, lifted up his hand, like a drunken man, and gave the Barmecide such a box on the ear as made him fall down. He was going to give him another blow; but the Barmecide, holding up his hand to ward it off, cried: "Are you mad?"

Then my brother, making as if he had come to himself again, said, "My lord, you have been so good as to admit your slave into your house, and give him a treat. You should have been content with making me eat, and not have forced me to drink wine; for I told you that it might cause me to fail in my respect to you. I am very sorry for it, and beg you a thousand pardons."

When he had finished these words, the Barmecide, instead of being angry, began to laugh with all his might. "I have been long," said he, "seeking a man of your sort. I not only forgive you the blow you have given me, but I desire that we may be friends from this time forth, and that you take my house for your home. You have had the good nature

他說：“老爺，這酒好極了，但我覺得淡了點。”

巴米賽德答道：“如果你想喝烈酒，只管說，我地窖裏有好幾種呢。再嚐嚐這個怎麼樣。”

然後，他裝着又給自己斟上一杯，給我弟弟也倒了一杯。這樣幾次以後，夏克巴假裝酒上了頭，像個醉漢似的舉手重重地給了巴米賽德一個耳光，把他打倒在地。他正要再給他一巴掌，巴米賽德急忙舉手擋開，喊道：“你瘋啦？”

然後我弟弟假裝清醒過來，說：“老爺，您好意讓我這奴才進了府上，還請我吃飯。您本應只讓我吃飯，而不要強勸我喝酒，因為我告訴過您我怕酒後失態。這，實在對不起了，求您千萬原諒。”

他說完後，巴米賽德非但沒有生氣，反而哈哈大笑起來，一面說：“我找你這樣的人找了很長時間了。我不但原諒你打了我一巴掌，而且還希望從此以後我們成為朋友，你可以把我這裏當作自己的家。你脾氣好，能投我所

to adapt yourself to my humors, and the patience to keep the jest up to the last. We will now eat in good earnest."

Then he clapped his hands and commanded his servants, who appeared at once, to cover the table, and my brother was really treated with all the dishes of which before he had eaten only in fancy. Wine and music followed, and the Barmecide's goodness to my brother did not stop there, for finding him to be a man of wit and sense, he soon gave him the care of his household, and for twenty years, until the Barmecide's death, Shacabac performed his duties well.

好，而且有耐性把這場玩笑開到底。現在，我們真的吃飯吧。”

說完，他拍拍手，命僕人馬上擺桌上菜。這一回我弟弟真的吃到了剛才只是假裝吃的那些菜了。飯後還有酒和音樂助興。巴米賽德對我弟弟的關照還不止於此；他認為我弟弟是個才識兼備的人材，不久任命他為自己的管家，而夏克巴也盡心盡職地為他服務了二十年，直到巴米賽德逝世。

## 44 The Barmecide and the Poor Man

Yehya ben Khalid the Barmecide was returning home, one day, from the Khalif's palace, when he saw a man at the gate of his house, who rose at his approach and saluted him, saying, "O Yehya, I am in need of that which is in thy hand, and I make God my intermediary with thee." So Yehya caused set apart a place for him in his house and bade his treasurer carry him a thousand dirhems every day and that his food should be of the choicest of his own meat. The man abode thus a whole month, at the end of which time, having received in all thirty thousand dirhems, he departed by stealth, fearing lest Yehya should take the money from him, because of the greatness of the sum; and when they told Yehya of this, he said, "By Allah, though he had tarried with me to the end of his days, yet had I not scanted him of my largesse nor cut off from him the bounties of my hospitality!" For, indeed, the excellences of the Barmecides were past count nor can their virtues be told; especially those of Yehya ben Khalid, for he abounded in noble qualities, even as saith[1] the poet of him:

---

1. saith：（古）= says。

## 四十四　富人與窮漢

一天，富翁葉亞·卡列德從王宮回家，看到一個人在他家門口。他走近時，那人站起來向他打招呼說：“葉亞，我需要你的幫助，是上帝介紹我來見你的。”葉亞命人給他在家裏安排地方並吩咐賬房每天給他一千塊錢，並用他本人專用的最好食品招待他。這人住了整整一個月，到月末他已積蓄了三萬塊錢。因為這是一筆巨款，他害怕葉亞又要回去，便偷偷溜走了。僕人將此事報告了葉亞，他說：“真主作證，即使在我這裏住一輩子，我給他的錢也不會減少，更不會停止我對他的款待！”巴米賽德家族的美德，特別是葉亞的高尚品德，真是數不清，講不完啊！有詩為證：

*I asked munificence, "Art free?" It answered, "No, perdie[2]! Yehya ben Khalid's slave am I; my lord and master he."*
*"A boughten[3] slave?" asked I; but, "Nay, so heaven forfend[4]!" quoth it. "From ancestor to ancestor he did inherit me."*

---

2. perdie：（古）= pardi，當然。
3. boughten：（古）= bought。
4. forfend：（古）禁止；這裏也可直譯為“不，天意不准這樣説。”

我向慷慨問："你可自由？"

它回答："當然不，我是葉亞的奴；他是我的主"。

我又問："一個買來的奴僕？"

它答道："絕對不是，我是他家代代相傳的家奴。"

# 45 The Sons of Yehya Ben Khalid

I was once, in very narrow case and greatly oppressed with debts, that had accumulated upon me and that I had no means of discharging. My doors were blocked up with creditors and I was without cease importuned for payment by claimants, who dunned me in crowds, till I was at my wits' end what to do. At last, being sore perplexed and troubled, I betook myself to Abdallah ben Malik el Khuzai and besought him to aid me with his judgment and of his good counsel direct me to the door of relief; and he said, "None can quit thee of this thy strait but the Barmecides." Quoth I, "Who can brook their pride and put up with their arrogance?" And he answered, "Thou must put up with it, for the sake of amending thy case." So I left him and went straight to El Fezl and Jaafer, sons of Yehya ben Khalid, to whom I related my case. "God give thee His aid," answered they, "and enable thee by His bounties to dispense with the aid of His creatures and vouchsafe thee abundant good and bestow on thee what shall suffice thee, without the need of any but Himself; for He can what He will and is gracious and provident with His servants."

## 四十五　絕境遇貴人

我曾一度窮困潦倒，債台高築，無法償還。討債的人堵住了我的門，或在大庭廣眾之中不斷地纏住我要我還錢，我走投無路，一籌莫展。最後我被弄得傷透了腦筋，才去找阿卜杜拉·庫柴，求他想個好辦法幫我解困。他說：“只有巴米賽德家族才能幫你度過難關”。我說：“誰受得了他們那種趾高氣揚的傲慢態度啊？”他答道：“為了挽救你自己，你必須忍受。”於是我起身告辭，徑直去找葉海亞·哈里德的兒子埃佛茲爾和賈凡爾，向他們講了我的處境。“真主會幫助你的”，他們說，“祂的恩賜足以使你無需求別人幫助，並且讓你豐衣足食，而不必仰他人的鼻息，因為凡是祂要做的，祂都能做到，而且祂對祂的僕人向來是慈悲為懷的。”

I went out from them and returned to Abdallah, disappointed and perplexed and heavy at heart, and told him what they had said. Quoth he, "Thou wouldst do well to abide with us this day, that we may see what God the Most High will decree." So I sat with him awhile, and lo, up came my servant, who said to me, "O my lord, there are at our door many laden mules, and with them a man, who says he is the agent of Fezl and Jaafer ben Yehya." Quoth Abdallah, "I trust that relief is come to thee: go and see what is to do." So I left him and running to my house, found at the door a man, who gave me a letter, wherein was written the following: "Know that, after thou hadst been with us and acquainted us with thy case, we betook ourselves to the Khalif and informed him that the case had reduced thee to the humiliation of begging; whereupon he ordered thee a million dirhems from the Treasury. We represented to him that thou wouldst spend this money in paying thy creditors and said, 'Whence shall he provide for his subsistence?' So he ordered thee other three hundred thousand, and we have sent thee, of our own money, a million dirhems each, so that thou hast now three million and three hundred thousand dirhems, wherewithal to order thine affair and amend thine estate."

See, then, the munificence of these generous men: may God the Most High have mercy on them!

我辭別他們，回到阿卜杜拉家中，垂頭喪氣，憂心如焚，把他們的話告訴阿卜杜拉。他說：“你今天應當呆在我家中，讓我們看看真主的安排”。我就和他坐了一會兒，這時，我的僕人突然來到，對我說：“主人，我們門口來了許多裝有馱子的騾馬，趕馬的人說他是埃佛茲爾和賈凡爾派來的人。”阿卜杜拉說：“我看這是你的救星到了，快去看看吧！”於是我告別了阿卜杜拉，一路跑回家，到了家門口，有個人遞給我一封信，上面寫着：“你到我們家談了你的困境後，我就去見了國王，向他奏明你現在的處境已使你幾乎淪為乞丐，他聽後命令從國庫中撥出一百萬迪拉姆給你。我們報告說，這筆錢只能還債，生活問題仍不能解決。於是他吩咐再加三十萬。此外，我們兄弟每人送你一百萬迪拉姆，如今你就得到共計三百三十萬迪拉姆，供你作還債及生活之用。”

瞧！這些慷慨的人多麼大量。願真主保佑他們！

# 46 The Poor Man and His Generous Friend

There was once a rich man, who lost all he had and became poor, whereupon his wife counselled him to seek aid of one of his friends. So he betook himself to a certain friend of his and acquainted him with his strait; and he lent him five hundred dinars to trade withal. Now he had aforetime been a jeweller; so he took the money and went to the jewel-bazaar, where he opened a shop to buy and sell. Presently, three men accosted him, as he sat in his shop, and asked for his father. He told them that he was dead, and they said, "Did he leave any offspring?" Quoth the jeweller, "He left a son, your servant." "And who knoweth thee for his son?" asked they. "The people of the bazaar," replied he; and they said, "Call them together, that they may testify to us that thou art his son." So he called them and they bore witness of this; whereupon the three men delivered to him a pair of saddle-bags, containing thirty thousand dinars, besides jewels and bullion, saying, "This was deposited with us in trust by thy father." Then they went away; and presently there came to him a woman, who sought of him certain of the jewels, worth five hundred dinars, and paid him three thousand for them.

## 四十六　窮人和他慷慨的朋友

從前有個富人，他後來失去了一切，變得一貧如洗。他的妻子要他去找朋友幫忙。他就去找了一位朋友，對他說了困難，朋友借給他五百第納爾去做生意。他以前曾是個珠寶商，所以他拿着錢到了珠寶集市，在那裏開了一個店鋪做買賣。不久，當他坐在店子裏有三個人來到他面前找他的父親。他告訴他們父親已死了。他們問："他有子女嗎？"珠寶商答道："他有個兒子，就是在下。"他們問："誰知道你就是他的兒子呢？""集市裏的人都知道。"他答道。他們說："那把他們叫來，好證明你是他的兒子。"他就把他們叫來並且都作了證。於是這三個人交給他一對鞍囊，裏面裝有三萬第納爾，還有珠寶和金塊，說："這是你父親存在我們那裏的。"然後他們就走了。過了一會兒，來了一位婦人，她選購了一些珠寶，值五百第納爾，但付給他三千第納爾。

So he took five hundred dinars and carrying them to his friend, who had lent him the money, said to him, "Take the five hundred dinars I borrowed of thee; for God hath aided and prospered me." "Not so," quoth the other. "I gave them to thee outright, for the love of God; so do thou keep them. And take this paper, but read it not, till thou be at home, and do according to that which is therein." So he took the paper and returned home, where he opened it and read therein the following verses:

*The men who came to thee at first my kinsmen were, my sire*[1]*,*
*His brother and my dam's, Salih ben Ali is his name.*
*Moreover, she to whom thou soldst the goods my mother was,*
*And eke the jewels and the gold, from me, to boot, they came;*
*Nor, in thus ordering myself to thee, aught did I seek*
*Save of*[2] *the taking it*[3] *from me to spare thee from the shame.*

---

1. sire：（古）＝ father，senior。
2. Save of：（古）按現代英文文法應為 to save。
3. the taking it：（古）按現代英文文法應為 the taking of it。

後來他拿了五百第納爾去找借錢給他的朋友，對他說：“請收下我向你借的那五百第納爾，主已經幫助了我，使我發了財。”“不要這樣，”他朋友說，“出於對主的愛，我已把錢給了你，你就留着吧！把這張紙條拿去，但先不要看，等你到家時再看，然後照上面寫的辦。”他拿了紙條，回到家裏，打開紙條，上面寫着如下詩句：

初訪者家嚴，
沙里是其名，
隨同有叔舅，
買珠乃母親，
贈金本我願，
免君難為情。

# 47 Jaafer and the Beanseller

When Haroun er Reshid put Jaafer to death, he commanded that all who wept or made moan for him should be crucified; so the folk abstained from this. Now there was a Bedouin from a distant desert, who used every year to make and bring to Jaafer an ode in his honour, for which he rewarded him with a thousand dinars; and the Bedouin took them and returning to his own country, lived upon them, he and his family, for the rest of the year. Accordingly, he came with his ode at the wonted time and finding Jaafer done to death, betook himself to the place where his body was hanging, and there made his camel kneel down and wept sore and mourned grievously. Then he recited his ode and fell asleep. In his sleep Jaafer appeared to him and said, "Thou hast wearied thyself to come to us and findest[1] us as thou seest; but go to Bassora and ask for such a man there of the merchants of the town and say to him, 'Jaafer salutes thee and bids thee give me a thousand dinars, by the token of the bean.'"

---

1. findest：（古）＝ find〔-(e)st 是動詞後綴，構成陳述語氣第二人稱單數形式，如下文中的 seest〕。

## 四十七　嘉佛與賣豆人

當哈隆・雷切德國王判處嘉佛死罪時，他命令凡是為嘉佛哭喪的人要被釘死在十字架上。所以老百姓都不敢為他哭喪。這時，從遠方的沙漠來了一個貝督因人。他過去每年都來為嘉佛作頌詞，嘉佛就獎他一千第納爾。他把錢拿回去作為他全家一年的生活費。這次他又按時帶了頌詞來，方知嘉佛已被處死。他來到嘉佛屍體被吊的地方，讓他的駱駝跪下，就痛哭盡哀。然後他吟誦了頌詞就睡着了。睡夢中嘉佛來到他面前對他說，“你不辭勞累一趟來找我們，看到我們已成這樣。不過你可到巴索拉去找那裏的一個商人，對他說，‘嘉佛向你致意，並要你給我一千第納爾，以豆子為憑。’”

When the Bedouin awoke, he repaired to Bassora, where he sought out the merchant and repeated to him what Jaafer had said in the dream; whereupon he wept sore, till he was like to depart the world. Then he welcomed the Bedouin and entertained him three days as an honoured guest; and when he was minded to depart, he gave him a thousand and five hundred dinars, saying, "The thousand are what is commanded to thee, and the five hundred are a gift from me to thee; and every year thou shalt have of me a thousand dinars." When the Bedouin was about to take leave, he said to the merchant, "I conjure thee, by Allah, tell me the story of the bean, that I may know the origin of all this."

"In the early part of my life," replied the merchant, "I was miserably poor and hawked hot boiled beans about the streets of Baghdad for a living.

"I went out one cold, rainy day, without clothes enough on my body to protect me from the weather, now shivering for excess of cold and now stumbling into the pools of rain-water, and altogether in so piteous a plight as would make one shudder to look upon. Now it chanced that Jaafer was seated that day, with his officers and favourites, in an upper chamber overlooking the street, and his eye fell on me; so he took pity on my case and sending one of his servants to fetch me to him, said to me, 'Sell thy beans to my people.' So I

貝督因人醒來後就去了巴索拉，找到了那個商人，把嘉佛在夢中對他說的話向商人說了一遍，商人聽後，哭得死去活來。然後商人歡迎貝督因人，把他當上賓款待了三天。他要走時，商人給了他一千五百第納爾，說，“一千是嘉佛要我給你的，另外五百是我送你的，而且今後每年你都會從我這裏得到一千第納爾。”貝督因人告別時，對商人說，“求你告訴我豆子的故事，我好知道這一切的原委。”

商人答道：“早年我很窮，在巴格達沿街叫賣熱煮豆謀生。有一天我出外叫賣，天氣寒冷，還下着雨，我衣服單薄，凍得直發抖，在雨水坑裏蹣跚，那副可憐相真叫人慘不忍睹。湊巧那天嘉佛和他的管事和妻妾們坐在臨街的樓房裏，看見了我。他很可憐我，就吩咐他的僕人把我帶到他面前，對我說：‘把豆子賣給我們吧！’我就用隨身

began to mete out the beans with a measure I had with me, and each who took a measure of beans filled the vessel with gold pieces, till the basket was empty. Then I gathered together the money I had gotten, and Jaafer said to me, 'Hast thou any beans left?' 'I know not,' answered I and sought in the basket, but found only one bean. This Jaafer took and splitting it in twain[2], kept one half himself and gave the other to one of his favourites, saying, 'for how much wilt thou buy this half-bean?' 'For the tale[3] of all this money twice-told[4],' replied she; whereat I was confounded and said in myself, 'This is impossible.' But, as I stood wondering, she gave an order to one of her handmaids and the girl brought me the amount twice-told. Then said Jaafer, 'And I will buy my half for twice the sum of the whole. Take the price of thy bean.' And he gave an order to one of his servants, who gathered together the whole of the money and laid it in my basket; and I took it and departed. Then I betook myself to Bassora, where I traded with the money and God prospered me, to Him be the praise and the thanks! So, if I give thee a thousand dinars a year of the bounty of Jaafer, it will in no wise irk me."

---

2. twain：（古）= two。
3. tale：總數，數目。
4. twice-told：= twofold，double。

帶的缶子把豆子量出去。每位拿了一缶豆子的人都往缶子裏裝滿金幣。最後籃子空了，我就把得到的金幣聚攏來。嘉佛對我說‘你還有豆子嗎？’‘不知道。’我答道。我在籃子裏找，只找到一粒豆。嘉佛把豆子拿去，分成兩半，自己留了一半，另一半給了他的一位侍妾，說‘你給多少錢買這半粒豆了？’‘全部錢數的兩倍，’她答道。我聽見後惶恐不安，心想，‘這不可能。’但我正在不知所措時，她已令她的一個女侍拿來了兩倍的錢，然後嘉佛說，‘我要用總數的兩倍價錢買下這半粒豆，你把賣豆的錢都拿去吧！’他命令一個僕人把所有的錢收好，放在我的籃子裏，我拿了籃子就離開了。後來，我到了巴索拉，用這筆錢做生意，謝天謝地，真主保佑我發了財。為了報答嘉佛的恩情，我每年給你一千第納爾，我是毫不吝嗇的。”

Consider then the munificence of Jaafer's nature and how he was praised both alive and dead, the mercy of God the Most High be upon him!

你想想嘉佛生性多麼慷慨大方，不論活着還是死後，他都受人讚揚，願真主憐憫他！

## 48 Generosity after Death

It is told of Hatim et Tai[1], that when he died, they buried him on the top of a mountain and set over his grave two troughs hewn out of two rocks and stone figures of women with dishevelled hair. At the foot of the hill was a stream of running water, and when wayfarers camped there, they heard loud crying in the night, from dark till daybreak; but when they arose in the morning, they found nothing but the girls carved in stone. Now when Dhoulkeraa, King of Himyer, going forth of his tribe, came to the valley, he halted to pass the night there and drawing near the mountain, heard the crying and said, "What lamenting is that on yonder hill?" They answerd him, saying, "This is the tomb of Hatim et Tai and all who camp in this place by night hear this crying and lamenting." So he said jestingly, "O Hatim et Tai, we are thy guests this night, and we are lank with hunger." Then sleep overcame him, but presently he awoke in affright and cried out, saying, "Help, O Arabs! Look at my beast!" So they came to him and finding his she-camel struggling in the death-

1. Hatim et Tai：海蒂姆・泰是六世紀下半葉的一個著名阿拉伯酋長，因其慷慨好客而遠近聞名，死於穆罕默德出世數年後。

# 四十八　死後的慷慨

傳說海蒂姆·泰死後人們把他埋在山頂上，並在墳墓上安放兩個石槽和一些頭髮蓬亂的石雕女人像。山腳下有淙淙流淌的溪水，徒步旅行者在這裏宿營時，夜間會聽見很響的哭啼聲，從天黑直到天明；但當他們早晨起來，卻甚麼也沒有，只有石雕女像。後來希米爾王道凱拉帶領他的部落來到這個山谷，他停下來要在這裏過夜。當他走近這山時，聽見了哭啼聲，便問，“那邊山上出了甚麼事這麼悲痛？”他們回答道，“這是海蒂姆·泰的墳地，晚上在這裏宿營的人都會聽到這種悲哭聲。”道凱拉開玩笑說，“海蒂姆·泰，我們今晚做你的客人，我們都餓壞了！”然後他就睡着了，但不久他就驚醒起來，大叫，“救命！阿拉伯人！快來看我的駱駝！”隨從們來到他那裏，見到他的母駱駝正在痛苦地垂死掙扎，於是他們就殺

agony, slaughtered it and roasted its flesh and ate. Then they asked him what had happened and he said, "When I closed my eyes, I saw in my sleep Hatim et Tai, who came to me with a sword in his hand and said to me, 'Thou comest to us and we have nothing by us.' Then he smote my she-camel with his sword, and she would have died, though ye had not come to her and cut her throat." Next morning the prince mounted the beast of one of his companions and taking the latter up behind him, set out and fared on till midday, when they saw a man coming towards them, mounted on a camel and leading another, and said to him, "Who art thou?" "I am Adi, son of Hatim et Tai," answered he. "Where is Dhoulkeraa, Prince of Himyer?" "This is he," replied they, and he said to the prince, "Take this camel in place of thine own, which my father slaughtered for thee." "Who told thee of this?" asked Dhoulkeraa, and Adi answered, "My father appeared to me in a dream last night and said to me, 'Hark ye, Adi; Dhoulkeraa, King of Himyer, sought hospitality of me and I, having nought to give him, slaughtered him his she-camel, that he might eat; so do thou carry him a she-camel to ride, for I have nothing.'" And Dhoulkeraa took her, marvelling at the generosity of Hatim et Tai, alive and dead.

了駱駝，把肉烤着吃了。然後他們問他出了甚麼事，他説，“我閉上眼睛後，睡夢中看見海蒂姆．泰向我走來，手中拿着一把劍，對我說，‘你到我這裏來了，可是我們甚麼也沒有。’然後他就用劍狠狠擊打我的駱駝，即使你們不來割斷她的喉嚨，她也會死的。”第二天早晨，國王只好騎着同伴的駱駝上路，帶着身後的隨從；他們一直走到中午，見到一個人向他們走來。這人騎着一頭駱駝，另外還牽着一頭。他們問他，“你是誰？”“我叫阿迪，是海蒂姆．泰的兒子，”他答道，“誰是希米爾王道凱拉？”“他就是，”他們回答。他就對國王說，“把這頭駱駝拿去，代替我父親為你殺掉的你的那頭駱駝。”道凱拉問，“誰告訴你這件事的？”阿迪答道，“昨夜我父親託夢給我，對我說，‘聽着，阿迪，道凱拉要我請客，可我甚麼也沒有，只好殺了他自己的駱駝請他們吃。所以你一定要送一頭母駱駝去給他騎，因為我一無所有。’”於是道凱拉收下了這頭駱駝。對於海蒂姆．泰不論是生前死後依然這樣慷慨驚訝讚嘆不已。”

# 49 Iskender Dhoulkernein and a Certain Tribe of Poor Folk

It is related that Iskender Dhoulkernein[1] came once, in his travels, upon a tribe of poor folk, who owned nought of the goods of the world and who dug their graves over against the doors of their houses and were wont at all times to frequent them and sweep the earth from them and keep them clean and visit them and worship God the Most High in them; and they had no food save herbs and the fruits of the earth. Iskender sent a man to them, to bid their king to him, but he refused to come, saying, "I have no occasion to him." So Iskender went to him and said to him, "How is it with you and what manner of folk are you? For I see with you nothing of gold or silver nor aught of the good things of the world." "None hath his fill of the goods of the world," answered the king. "Why do you dig your graves before the doors of your houses?" asked Iskender. "That they may be the cynosure of our eyes," replied the king, "so we may look on them and still take thought unto death neither forget the world to come.

---

1. Iskender Dhoulkernein：即雙角亞歷山大，東方作家給亞歷山大大帝的稱號，可能是由於他自稱為丘比特阿蘭之後代，而丘比特的顯著特徵就是在鬢角兩邊各有一隻角。

## 四十九　國王與窮人部落

傳說國王伊斯坎德爾一次旅行時碰到一個窮人的部落。他們一無所有，他們在自己的家門口掘自己的墳墓，且經常進出其中，掃除灰塵，保持清潔，並在那裏向主禮拜。他們沒有食品，只吃地上長的野草和果實。伊斯坎德爾派人去訪他們的首領，但他不肯來，說："我不想見他。"於是伊斯坎德爾就去看他，對他說："你是甚麼人？我看你們沒有金銀財寶，也沒有世界上的好東西。""物慾難填，"首領回答。"你們為甚麼在家門前掘墓呢？"伊斯坎德爾問。"它們是眾人注意的目標，"首領回答，"我們看到它們就想到死亡，也想到來世。我們心

Thus is the love of the world banished from our hearts and we are not distracted thereby from the service of our Lord, exalted be His name!" Quoth Iskender, "Why do ye eat herbs?" And the other answered, "Because it misliketh us to make our bellies the tombs of beasts and because the pleasure of eating overpasseth not the gullet."

Then he brought out a human skull and laying it before Iskender, said to him, "O Dhoulkernein, knowest thou whose was this skull?" "Nay," answered Iskender; and the other rejoined, "He whose skull this is was a king of the kings of the world, who dealt tyrannously with his subjects, oppressing the weak and passing his days in heaping up the perishable goods of the world, till God took his soul and made the fire his abiding-place; and this is his head."

Then he produced another skull and laying it before Iskender, said to him, "Knowest thou this?" "No," answered the prince; and the other rejoined, "This is the skull of another king, who dealt justly by his subjects and was tenderly solicitous for the people of his realm and his dominions, till God took his soul and lodged him in His Paradise and made high his degree." Then he laid his hands on Iskender's head and said, "Whether of these twain art thou?" Whereupon Iskender wept sore and straining the king to his bosom, said,

中就會排除對現世的眷戀，就能專心致意侍奉我主，榮耀祂的聖名。”伊斯坎德爾問，“那你們為甚麼去吃野草呢？”首領答道，“讓我們的肚腹成為牲畜的墳墓令我們厭惡，而且因為食的樂趣只不過到咽喉為止。”

然後他拿出一個人的顱骨放在伊斯坎德爾面前，對他說“你知道這是誰的顱骨嗎？”“不知道，”伊斯坎德爾說。首領說，“他是世界上的一個王中之王，他像暴君一樣對待他的臣民，壓迫弱者，整天在聚斂那世界上並不恆久的東西，直到一天上帝取走了他的靈魂，使煉獄之火成了他的住所，這就是他的頭。”

然後他又拿出另一個顱骨放在伊斯坎德爾面前說“你知道這是誰的嗎？”“不知道。”“這是另一個國王的顱骨，他對他的臣民很公正，對他國土及領地上的人民關心體貼，後來上帝取走了他的靈魂，把他放在天堂裏，給他很高的身份。”然後他把手放在伊斯坎德爾的頭上，問他：“你是這兩者中的那一種？”伊斯坎德爾聽後，痛哭

"An[3] thou be minded to consort with me, I will commit to thee the government of my affairs and share with thee in my kingdom." "Away! away!" replied the other. "I have no mind to this." "Why so?" asked Iskender, and the King answered, "Because all men are thine enemies by reason of the wealth and possessions thou hast gotten, and all men are my friends in verity, because of my contentment and poverty, for that I possess nothing, neither covet aught of the goods of the world." So Iskender pressed him to his bosom and kissed him between the eyes and went his way.

---

3. An：（古）＝If。

起來，把首領擁抱在胸前說：“如果你願意與我合作，我將委託你管理政務，與你分享國土。”“走開，”他說，“我才不想幹呢！”“為甚麼？”伊斯坎德爾問道。首領回答說：“由於你佔有了財富，所有的人都是你的敵人。而我卻因為安貧樂道，一無所有，毫不貪婪世間財富，所有的人都是我的真實朋友。”於是伊斯坎德爾擁抱了他，吻了他的額頭就走了。

# Love, Marriage and the Family
# 愛情、婚姻、家庭

## 50 The Freedman of Al-Datma

*— Prince Behram and Princess Al-Datma (1)*

There was once a king's daughter called Al-Datma who, in her time, had no equal in beauty and grace. In addition to her lovely looks, she was brilliant and feisty and took great pleasure in ravishing the wits of the male sex. In fact, she used to boast, "There is nobody who can match me in anything." And the fact is that she was most accomplished in horsemanship and martial exercises, and all those things a cavalier should know.

Given her qualities, numerous princes sought her hand in marriage, but she rejected them all. Instead, she proclaimed, "No man shall marry me unless he defeats me with his lance and sword in fair battle. He who succeeds I will gladly wed. But if I overcome him, I will take his horse, clothes, and arms and brand his head with the following words: 'This is the freedman of Al-Datma.'"

Now the sons of kings flocked to her from every quarter far and near, but she prevailed and put them to shame, stripping them of their arms and branding them with fire. Soon, a son of the king of Persia named Behram ibn Taji heard about her and journeyed from afar to her father's court. He brought men and horses with him and a great deal of

# 五十　公主比武招親

*——貝拉姆王子和艾爾達瑪公主（一）*

從前有位公主，名叫艾爾達瑪。她年輕時的容貌和儀態舉世無雙。她不但美貌而且聰明活潑，以把男性弄得無計可施為樂。事實上，她常常誇口："沒有人能在任何事情上跟我相比。"她也的確精通騎術、武藝以及一個騎士應當具備的本領。

她這些的優點吸引了許多王子前來求婚，但她都拒絕了，反而宣稱："哪個男人能在公平的戰鬥中用矛和劍打敗我，我就跟他結婚。但是，要是我贏了，我就要拿走他的馬、衣服和武器，還要在他的額頭烙上幾個字：'這是艾爾達瑪釋放的奴隸'。"

王子們從四面八方前來跟她比武，但她總是獲勝，使他們蒙羞，奪走他們的武器，並施以烙刑。不久，波斯王子貝拉姆也慕名遠道來到她父王的宮庭。他帶來了人和馬

wealth and royal treasures. When he drew near the city, he sent her father a rich present, and the king came out to meet him and bestowed great honors on him. Then the king's son sent a message to him through his vizier and requested his daughter's hand in marriage. However, the king answered, "With regard to my daughter Al-Datma, I have no power over her, for she has sworn by her soul to marry no one but him who defeats her in the listed field."

"I journeyed here from my father's court with no other purpose but this," the prince declared. "I came here to woo her and to form an alliance with you."

"Then you shall meet her tomorrow," said the king.

So the next day he sent for his daughter, who got ready for battle by donning her armor of war. Since the people of the kingdom had heard about the coming joust, they flocked from all sides to the field. Soon the princess rode into the lists, armed head to toe with her visor down, and the Persian king's son came out to meet her, equipped in the fairest of fashions. Then they charged at each other and fought a long time, wheeling and sparring, advancing and retreating, and the princess realized that he had more courage and skill than she had ever encountered before. Indeed, she began to fear that he might put her to shame before the bystanders and defeat her. Consequently, she decided to trick him, and raising

匹、大量財富以及王室珍寶。當他快到達這個城市時，他派人送給她父親一份豐厚的禮物。國王出來迎接並賜給他很大的榮譽。然後，王子通過大臣給國王送信，向他的女兒求婚。但是，國王回信說："至於我的女兒艾爾達瑪，我可作不了主，因為她發誓非能在比武場上打敗她的男子不嫁。"

王子說："我從我父王的宮廷遠道而來正是為此目的。我是來向她求愛並與陛下結盟的。"

"那麼你明天就與她會會吧。"國王說。

第二天，他把女兒召來；公主全身披甲，準備戰鬥。全國人民聽說要舉行比武，紛紛從各地趕到校場。不一會兒，公主全副武裝，拉下了面罩，縱馬進入校場。波斯王子出來迎戰，裝束極其時髦華麗。然後，他們互相衝殺，戰鬥了很長時間，盤旋試探，進進退退。公主發現他比以前的對手更為勇敢，武藝也更高強。她真的開始害怕他可能使她當眾出醜，把她打敗。因此，她決定智取。她推上

her visor, she showed her face, which appeared more radiant than the full moon, and when he saw it, he was bewildered by her beauty. His strength failed, and his spirit faltered. When she perceived this moment of weakness, she attacked and knocked him from his saddle. Consequently, he became like a sparrow in the clutches of an eagle. Amazed and confused, he did not know what was happening to him when she took his steed, clothes, and armor. Then, after branding him with fire, she let him go his way.

面罩，露出她那羞花閉月的容貌。王子一看，頓時被她的美貌弄得神魂顛倒，全身無力，失去了勇氣。她就乘機進攻，把他打下馬來。結果，他變得像老鷹爪子中的一隻麻雀。她拿走了他的馬匹、衣服和盔甲，而他還稀里糊塗，不知道自己是怎麼回事兒。然後，她對他施以烙刑，打發他走了。

## 51 The Prince Thought of Different Ways to Attain His Goal

*— Prince Behram and Princess Al-Datma (2)*

In the meantime, the prince thought of different ways to attain his goal, and soon he decided to disguise himself as a decrepit old man. So he put a white beard over his own black one and went to the garden where the princess used to walk most of the days.

...

One day, as he was occupied with some work, he saw some slaves enter the garden leading mules and carrying carpets and vessels, and he asked them what they were doing there.

"The princess wants to spend an enjoyable afternoon here," they answered.

When he heard these words, he rushed to his lodging and fetched some jewels and ornaments he had brought with him from home. After returning to the garden, he sat down and spread some of the valuable items before him while shaking and pretending to be a very old man.

After an hour or so a company of damsels and eunuchs entered the garden with the princess, who looked just like the radiant moon among the stars. They ran about the garden,

## 五十一　王子計賺新娘

*—— 貝拉姆王子和艾爾達瑪公主（二）*

這時，王子想方設法要達到目的；他很快決定假裝成一個衰弱不堪的老頭兒。他戴上了白鬍子，來到了公主經常去散步的花園。

……

一天，他正忙着幹這幹那，忽然看見幾個奴隸牽着騾子走進花園，上面馱着地毯和器皿。他問他們來幹甚麼。

“公主下午要來這裏玩兒，”他們答道。

他一聽這話，就急忙跑回住處，拿了一些從家裏帶來的珠寶首飾。跑到花園之後，他就坐下來把一些值錢的東西擺放在面前，同時顫顫巍巍，假裝老朽。

過了一個鐘頭光景，一羣少女和太監陪着公主走進花園，猶如眾星捧月。他們在花園裏到處奔跑，摘果玩耍，

plucking fruits and enjoying themselves, until they caught sight of the prince disguised as an old man sitting under one of the trees. The man's hands and feet were trembling from old age, and he had spread a great many precious jewels and regal ornaments before him. Of course, they were astounded by this and asked him what he was doing there with the jewels.

"I want to use these trinkets," he said, "to buy me a wife from among the lot of you."

They all laughed at him and said, "If one of us marries you, what will you do with her?"

"I'll give her one kiss," he replied, "and then divorce her."

"If that's the case," said the princess, "I'll give this damsel to you for your wife."

So he rose, leaned on his staff, staggered toward the damsel, and gave her a kiss. Right after that he gave her the jewels and ornaments, whereupon she rejoiced and they all went on their way laughing at him.

The next day they came again to the garden, and they found him seated in the same place with more jewels and ornaments than before spread before him.

"Oh sheikh," they asked him, "what are you going to do with all this jewelry?"

"I want to wed one of you again," he answered, "just as I did yesterday."

直到她們看到假扮老頭兒的王子坐在樹下。那人手腳發顫，老朽不堪，面前卻擺放着許多貴重的珠寶和王族的首飾。當然，她們十分驚奇，就問他在那兒擺着珠寶做甚麼。

“我要用這些珠寶買你們中的一個人做老婆，”他說。

她們都笑他說，“如果我們中有人跟你結婚，你拿她怎麼辦？”

“那我就給她一個吻，然後跟她離婚，”他答道。

公主說，“要是這樣，我就把這個女孩給你做老婆。”

他站了起來，倚着拐杖，跌跌撞撞地走向那個女孩，吻了她一下，隨即把珠寶首飾給了她。女孩大喜過望，她們都大笑着走了。

第二天，她們又到花園來了，又看到老頭坐在原來的地方，面前放着更多的珠寶首飾。

“老大爺，您要用這些珠寶幹甚麼？”她們問。

“我要像昨天一樣再娶你們中的一位，”他答道。

So the princess said, "I'll marry you to this damsel."

And the prince went up to her, kissed her, and gave her the jewels, and they all went their way.

After seeing how generous the old man was to her slave girls, the princess said to herself, "I have more right to these fine things than my slaves, and there's surely no danger involved in this game." So when morning arrived, she went down by herself into the garden dressed as one of her own damsels, and she appeared all alone before the prince and said to him, "Old man, the king's daughter has sent me to you so that you can marry me."

When he looked at her, he knew who she was. So he answered, "With all my heart and love," and he gave her the finest and costliest of jewels and ornaments. Then he rose to kiss her, and since she was not on her guard and thought she had nothing to fear, he grabbed hold of her with his strong hands and threw her down on the ground, where he deprived her of her maidenhead. Then he pulled the beard from his face and said, "Do you recognize me?"

"Who are you?"

"I am Behram, The King of Persia's son," he replied. "I've changed myself and have become a stranger to my people, all for your sake. And I have lavished my treasures for your love."

公主就說，“我就把這個姑娘嫁給你。”

王子又走上前去吻了她，並給了她珠寶。她們又都走了。

看到老頭兒對她的女奴如此大方，公主心想，“我比那些奴隸更有資格得到這些好東西。再說，這遊戲也沒有甚麼危險。”所以，次日早晨，她打扮成女奴獨自來到花園，走到王子面前說道，“老大爺，公主叫我來嫁給你。”

他一下就看出她是誰，就回答道，“我把全部的愛獻給你。”於是，他給了她最漂亮、最貴重的珠寶。然後，他站起來吻她，並趁她自以為沒有危險，毫無戒備之際，用粗壯的雙手將她一把抱住，並按倒在地，奪去了她的童貞。接着，他扯掉臉上的鬍子，說：“你認識我嗎？”

“你是誰？”

“我是波斯王子貝拉姆，”他答道。“為了你，我喬裝打扮，連我的家人都不認識了。為了得到你的愛，我揮霍了我的財富。”

She rose from him in silence and did not say a word to him. Indeed, she was dazed by what had happened and felt that it was best to be silent, especially since she did not want to be shamed. All the while she was thinking to herself, "If I kill myself, it will be senseless, and if I have him put to death, there's nothing that I'd really gain. The best thing for me to do is to elope with him to his own country."

So, after leaving him in the garden, she gatherd together her money and treasures and sent him a message informing him what she intended to do and telling him to get ready to depart with his possessions and whatever else he needed. Then they set a rendezvous for their departure.

At the appointed time they mounted racehorses and set out under cover of darkness, and by the next morning they had traveled a great distance. They kept traveling at a fast pace until they drew near his father's capital in Persia, and when his father heard about his son's coming, he rode out to meet him with his troops and was full of joy.

她默默地站起身來，一句話也說不出來。的確，她被剛才發生的事弄得不知所措，覺得最好還是保持沉默，尤其因為她不希望被恥笑。她心裏一直在想："如果自殺，那毫無意義。如果把他處死，我其實也一無所得。我最好還是跟他私奔到他的國家去。"

就這樣，她在花園離開他後，就收拾好自己的金銀細軟，並給他送信，告訴他自己的打算，要他準備好帶着財物和所需的一切動身。然後，他們約定了動身的會合地點和時間。

在約定的時間，他們騎上快馬，在夜色的掩護下出發了。到了次日早晨，他們已經走了很遠。他們繼續快速前進，直到靠近了波斯首都。波斯國王聽說兒子回來的消息，親自帶了軍隊騎馬出迎，高興得不得了。

## 52 The King and His Vizier's Wife

There was once a king, who was given to the love of women, and one day, being alone in his palace, he espied a beautiful woman on the roof of her house and could not contain himself from falling in love with her. He asked [his servants] to whom the house belonged and they said, "To thy vizier such an one." So he called the vizier in question and despatched him on an errand to a distant part of the kingdom; then, as soon as he was gone, he made an excuse to gain access to his house. When the vizier's wife saw him, she knew him and springing up, kissed his hands and feet and welcomed him. Then she stood afar off, and said to him "O our lord, what is the cause of thy gracious visit? Such an honour is not for the like of me." Quoth he, "Love of thee and desire to thee hath moved me to this." Whereupon she kissed the earth before him a second time and said, "O our lord, indeed I am not worthy to be the handmaid of one of the king's servants; whence then have I the great good fortune to be in such favour with thee?" Then the king put out his hand to her, but she said, "This thing shall not escape us; but take patience, O king, and abide with me all this day, that I may make ready for thee somewhat of victual." So the king

## 五十二　國王和大臣的妻子

從前有個國王，很喜歡拈花惹草。一天他獨自在宮中，看見一個漂亮的婦人在她的房頂上，就禁不住愛上了她。他問〔僕人〕這房子是誰的，他們回答說：“是某大臣的。”於是他就召見那個大臣，把他派到很遠的地方去辦事；然後等大臣一走，國王就找了個藉口進了大臣的家。大臣的妻子見到了他，認出是國王來，就趕快起身，吻他的手腳歡迎他。然後她站得遠遠的，問國王：“陛下光臨，不知有何貴幹？這樣的榮幸我真擔當不起。”他說：“是對你的愛和想要你的慾望把我帶到了這裏。”她一聽就又一次吻國王面前的土地，說：“陛下，我連做國王僕人的侍女都不配，怎麼會有幸受國王的恩寵呢？”國王把手伸給她，但她說：“這事一定能成，但您要有耐心。陛下，請您今天陪着我，我去為您準備些食物。”於

sat down on his vizier's couch and the lady brought him a book wherein he might read, whilst she made ready the food. He took the book and beginning to read, found therein moral instances and exhortations, such as restrained him from adultery and broke his intent to commit sin.

After awhile, she returned and set before him a collation of ninety dishes of different kinds and colours, and he ate a spoonful of each and found that the taste of them was one. At this, he marvelled exceedingly and said to the lady, "O damsel, I see these meats to be many [and various of hue], but the taste of them is one." "God prosper the king!" replied she. "This is a parable I have set for thee, that thou mayst be admonished thereby." "And what is its meaning?" asked he. "May God amend the case[1] of our lord the king!" answered she.

"In thy palace are ninety concubines of various colours, but their taste is one." When the king heard this, he was ashamed and rising hastily, went out and returned to his palace, without offering her any affront; but, in his haste and confusion, he forgot his signet-ring and left it under the cushion where he had been sitting.

---

1. May God amend the case：原義為“願真主匡正（吾王）的過失！”

是國王就坐在大臣的躺椅上，婦人給他拿來一本書讓他看，她又去弄吃的。國王看起書來，發現書裏有許多講道德的實例和規勸，就抑制了自己不去和婦人通姦，打消了邪惡的企圖。

過了一會兒，婦人回來了，在國王面前擺下了九十種不同種類和顏色的菜肴，國王每道都吃了一勺，但發現它們都是一個味道。他十分驚奇，對婦人說："年輕的女人，我看這肉有這麼多種〔而且顏色也各不相同〕，可味道都一樣。""主保佑陛下！"她說，"這是我為您準備的一個比喻，您從中會得到告誡。""甚麼意思？"他問。"願主保佑陛下，"她回答道。

"您的宮中有九十個各種膚色的嬪妃，可她們的味道都相同。"國王聽後感到羞愧，不敢對她有所冒犯就匆匆起身回宮去了。但在匆忙和慌亂中他忘了他的玉璽戒指留在他坐過的墊子下面。

Presently the vizier returned and presenting himself before the king, kissed the earth and made his report to him of the state of the province in question. Then he repaired to his own house and sat down on his couch, and chancing to put his hand under the cushion, found the king's seal-ring. So he looked at it and knew it and taking the matter to heart, held aloof from his wife nor spoke with her for a whole year, while she knew not the reason of his anger. At last, being weary of estrangement, she sent for her father and told him the case, whereupon quoth he, "I will complain of him to the king, some day when he is in presence."

So, one day, he went in to the king and finding the vizier and the cadi of the army before him, made his complaint in the following words. "May God the Most High amend the king's case! I had a fair garden, which I planted with my own hand and spent my substance thereon, till it bore fruit and its fruit was ripe, when I gave it to this thy vizier, who ate of it what seemed good to him, then forsook it and watered it not, so that its flowers withered and its beauty departed and it became waste." Then said the vizier, "O king, what this man says is true. I did indeed care for the garden and ate thereof, till, one day, going thither, I saw the track of the lion there, wherefore I feared him and withdrew from the garden." The king understood the parable and knew that, by the track of

不久大臣回來了，他去見國王，吻國王面前的土地並向國王報告了他去那個省的情況。然後他回到家裏，坐到躺椅上，偶而把手放在墊子下，發現了國王的玉璽戒指。他看看這隻戒指，認出是國王的戒指，並對此事耿耿於懷。他躲避着他的妻子，一年都不和她講話，而他妻子卻不知道他為甚麼生氣。後來妻子厭煩了這種疏遠，就把情況告訴了父親，她父親說：“我要到國王那兒當他的面告他。”

於是，有一天，他去見國王，發現大臣和軍法官都在場，就向國王指控大臣，說：“願主保佑陛下！我有一個美麗的花園，我親手種花養草耗盡心血，直到果實成熟，我就把花園交給了您的這位大臣，他吃了果實，也認為不錯，然後他又拋棄了它，不給它澆水，以致花兒凋謝，美景不再，花園荒蕪。”大臣說：“陛下，這人說的都是真的。我原先確實很喜愛這個花園，也吃了它的果實。直到有一天我到花園去，看見了獅子的蹤迹，我害怕獅子，所以不再去花園了。”國王明白了這個比喻知道大臣所說的

the lion, he meant his own seal-ring, which he had forgotten in his house; so he said, "Return to thy garden, O vizier, and fear nothing, for the lion came not near it. It hath been told me that he went thither, but by the honour of my fathers and forefathers, he offered it no hurt." "I hear and obey," answered the vizier, and returning home, made his peace with his wife and thenceforth put faith in her chastity.

獅子蹤迹是指他留在大臣家的玉璽戒指。因此他說：“愛卿，回到你的花園中去吧！不用怕，獅子並沒有走近它。我聽說獅子曾去過那花園裏，但朕以列祖列宗的名譽發誓，獅子沒有造成任何傷害。”“遵命！”大臣答道。大臣回家後與妻子和好如初，從此以後再沒懷疑過妻子的貞潔。

## 53 The Miller and His Wife

There was a miller, who had an ass to turn his mill; and he was married to a wicked wife, whom he loved; but she hated him and loved a neighbour of hers, who liked her not and held aloof from her. One night, the miller saw, in his sleep, one who said to him, "Dig in such a spot of the ass's circuit in the mill, and thou shalt find a treasure." When he awoke, he told his wife the dream and charged her keep it secret; but she told her neighbour, thinking to win his favour, and he appointed with her to come to her by night. So he came and they dug in the mill and found the treasure and took it forth. Then said he to her, "How shall we do with this?" "We will share it equally between us," answered she; "and do thou leave thy wife and I will cast about to rid me of my husband. Then shalt thou marry me, and when we are united, we will add the two halves of the treasure, one to the other, and it will be [all] in our hands." Quoth he, "I fear lest Satan seduce thee and thou take some man other than myself; for gold in the house is like the sun in the world. Meseems,

## 五十三　磨坊主和他的妻子

從前有個磨坊主，他有頭驢來推磨，他娶了一個惡妻。他很愛她，但這女人卻恨他而愛上他們的一個鄰居，但這鄰居並不愛她，總是跟她疏遠。一天夜裏，磨坊主在夢中見到一個人對他說：“在磨坊裏驢子路經的某一個地方挖下去就會找到財寶”。他醒後便把夢告訴了妻子，並吩咐她一定要保密；但她卻告訴了鄰居想贏得他的好感，鄰居與她約好晚上來找她。晚上鄰居來了，他們在磨坊裏挖到了財寶，並取了出來。鄰居對她說，“我們拿這財寶怎麼辦呢？”她回答道：“我們兩人平分。你要離開你的妻子，我則想法離開我的丈夫。然後你娶我，我們再把兩份財寶加在一起，那麼全部都在我們手中了”。他說，“我害怕萬一魔鬼引誘你，你要了別個男人而不要我，因為屋子裏的金子就像世界上的太陽一樣貴重。所以我以為

therefore, it were better that the money be all in my hands, so thou mayst[1] study to win free of thy husband and come to me." "I fear the like of thee," rejoined she, "and I will not yield up my part to thee; for it was I directed thee to it." When he heard this, covetise prompted him to kill her; so he killed her and threw her body into the empty hole; but the day overtook him and hindered him from covering it up; so he took the treasure and went away.

Presently, the miller awoke and missing his wife, went into the mill, where he fastened the ass to the beam and shouted to it. It went on a little, then stopped; whereupon he beat it grievously; but the more he beat it, the more it drew back; for it was affrighted at the dead woman and could not go on. So he took out a knife and goaded it again and again, but still it would not budge. Then he was wroth with it, knowing not the cause of its obstinacy, and drove the knife into its flanks, and it fell down dead. When the sun rose, he saw his wife lying dead, in the place of the treasure, and great was his rage and sore his chagrin for the loss of the treasure and the death of his wife and his ass. All this came of his letting his wife into his secret and not keeping it to himself.

---

1. mayst：（古）may 的第二人稱單數。

最好這些錢全部放在我這裏，你想辦法脱離你的丈夫到我這裏來。”她回答：“我的擔心和你一樣。我決不把我那份給你；因為是我帶你來的”。他聽見此話後，貪婪促使他起殺機，於是他殺了她，把她丢在空的坑裏，但天已亮了，他來不及掩蓋好坑，就拿起財寶走了。

不久，磨坊主醒過來，沒有見到他的妻子，他就去了磨坊，把驢子拴緊在磨杆上，對驢子呼喝要牠推磨，驢子走了一會兒就停了下來，他就使勁鞭打牠，但他越打，驢子越後退，因為牠害怕那女屍，不敢往前走。磨坊主拿出一把刀子，一再刺驢子的脊，但牠還是不肯走。他不明白為甚麼驢子這麼頑固，對牠十分生氣，就把刀子插入牠的腰部，驢子就倒下死了。當太陽升起之後，他看見妻子的屍體躺在藏財寶的地方。他憤怒異常又懊惱萬分，他失去了財寶，還死了妻子和驢子。這一切都因為他讓妻子知道了秘密而沒有自己嚴守秘密。

## 54 The Husband and the Parrot

There lived once a good man, who had a beautiful wife, whom he loved so much that he could scarcely bear to have her out of his sight. One day, when obliged to leave her, he purchased a parrot, which possessed the rare gift of telling everything that was done in its presence. The husband took it home in a cage, and begged his wife to keep it in her chamber, and take great care of it during his absence; after this he set out on his journey.

On his return, he did not fail to interrogate the parrot on what had passed while he was away; and the bird very expertly related a few circumstances which occasioned the husband to reprimand his wife. She supposed that some of her slaves had exposed her, but they all assured her they were faithful, and agreed in charging the parrot with the crime. Desirous of being convinced of the truth of this matter, the wife devised a method of quieting the suspicions of her husband, and at the same time of revenging herself on the parrot, if he were the culprit. The next time the husband was absent, she ordered one of her slaves, during the night, to turn a handmill under the bird's cage, and another to throw water over it like rain, and a third to wave a looking-glass

## 五十四　丈夫與鸚鵡

從前有個好人，他有個美麗的妻子。他很愛她，幾乎到了一眼看不見就受不了的程度。一天，他因故不得不出門，就買了一隻鸚鵡，因為這鳥有一種難得的本領，能說出曾經在牠面前發生過的一切。那丈夫把鳥裝在籠子裏拿回家來，吩咐妻子把牠放在她的房裏，並在他出門期間好好照看牠。安排好以後，他就動身去旅行了。

他一回到家就去盤問鸚鵡，想了解他不在的時候發生了甚麼事情。鳥兒很流利地講了一些情況使他責打了妻子。她以為是幾個奴隸告發了她，但他們都向她保證自己是忠實的，而且一致認為是那隻鸚鵡搗的鬼。妻子想弄清事實真相，就想了個辦法來消除丈夫的疑心，同時向鸚鵡報讎，如果是牠犯事的話。在丈夫下一次出門的時候，她吩咐一個奴隸夜間在鳥籠下面推磨，另一個在上面像下雨似的灑水，第三個則映着燭光在鸚鵡面前晃動鏡子。那天

before the parrot by the light of a candle. The slaves were employed the greatest part of the night in doing as their mistress had ordered them.

The following day, when the husband returned, he again applied to the parrot to say what had taken place. The bird replied, "My dear master, the lightning, the thunder, and the rain have so disturbed me the whole night, that I cannot tell you how much I have suffered." The husband, who knew there had been no storm that night, became convinced that the parrot did not always relate facts; and that having told an untruth in this particular, he had also deceived him with respect to his wife: being, therefore, extremely enraged with it, he took the bird out of the cage, and, dashing it on the floor, killed it. He, however, afterward learnt from his neighbors that the poor parrot had told no falsehood in reference to his wife's conduct, which made him repent of having destroyed it.

夜裏，奴隸們就照着女主人的吩咐鬧騰了大半宿。

第二天，丈夫回家後又去問鸚鵡發生了甚麼情況。鳥兒說：“我親愛的主人，我被電閃、雷鳴和雨水折騰了整整一夜，沒法說有多難受了。”丈夫知道那晚沒有暴雨，就相信鸚鵡講的並不總是事實；而且既然這次撒了謊，牠以前關於妻子的話也一定是騙他的。因此，他一怒之下就從籠子裏把鳥兒抓出來，摔死在地上了。但是，他後來從鄰居那兒得知他妻子的不軌行為，證明那隻可憐的鸚鵡講的並非謊話，但是已後悔不及了。

## 55 The Debauchee and the Three-year-old Child

A certain profligate man, who was addicted to women, once heard of a beautiful and graceful woman who dwelt in a town other than his own. So he journeyed thither, taking with him a gift, and wrote her a letter, seeking access to her and setting out all that he suffered for longing and desire for her and how the love of her had driven him to forsake his native land and come to her. She gave him leave[1] to visit her and received him with all honour and worship, kissing his hands and entertaining him with the best of meat and drink. Now she had a little three-year-old son, whom she left and busied herself in cooking rice. Presently the man said to her, "Come, let us go to bed;" and she said, "My son is sitting looking at us." Quoth the man, "He is a little child, understanding not, neither knowing how to speak." "Thou wouldst not say thus," answered the woman, "if thou knewest his intelligence." When the boy saw that the rice was done, he fell to weeping bitterly, and his mother said to him, "What ails thee[2] to weep, O my son?" "Give me some rice," answered

1. gave him leave： gave him permission。

2. what ails thee：原義"甚麼使你苦惱"。

## 五十五　浪子和三齡童

從前，一個浪子好色成性。他聽說在另一座城市住着一個美麗窈窕的女人，便帶了禮物動身上她那兒去。他還給她寫了一封信，要求和她見面，訴說對她的渴慕之苦以及為了愛情而背井離鄉前來找她之情。她允許他來訪並十分尊敬地接待他，吻他的手並用豐盛的飲食招待他。她有一個三歲的兒子。她因為忙着做飯，就把孩子放在一邊了。一會兒那人對她說，“來吧，我們上牀吧。”她說，“我的兒子正坐着看我們呢。”男子說，“他是個小孩，既不懂事又不會說話。”女人答道，“如果你知道他多麼聰明就不會這樣說了。”孩子看到飯煮好了，便大哭起來，他母親問他，“兒子，你哭甚麼？”他答道，“給我

he, "and put butter in it." So she ladled him out somewhat[3] of rice and put butter therein; and he ate a little, then began to weep again. Quoth she, "What ails thee now?" and he answered, saying, "O my mother, I want some sugar with my rice." At this the man was angered and said to him, "Thou art none other than a curst[4] child." "It is thou who art curst," answered the boy, "seeing thou weariest thyself and journeyest from city to city, in quest of lewdness[5]. As for me, I wept because I had somewhat in my eye, and my weeping brought it out; and now I have eaten rice with butter and sugar and am content; so which is the curst of us twain?" The man was confounded at this rebuke from a little child and grace entered him[6] and he repented. Wherefore he laid not a finger on the woman, but went out from her forthright and returned to his own country, where he lived a contrite life till he died.

---

3. somewhat：（古）= something。
4. curst：（古）= cursed（adj）。
5. in quest of lewdness：為了尋花問柳。
6. grace entered him：善念進了他的心。

飯吃，還要往飯裏加點兒奶油。”她給他盛了一碗飯，加了奶油；可是他吃了一點兒，又哭了起來。她說，“又怎麼啦？”他答道，“媽媽，飯裏再加些糖。”聽了這話那男人惱了，對孩子說，“你這孩子真可惡。”孩子說，“你才可惡呢，你為了玩女人不惜勞頓從一個城市跑到另一個城市。而我呢，我哭是因為眼睛裏飛進了東西，我一哭那東西就隨眼淚流出來了；現在我已經吃了加奶油和糖的飯就滿足了；那末我們倆到底誰可惡？”男人讓孩子罵得十分難堪，心裏重新萌發了羞恥感，他感到後悔，因此對女人絲毫沒有侵犯就馬上離開她家回自己家鄉去了。從此，他痛改前非，生活檢點，直至壽終。

# 56 The Khalif El Mutawekkil and His Favourite Mehboubeh

There were in the palace of the Khalif El Mutawekkil ala Allah[1] four thousand concubines. Among these latter was a girl of Bassora, Mehboubeh by name, who was of surpassing beauty and elegance and voluptuous grace. Moreover, she played upon the lute and was skilled in singing and making verses and wrote excellent well; so that El Mutawekkil fell passionately in love with her and could not endure from her a single hour. When she saw this, she presumed upon his favour to use him haughtily and capriciously, so that he waxed exceeding wroth with her and forsook her, forbidding the people of the palace to speak with her.

On this wise she abode some days, but the Khalif still inclined to her; and he arose one morning and said to his courtiers, "I dreamt, last night, that I was reconciled to Mehboubeh." "Would God this might be on wake!" answered they. As they were talking, in came one of the Khalif's maidservants and whispered him that they had heard a noise of singing and luting in Mehboubeh's chamber and knew not

---

1. El Mutawekkil ala Allah：阿伯賽（Abbaside）王朝第十任國王，公元 849－861 年。

## 五十六　國王與愛妃

國王埃穆塔魏基的宮中有嬪妃四千，其中有一個來自巴索拉的姑娘，名叫梅波白。她美麗絕頂，艷光照人。她會彈弦琴，會唱歌，又擅長賦詩作文。因此國王對她萬分寵愛，一刻也不願離開她。但她卻恃寵而驕，動不動就對國王使性子，國王一怒之下，便拋棄了她，而且禁止宮中的人跟她說話。

這樣過了些日子，國王還是想念她。一天他起牀後對朝臣說，“昨夜我作了一個夢，與梅波白和好了。”朝臣答道：“但願上帝讓這事發生在您醒着的時候就好了。”他們正談着，國王的一個女侍進來，悄悄對國王說他們聽見梅波白的房裏有彈琴唱歌聲，不知是怎麼回事。國王起

what this meant. So he rose and entering the harem, went straight to Mehboubeh's apartment, where he heard her playing wonder-sweetly upon the lute and singing the following verses:

*I wander through the halls, but not a soul I see,*
*To whom I may complain or who will speak with me.*
*It is as though I'd wrought so grievous an offence,*
*No penitence avails myself therefrom to free.*
*Will no one plead my cause with a king, who came to me*
*In sleep and took me back to favour and to gree;*
*But with the break of day to rigour did revert*
*And cast me off from him and far away did flee?*

When the Khalif heard these verses, he marvelled at the strange coincidence of their dreams and entered the chamber. As soon as she was ware of him, she hastened to throw herself at his feet, and kissing them, said, "By Allah, O my lord, this is what I dreamt last night; and when I awoke, I made the verses thou hast heard." "By Allah," replied El Mutawekkil, "I also dreamt the like!" Then they embraced and made friends and he abode with her seven days and nights.

When El Mutawekkil died, all his women forgot him, save Mehboubeh, who ceased not to mourn for him, till she died.

身進入後宮，直接來到梅波白的門外，果然聽見了她悠揚甜美的琴聲和歌聲，她在唱：

我在宮殿徘徊，不見人影；
我無人可細訴，無人願傾聽；
好像我犯了彌天大罪，怎麼懺悔也無法解脫；
難道無人為我向國王求情？
昨夜夢中國王向我走來，
帶來寵愛，帶來歡慶；
但白晝一到，我重回冷酷的世界，
難道他非要把我遠遠地拋棄不行？

國王聽到她的歌，非常驚異他們的夢境竟如此巧合，就進了她的房間。她見國王來了，急忙跪下，吻他的雙腳，說，“陛下，這是我昨夜夢見的，今天醒來就作了這段歌詞，您已聽到。”“真主啊！”國王說，“我也做了這樣的夢。”於是他們相互擁抱，和好如初，國王陪了她七天七夜。

埃穆塔魏基去世後，他所有的嬪妃都忘了他，只有梅波白不停悼念他直至去世。

## 57 The Lovers of the Benou Tai

I went out one day and coming to the waters of the Benou Tai, saw two companies of people, near one another, and those of each company were disputing among themselves. So I watched them and observed, in one of the companies, a young man, wasted with sickness, as he were a worn-out water-skin. As I looked on him, he repeated the following verses:

*What ails the fair that she returneth not to me?*
*Is't grudgingness in her or inhumanity?*
*I sickened, and my folk to visit me came all.*
*Why 'mongst the visitors wast thou then not to see?*
*Hadst thou been sick, I would have hastened to thy side;*
*Nor menaces nor threats had hindered me from thee.*
*I miss thee midst the rest, and desolate am I:*
*Thy loss, my heart's abode, is grievous unto me.*

A damsel in the other company heard his words and hastened towards him. Her people followed her, but she repelled them with blows. Then the youth caught sight of

## 五十七　貝諾泰河邊的情人

一天我外出，來到貝諾泰河邊，見到相距不遠的兩夥人，各自爭論着甚麼。我就看着，觀察着，其中 夥中有個青年，被病魔折磨得虛弱不堪，活像個用舊了的水囊。我看他時，他口中反覆吟着下面的詩句：

我心愛的姑娘為甚麼不回來我這裏？
是因你的讎恨還是不仁不義？
我生病了，大家都來看我，
但看望的人中為甚麼沒有你？
如果你生病，我會立刻趕到你身邊，
任何恫嚇威脅都不能使我與你分離。
我想念你，我孤獨寂寞，我的心在期盼，
而你的消失使我悲傷無比。

另一夥人中一個年輕姑娘聽見這些話後趕快向他跑去。她那夥人就追她，她卻揮拳趕他們回去。青年看見

her and ran towards her, whilst his people ran after him and laid hold of him. However, he struggled, till he freed himself from them, and she in like manner loosed herself; and they ran to each other and meeting between the two parties, embraced and fell down dead.

Thereupon there came out an old man from one of the tents and stood over them, weeping sore and exclaiming, "May God the Most High have mercy on you both!" said he. "By Allah, though you were not united in your lives, I will at least unite you after death." And he bade lay them out. Then I questioned the old man of them, and he said, "She was my daughter and he my brother's son; and love brought them to this pass." "But why didst thou not marry them to one another?" Quoth he, "I feared reproach and dishonour; and now I am fallen upon both."

她，也向她跑去，他那幫人也來追他，並抓住了他。但他奮力掙脫了。姑娘也一樣擺脫了那一幫人。二人相互迎面跑來，在兩幫人之間相遇，他們擁抱着倒地死了。

這時從一個帳篷中走出一位老者，站在兩個年輕人身邊，失聲痛哭。他說，“願主憐憫你們二人！你們生時不能結為夫妻，我至少要讓你們死後團聚。”於是他吩咐把他們的屍體收拾好以備埋葬。我問老者年輕人是誰，他說，“她是我的女兒，他是我兄弟的兒子。是愛情使他們落到這個下場的。”“你為甚麼不讓他們結婚呢？”他說，“我怕挨罵丟臉，現在偏要挨罵丟臉了。”

# 58 The Three Unfortunate Lovers

I was sitting one day with a company of men of culture, telling stories of the folk, when the talk turned upon anecdotes of lovers and each of us said his say thereon. Now there was in our company an old man, who remained silent, till we had all spoken and had no more to say, when he said, "Shall I tell you a thing, the like of which you never heard?" "Yes," answered we; and he said, "Know, then, that I had a daughter, who loved a youth, but we knew it not. The youth in question loved a singing-girl, who, in her turn, was enamoured of my daughter. One day, I was present at an assembly, where were also the young man and the girl; when the latter sang the following verses:

*Tears are the token by which, for love,*
*Abjection in lovers still is shown,*
*And more by token in one who finds*
*No friend, to whom he may make his moan.*

'By Allah, thou hast said well, O my lady!' exclaimed the youth. 'Dost[1] thou bid me die?' 'Yes,' answered the girl

---

1. Dost：（古）= do。

## 五十八　殉情

有一天，我與一幫文化人坐在一起擺龍門陣，後來話題轉到了愛情故事，每個人都暢所欲言，只有一個老人始終緘默不語，直到我們大家都無話可談時，他才說：“我講一個你們從未聽過的故事，好嗎？”“好極了，”我們答道。他說道：“我有一個女兒，她愛上了一個青年，而我們卻不知道。但這個青年卻愛着一個歌女，而那個歌女卻傾心於我的女兒。有一天，我參加了一個集會，那個青年和歌女也在場，當時那歌女唱道：

眼淚表示單戀情人感受的羞辱，

那沒有朋友可以傾訴的人的眼淚更是苦澀。

‘天哪，你唱的真好，小姐！’那青年叫道，‘你是要我去死嗎？’‘是的，’歌女在幕後回答，‘如果你真在

from behind the curtain, 'if thou be in love.' So he laid his head on a cushion and closed his eyes; and when the cup came round to him, we shook him and found that he was dead. Therewith we all flocked to him, and our joy was troubled and we grieved and broke up forthright. When I came home, my people taxed me with returning before the appointed time, and I told them what had befallen the youth, thinking to surprise them. My daughter heard my words and rising, went into another chamber, whither I followed her and found her lying, with her head on a cushion, as I had told of the young man. I shook her and behold, she was dead. So we laid her out and set forth next morning with her funeral, whilst the friends of the young man carried him out, likewise, to bury him. As we were on the way to the burial-place, we met a third funeral and enquiring whose it was, were told that it was that of the singing-girl, who, hearing of my daughter's death, had done even as she and was dead. So we buried them all three on one day, and this is the rarest story that ever was heard of lovers."

戀愛，你就死吧！’於是青年把頭靠在墊子上，閉上了眼睛，直至輪到他喝酒時，我們搖他不醒，才發現他已氣絕身亡。我們圍在他身旁，歡樂的場面頓時被擾亂，大家心情沉重，不歡而散。我回到家中，家人問我為甚麼比約定時間早回來，我告訴他們那青年的事，想讓他們大吃一驚。我女兒聽了我的話，起身進了另一個房間。我隨她走進那房間，只見她躺着，頭靠在墊子上，和那青年一樣。我伸手去搖她，發現她已死了。於是我們為她入殮做準備，次日舉行葬禮。同時青年的朋友也把他抬出去埋葬，在我們去墓地的途中，碰見了第三樁出殯，我們問死者是誰。他們告訴我們死者就是那歌女，她一聽說我女兒死了，就和我女兒一樣靠着墊子斷了氣。這樣在一天之內我們埋葬了三個人。這是我聽到的愛情故事中最希奇的。”

# 59 El Mutelemmis and His Wife Umeimeh

It is related that El Mutelemmis[1] once fled from En Numan ben Mundhir[2] and was absent so long that the folk deemed him dead. Now he had a handsome wife, Umeimeh by name, and her family pressed her to marry again; but she refused, for that she loved her husband El Mutelemmis very dearly. However, they were instant with her, because of the multitude of her suitors, and importuned her till she at last reluctantly consented and they married her to a man of her own tribe.

On the night of the wedding, El Mutelemmis came back and hearing in the camp a noise of pipes and tabrets and seeing signs of festival, asked some of the children what was toward, to which they replied, "They have married Umeimeh, widow of El Mutelemmis, to such an one, and he goes in to her this night." When he heard this, he made shift to enter the house with the women and saw there the bride seated on

1. El Mutelemmis：穆罕默德前的著名詩人。
2. En Numan ben Mundhir：迦勒底（Chaldea）地區希萊赫國（Hireh）國王，詩人諷刺過的嗜血成性的暴君。

## 五十九　破鏡重圓

傳說穆塔蘭米逃出紐曼·門德爾國王的魔掌之後多年流亡在外，家人都以為他已不在人世了，他有個美麗的妻子，名叫烏美梅。她家人逼她再嫁，但她不從，因為她深愛自己的丈夫。可是，由於追求她的人很多，他們就跟她糾纏不休，非要她嫁人不可。最後她只好勉強同意了。於是他們就把她嫁給了同族的一個男人。

就在結婚的那天晚上，穆塔蘭米回來了。他聽到營地裏有排簫和手鼓的聲音並看到喜慶的迹象，就問幾個孩子發生了甚麼事。他們回答：“他們把穆塔蘭米的寡婦烏美梅嫁了人，那個男人今夜要來跟她洞房。”他一聽這話就

her throne. By and by, the bridegroom came up to her, whereupon she sighed heavily and weeping, recited the following verses:

*Ah would, (but many are the shifts of good and evil fate),*
*I knew in what far land thou art, O Mutelemmis mine!*

Now El Mutelemmis was a renowned poet: so he answered her with the following verse:

*Right near at hand, Umeimeh! Know, whene'er the caravan*
*Halted, I never ceased for thee with longing heart to pine.*

When the bridegroom heard this, he guessed how the case stood and went forth from among them in haste, repeating the following verse:

*I was in luck, but now I'm fall'n into the contrary.*
*A hospitable house and room your reknit loves enshrine!*

So El Mutelemmis took his wife again and abode with her in all delight and solace of life, till death parted them.

馬上跟女人們進屋，看見新娘坐在高座上。不久，新郎向她走去，她就長嘆一聲，流下了眼淚，吟出如下詩句：

（世事多翻覆，命運作弄人；）
良人今何在，關山遠隔處。

穆塔蘭米是著名詩人，立即吟詩作答：

篷車行停時，此心長相思，
今日歸故園，近在咫尺間。

新郎聽了這些詩句，猜到眼前的情況，就急忙從他們中間走開了，吟着如下詩句：

運正交桃花，頃刻又成空。
新房現成在，供爾重團圓。

就這樣，穆塔蘭米又跟妻子團圓了，並從此長相廝守，享盡了人生之樂，直至壽終。

# Reward and Retribution
# 因果報應

# 60 The Woman Whose Hands Were Cut Off

A certain King once made proclamation to the people of his realm, saying, "If any of you give alms of aught, I will assuredly cut off his hand;" wherefore all the people abstained from alms-giving, and none could give to any.

One day a beggar accosted a certain woman (and indeed hunger was sore upon him) and said to her, "Give me an alms." "How can I give thee aught," answered she, "when the King cutteth off the hands of all who give alms?" But he said, "I conjure thee by God the Most High, give me an alms." So, when he adjured her by God, she had compassion on him and gave him two cakes of bread. The King heard of this; so he called her before him and cut off her hands, after which she returned to her house.

A while after, the King said to his mother, "I have a mind to take a wife; so do thou marry me to a fair woman." Quoth she, "There is among our female slaves one who is unsurpassed in beauty; but she hath a grievous blemish." "What is that?" asked the King; and his mother answered, "She hath had both her hands cut off." Said he, "Let me see her." So she brought her to him, and he was ravished by her and married her; and she brought him a son.

# 六十　被砍掉雙手的女人

從前有一個國王，他向人民發出了公告，上面說，“任何人若向別人施捨，我就砍斷他的手。”因此所有人都不敢施捨東西給別人。

一天，一個乞丐走到一位婦人面前，(因他飢餓難耐)對她說，“請施捨吧！”“我怎麼能給你甚麼呢？”她回答，“國王會把施捨人的雙手砍掉的。”但他說，“我以真主的名義求你，給我施捨吧！”當乞丐用主的名義求她時，她動了同情心，給了他兩塊麵包。國王聽說後便把這婦人叫來，砍掉了她的雙手，然後她就回家了。

過了不久，國王對母后說，“我想娶個妻子，你給我找個漂亮女人吧。”她說，“我們的女奴中有一個絕頂漂亮，不過她有一個嚴重的缺陷。”“是甚麼？”國王問道。他母親說，“她的兩隻手都被砍掉了。”他說，“讓我看看她。”於是母后便把這女人帶到國王面前，國王被她迷住了，就跟她結了婚。她為他生了一個兒子。

Now this was the woman, who had her hands cut off for alms-giving; and when she became queen, her fellowwives envied her and wrote to the King [who was then absent] that she was unchaste; so he wrote to his mother, bidding her carry the woman into the desert and leave her there. The old queen obeyed his commandment and abandoned the woman and her son in the desert; whereupon she fell to weeping and wailing exceeding sore for that which had befallen her. As she went along, with the child at her neck, she came to a river and knelt down to drink, being overcome with excess of thirst, for fatigue and grief; but, as she bent her head, the child fell into the water.

Then she sat weeping sore for her child, and as she wept, there came up two men, who said to her, "What makes thee weep?" Quoth she, "I had a child at my neck, and he hath fallen into the water." "Wilt thou that we bring him out to thee?" asked they, and she answered, "Yes." So they prayed to God the Most High, and the child came forth of the water to her, safe and sound. Quoth they, "Wilt thou that God restore thee thy hands as they were?" "Yes," replied she: whereupon they prayed to God, blessed and exalted be He! and her hands were restored to her, goodlier than before. Then said they,

她就是因施捨而被砍掉雙手的女人。她成了王后以後，王室的其他嬪妃都很嫉妒她。（國王外出時，）她們寄信給國王，告她不貞。於是國王給母后寫信，要母后把這個女人帶到沙漠並把她拋棄在那裏。太后遵從了他的吩咐把女人和她的兒子都丟棄在沙漠裏。女人悲痛欲絕，為目前的遭遇痛哭不止。她揹着孩子，向前走去，來到一條小河旁。這時，她疲勞又悲傷，口渴難忍，就跪下去喝水。但是，她一低頭，孩子就掉進了水裏。

於是她坐在河邊，哭她的孩子。她正哭着，來了兩個人，問她"你哭甚麼？"她說，"我揹着的孩子，掉到水裏去了。""你要我們把孩子撈上來給你嗎？"她答道，"要。"於是，他們向上天祈禱，孩子就從水中出來，安然無恙回到了她身旁。他們又說，"你要真主把你的雙手還給你嗎？""要，"她回答。於是他們又祈禱，她的雙手就回到了她的身上，比原先還要漂亮。然後他們問她，

"Knowst thou who we are?" "God [only] is all-knowing," answered she; and they said, "We are thy two cakes of bread, that thou gavest in alms to the beggar and which were the cause of the cutting off of thy hands. So praise thou God the Most High, for that He hath restored thee thy hands and thy child."

“你知道我們是誰嗎？”“只有主才無所不知，”她答道。他們説，“我們就是你給乞丐的那兩塊麵包，也就是你被砍掉雙手的原因。讚美至高無上的真主吧！是祂還給你了雙手和孩子。”

## 61 The Devout Israelite

There was once a devout man of the children of Israel[1], whose family span cotton; and he used every day to sell the yarn they span and buy fresh cotton, and with the profit he bought the day's victual for his household. One day, he went out and sold the day's yarn as usual, when there met him one of his brethren, who complained to him of want; so he gave him the price of the yarn and returned, empty-handed, to his family, who said to him, "Where is the cotton and the food?" Quoth he, "Such an one met me and complained to me of want; so I gave him the price of the yarn." And they said, "How shall we do? We have nothing to sell." Now they had a broken platter and a jar; so he took them to the market; but none would buy them of him.

Presently, as he stood in the market, there came up a man with a stinking, swollen fish, which no one would buy of him, and he said to the Jew, "Wilt thou sell me thine unsaleable ware for mine?" "Yes," answered the Jew and giving him the jar and platter, took the fish and carried it

1. a devout man of the children of Israel：即信回教的猶太人。

## 六十一　虔誠的以色列人

從前有一個虔誠的以色列人，他的一家都紡棉花；他每天都去賣紡好的棉紗再買回新的棉花，並用賺來的錢買回一家當天的食品。有一天他像往常一樣外出，賣掉了當天的棉紗。這時他遇見了一個兄弟，兄弟向他哭窮，他就把賣棉紗的錢給了這個兄弟，自己空手回到家裏。家人問他，“棉花和食物在哪裏？”他說，“我碰見了這麼一個人，他向我哭窮，我就把賣棉紗的錢給他了。”他們說，“那我們怎麼辦呢？我們沒有東西可賣了。”他們只有一個破盤子和一個罐子，他就把它們拿到市場去，但沒人願意買。

他站在市場不久來了一個人，提着一條腫脹發臭的魚，沒有人願意買他的魚，他就對這個猶太人說，“你願意把你那賣不出去的東西賣給我，換我的魚嗎？”“好吧！”猶太人回答，就把罐子和盤子給了那人，拿了魚回

home to his family, who said, "What shall we do with this fish?" Quoth he, "We will broil it and eat of it, till it please God to provide for us." So they took it and ripping open its belly, found therein a great pearl and told the Jew, who said, "See if it be pierced. If so, it belongs to some one of the folk; if not, it is a provision of God for us." So they examined it and found it unpierced.

The Jew took it to the jeweller, who said, "It is worth threescore and ten thousand dirhems and no more." Then he paid him that sum and the Jew hired two porters to carry the money to his house. As he came to his door, a beggar accosted him, saying, "Give me of that which God the Most High hath given thee." Quoth the Jew, "But yesterday, we were even as thou; take half the money." So he made two parts of it, and each took his half. Then said the beggar, "Take back thy money and God prosper thee in it; I am a messenger, whom thy Lord hath sent to try thee." Quoth the Jew, "To God be the praise and the thanks!" and abode with his family in all delight of life, till death.

到了家裏，家人說，“我們拿這魚怎麼辦呢？”他說，“把魚烤了，吃了牠，直到真主再給我們食物。”於是他們把魚開了膛，發現裏面有一顆大珍珠，他們告訴猶太人，他說，“看看珍珠上有沒有穿孔，若有孔，那就是別人的，若沒有孔，那就是真主賜予我們的。”他們檢查了珍珠，發現上面沒有穿孔。

猶太人把珍珠拿到珠寶商那裏，珠寶商說，“這珍珠值七萬迪拉姆，不能再多了。”他付給他這麼多錢，猶太人僱了兩個腳夫把錢運回家。他走到家門口時一個乞丐上前來對他說，“把至高無上的主給你的東西給我吧！”猶太人說，“就在昨天，我們還和你一樣，一無所有；這錢你拿一半去吧！”於是他把錢分成兩半，一人拿一半。後來乞丐對他說，“把你的錢拿回去吧，真主保佑你；我是一個使者，是真主派我來試探你的。”猶太人說：“讚美主，感謝主！”後來他和他的一家都過着快樂的日子直到壽終。

## 62 The Water-carrier and the Goldsmith's Wife

There was once, in the city of Bokhara, a water-carrier, who used to carry water to the house of a goldsmith and had done thus thirty years. Now the goldsmith had a wife of exceeding beauty and elegance and withal renowned for modesty, chastity and piety. One day, the water-carrier came, as of wont, and poured the water into the cisterns. Now the woman was standing in the midst of the court; so he went up to her and taking her hand, stroked it and pressed it, then went away and left her. When her husband came home from the bazaar, she said to him, "I would have thee tell me what thou hast done in the bazaar, to-day, to anger God the Most High." Quoth he, "I have done nothing." "Nay," rejoined she, "but, by Allah, thou hast indeed done something to anger God; and except thou tell me the truth, I will not abide in thy house, and thou shalt not see me, nor will I see thee." "I will tell thee the truth," answered he. "As I was sitting in my shop this day, a woman came up to me and bade me make her a bracelet. Then she went away and I wrought her a bracelet of gold and laid it aside. Presently, she returned and I brought her out the bracelet. She put out her hand and I

## 六十二　送水人和金匠的妻子

從前在博哈拉城有一個送水的人，他常給金匠家送水，已經送了三十年。金匠有個妻子，容貌美麗，舉止優雅，而且她的誠實、貞潔和虔誠遠近聞名。一天，送水人來了，和平常一樣，把水倒進了桶裏。這時女人正站在院子當中，他走了過去，拿起她的手，又摸又捏，然後他就離開了她走了。她丈夫從集市回到家裏時，她對他說，“你要告訴我你今天在集市做了些甚麼事，惹惱了至高無上的真主？”他說，“我沒做甚麼。”“不對，”她說，“真主作證！你一定做了甚麼事惹怒了主。除非你給我講實話，不然我不再呆在這個家裏，你從此見不到我，我也不再見你。”“我講實話吧，”他回答，“今天我坐在舖子裏，來了一個女人，她要我給她做一隻手鐲，然後她就走了，我給她做了一隻金手鐲，把它放在一邊。不久她回來了，我就把手鐲拿出來給她看。她伸出手來，我把手鐲

clasped the bracelet on her wrist; and I wondered at the whiteness of her hand and the beauty of her wrist. So I took her hand and pressed it and squeezed it."

"God is Most Great!" exclaimed the woman. "Why didst thou this ill thing? Know that the water-carrier, who has come to our house these thirty years, nor sawst[1] thou ever any treason in him, took my hand to day and pressed and squeezed it." Quoth her husband, "O woman, let us crave pardon of God! Verily, I repent of what I did, and do thou ask forgiveness of God for me." "God pardon me and thee," said she, "and vouchsafe to make good the issue of our affair!"

Next day, the water-carrier came in to the jeweller's wife and throwing himself at her feet, grovelled in the dust and besought pardon of her, saying, "O my lady, acquit me of that which Satan deluded me to do; for it was he that seduced me and led me astray." "Go thy ways," answered she; "the fault was not in thee, but in my husband, for that he did what he did in his shop, and God hath retaliated upon him in this world." And it is related that the goldsmith, when his wife told him how the water-carrier had used her, said, "Tit for tat! If I had done more, the water-carrier had done more."

---

1. sawst：（古）= saw。

戴在她手腕上。她的手可真白呀！手腕也真美呀！我都丟了魂了。我拿起她的手，握住了它，捏得緊緊的。”

“偉大的真主啊！”婦人叫道，“你為甚麼幹這件壞事啊？！你知道嗎，那個送水人，這三十年來一直來我們家，從未見他有甚麼不軌之處，今天卻拿起我的手，又摸又捏。”她丈夫說，“娘子，讓我們求真主饒恕吧！說真的，我真後悔我的所作所為，你一定要懇求真主饒恕我。”“願主饒恕我和你，”她說，“願真主讓我們這事有個好的結局。”

第二天，送水人來到珠寶商妻子面前，撲在她的腳下，趴在泥土裏請求她原諒。他說，“太太，饒恕我吧！那是魔鬼引誘我幹的，是魔鬼引誘我走上了邪路。”“做你的事去吧！”她說，“錯不在你，而在我丈夫，他在店裏做了那樣的事，真主就讓他得了現世報。”據說當金匠的妻子告訴他送水人如何調戲她時，金匠說，“真是以其人之道還治其人之身！如果我再多幹點壞事，送水人也會幹出更多壞事！”

# 63 The Devout Woman and the Two Wicked Elders

There was once, of old time, a virtuous woman among the children of Israel, who was pious and devout and used every day to go out to the place of prayer, first entering a garden, which adjoined thereto, and there making the ablution. Now there were in this garden two old men, its keepers, who fell in love with her and sought her favours; but she refused, whereupon said they, "Except thou yield thyself to us, we will bear witness against thee of fornication." Quoth she, "God will preserve me from your wickedness!" Then they opened the garden-gate and cried out, and the folk came to them from all sides, saying, "What ails you?" Quoth they, "We found this damsel in company with a youth, who was doing lewdness with her; but he escaped from our hands."

Now it was the use of the people of those days to expose an adulteress to public ignominy[1] for three days and after stone her. So they pilloried her three days, whilst the two old men came up to her daily and laying their hands on her head, said, "Praised be God who hath sent down His vengeance on thee!"

---

1. expose... to public ignominy：直譯為“……接受公眾的羞辱”。

## 六十三　貞潔婦人與淫老頭

從前，以色列人中有個貞婦，她十分虔誠，每天都到禮拜堂做禮拜。她總是先在隔鄰的花園中沐浴。花園裏有兩個老頭園丁愛上了她，向她求愛，但遭到了她的拒絕。他們就說："除非你順從我們，否則我們就作證，說你與人私通。"她說："真主會保護我不受你們的誣陷。"於是園丁打開園門，大聲喊起來。人們從四面八方趕來，他們問："你們怎麼了？"他們說："我們發現這個女人跟一個小伙子獨處，幹敗德的勾當，但他逃掉了。"

按當時的風俗習慣，女通姦者要示眾三天然後以亂石砸死。於是，他們把這女人上枷示眾了三天，兩個老頭每天都到她被示眾的地方去，伸手摸着她的頭說："讚美真主，這是祂降給你應得的處罰啊！"

On the fourth day, they carried her away, to stone her; but a lad of twelve years old, by name Daniel, followed them to the place of execution and said to them, "Hasten not to stone her, till I judge between them." So they set him a chair and he sat down and caused bring the old men before him separately. (Now he was the first that separated witnesses.) Then said he to the first, "What sawest thou?" So he repeated to him his story, and Daniel said, "In what part of the garden did this befall?" "On the eastern side," replied the elder, "under a pear-tree." Then he called the other old man and asked him the same question; and he replied, "On the western side of the garden, under an apple-tree." Meanwhile the damsel stood by, with her hands and eyes uplift to heaven, imploring God for deliverance. Then God the Most High sent down His vengeful thunder upon the two old men and consumed them and made manifest the innocence of the damsel.

This was the first of the miracles of the Prophet Daniel, on whom and on the Prophet be blessing and peace!

第四天，他們把她帶走，要以亂石砸死她，但有一個十二歲的少年，名叫丹尼爾，跟着他們到了行刑地，他說，“先別用石頭砸她，讓我先審問一下。”於是人們給他擺了一張椅子，他坐下後，命令把兩個老人分別帶來，單個盤問。（他是個別盤問證人的始作俑者。）他對第一個園丁說，“你看見了甚麼？”園丁重複了一遍他編造的說法。丹尼爾說，“通姦的事是在園中甚麼地方發生的？”“在靠東邊，”老頭答道，“在一棵梨樹下。”然後他叫來另一個老頭，問他同樣的問題。這個老頭說，“在花園西邊的蘋果樹下。”此時那女人站在一旁，兩眼凝視天空，兩手高高舉起，乞求上帝保佑，突然上帝發出了一陣晴天霹靂把兩個園丁頓時劈死，昭示了女人的清白無辜。

這是先知丹尼爾第一次顯示奇蹟，願真主保佑他平安！

## 64 The Justice of Providence

A certain prophet once worshipped on a high mountain, at whose foot was a spring of running water, and he was wont to sit by day on the mountain-top, where none could see him, calling upon the name of God the Most High and watching those who came to the spring. One day, as he sat looking on the spring, there came up a horseman, who dismounted thereby and taking a bag from his neck, laid it down beside him, after which he drank of the water and rested awhile, then mounted and rode away, leaving the bag behind him. Presently up came another man, to drink of the spring, who saw the bag and finding it full of gold, took it up and made off with it in safety, after he had drunken. A little after, came a woodcutter, with a heavy faggot on his back, and sat down by the spring to drink, when, behold, back came the horseman, in great concern, and said to him, "Where is the bag [with the thousand dinars] that was here?" "I know nothing of it," replied the woodcutter, whereupon the other drew his sword and smote him and killed him. Then he searched his clothes, but found nothing; so he left him and went away.

## 六十四　天意

從前，有個先知在一個高山上修行。山腳下有一眼泉水。他白天經常坐在山頂上，別人都看不見他。他默誦真主的名字並觀察來到泉邊的人。有一天，他正坐在山頂上看泉水，來了一位騎馬人，他在泉邊下了馬，卸下脖子上的錢袋，放在地上，然後喝水，休息了一會兒，就又上馬而去，但卻忘了帶走錢袋。過了不久，另一個人前來喝水，他看見錢袋，而且發現裏面裝滿了金子。他喝完水後拿着錢袋走了。又過了一會兒來了一個樵夫，揹着沉重的木柴，他也坐下來喝水。這時，騎馬人回來了，焦急萬分地對樵夫說："我忘在這裏的錢袋（裏面有一千第納爾）哪裏去了？""我不知道，"樵夫答道。騎馬人一聽這話，拔出寶劍一劍刺死了樵夫。然後他仔細搜查他的衣服，但甚麼也沒找到，只好走了。

When the prophet saw this, he said, "O Lord, this man hath been slain unjustly, for another had the thousand dinars." But God answered him, saying, "Busy thyself with thy service, for the ordering of the affairs of the universe is none of thine affair. Know that the horseman's father had despoiled the second man's father of a thousand dinars; so I gave the son possession of his father's money. As for the woodcutter, he had slain the horseman's father, wherefore I enabled the son to avenge himself." Then said the prophet, "Verily, there is none other god than Thou! Glory to Thee! Thou [alone] knowest the hidden things."[1]

---

1. 引自《古蘭經》108卷。

先知看到了這一切，説道：“真主啊！是另一個人拿走了他的一千第納爾，而這個人卻冤枉地被他殺死了”。真主回答他説：“你還是埋頭修煉吧！塵世的事不用你來安排。你要知道，騎馬人的父親搶劫了第二個人的父親一千第納爾，所以我把他父親的錢還給了他兒子。至於樵夫，他曾殺害了騎馬人的父親，所以今天我讓他兒子替他父親報了讎。”先知説：“真主啊！沒有人能比得上您！光榮歸於您！只有您才知道其中的奧秘啊！”

## 65 A Drop of Honey

A certain man used to hunt the wild beasts in the desert, and one day he came upon a grotto in the mountains, where he found a hollow full of bees' honey. So he took somewhat thereof in a water-skin he had with him and throwing it over his shoulder, carried it to the city, followed by a hunting dog which was dear to him. He stopped at the shop of an oilman and offered him the honey for sale and he bought it. Then he emptied it out of the skin that he might see it, and in the act a drop fell to the ground, whereupon the flies flocked to it and a bird swooped down upon the flies. Now the oilman had a cat, which pounced upon the bird, and the huntsman's dog, seeing the cat, sprang upon it and killed it; whereupon the oilman ran at the dog and killed it and the huntsman in turn leapt upon the oilman and killed him. Now the oilman was of one village and the huntsman of another; and when the people of the two places heard what had passed, they took up arms and rose on one another in anger, and there befell a sore battle; nor did the sword leave to play amongst them[1], till there died of them much people, none knoweth[2] their number save God the Most High.

# 六十五　一滴蜜

有個人常去沙漠獵野獸。一天，他在山裏發現一個巖洞，裏面有個裝滿蜂蜜的大坑。他就用隨身帶來的皮水袋裝了些蜂蜜，揹回城裏，身後跟着他心愛的獵犬。他在一家油店門前停了下來，問賣油的要不要蜜。賣油的説買。於是他把蜜從皮袋裏倒出來給他看。這時，有一滴蜜灑落在地上，立刻招來了一羣蒼蠅，一隻鳥就飛下來啄蒼蠅。賣油的有隻貓，牠撲上去抓鳥；獵人的狗看到了，又撲上去咬死了貓；賣油的一氣之下就衝過去打死了狗，獵人反過來把賣油的打死了。那兩人是來自兩個村的；兩村的村民得知消息大怒，立刻拿起武器去攻打對方；雙方展開了一場血戰，直殺得血流成河，方才罷手。倒底死了多少人只有天知道了。

---

1. the sword leave to play amongst them：停止揮刀互相砍殺。這裏 leave 作“停止”解。
2. knoweth：（古）= knows。

# The Commoners' Wisdom
# 平民的智慧

## 66 The Two Jesters

It is also related that there was once in the city of Damascus in Syria, a man noted for his droll and indelicate tricks; also there was another in Cairo, not less famous for the same quality. The Damascene jester had often heard tell of his Cairene rival and was the more anxious to meet him since his usual admirers were always saying: "There can be no doubt that the Egyptian is more spiteful and intelligent, cleverer and more amusing than you. To be with him is much more droll. If you do not believe us, go and see his work in Cairo and you will be forced to acknowledge his superiority." At last the man said to himself: "There is nothing for it, I must go to Cairo and see for myself." He made his luggage and left Damascus for Cairo; and Allah brought him safe and sound to that city. Immediately he inquired for the dwelling of his rival and paid him a visit; the jester of Cairo received him with a large hospitality and most cordial welcome. The two passed the night in agreeable conversation concerning the affairs of the great world.

## 六十六　兩個小丑

相傳，從前敘利亞大馬士革城有個人以滑稽和粗野的把戲出名。同時，開羅有另一個人也以此著稱。大馬士革的那位小丑時常聽說他的開羅對手的本領，很想會會他，因為他以前的崇拜者總是說："那個埃及人肯定要比你惡毒、機智、聰明和有趣。跟他在一起要好玩得多。你不信可以自己去開羅看看他的活兒，你就會不得不承認他比你強。"最後，那人心想："沒有別的辦法，我只好親自跑一趟開羅了。"他整理好行李就離開大馬士革到開羅去了；靠真主的保佑他平安抵達了那個城市。他馬上打聽對手的住址並去拜訪他。開羅的那位小丑熱烈歡迎並盛情款待了他。兩個人在一起縱論天下大事，融洽地談了一整夜。

Next morning the guest said to his host: "Dear companion, my sole reason for coming to Cairo was to judge for myself those excellent tricks and passes which I have heard that you play unceasingly upon your city. I would not like to return without instruction. Will you let me have a taste of your quality?" "Dear friend," answered the other, "they have been deceiving you. I am one of those slow fellows who can hardly distinguish his left hand from his right. How could I hope to teach a delicate Damascus spark like you? Still, since my duty as a host requires that I show you the fair things of our city, let us go out for a walk."

The Cairene led his guest to the mosque of Al-Ashar, so that he might tell the people of Damascus of the religious and scientific marvel which he had seen; but on the way he paused at a flower stall and bought a large bunch of aromatic herbs, carnations, roses, sweet basil, jasmin, mint, and marjoram. When they entered the court of the mosque they saw many persons satisfying their needs in the line of privies which faced the fountain of ablution; so the Cairo man said to his guest: "Now tell me, if you wanted to play a trick on this line of squatting persons, how would you set about it?"

"The method is obvious," answered the man from Damascus, "I would go behind them with a thorny broom and, while I swept, prick all their bums as if by accident."

第二天早晨，客人對主人說："親愛的朋友，我來開羅的唯一目的就是要親眼看看我聽說您不斷對您的城市玩過的絕技，務請不吝賜教，使我不虛此行。您可否讓我一飽眼福呢？"主人答道："親愛的朋友，你上當了。我是個笨人，連自己的左右手都分不清，怎麼敢教像您這樣聰明的大馬士革明星呢？不過，為盡地主之誼，我要領您去看看本城的美景。我們出去散散步吧。"

開羅小丑領客人去阿拉夏清真寺，以便他回去時能告訴大馬士革人民他所看到宗教和科學的奇蹟。但是，途中他在一家花店門前停了下來，買了一大束芳草、康乃馨、玫瑰花、羅勒、茉莉、薄荷和墨角蘭。他們走進清真寺的園子時，看到洗禮泉對面的一排廁所裏有許多人在解手。開羅人就對客人說："告訴我，如果你想對這些蹲在那裏解手的人開個玩笑，你會怎麼做？"

大馬士革人說："很明顯，我會拿着一把帶刺的掃帚走到他們身後，裝着不經意地掃過去，刺他們的屁股。"

"There is something a trifle heavy and gross to my mind about that pleasantry," said the Cairene, "Such jokes verge a little towards the indelicate. Now watch me!" He went up to the line of defecators with a friendly smile and offered a spray of flowers to each in turn, saying: "Allow me, good master." In confusion and fury, each replied: "Allah curse you, you son of a pimp! Where do you think we are, in the dining room?" All the people in the court of the mosque laughed most heartily at the expressions of these people.

Then the man from Damascus turned to his host, and said: "You have beaten me, O prince of jesters. It is a true proverb which says: *As fine as an Egyptian; for he can pass through the eye of a needle!"*

開羅人說：“我覺得這個玩笑開得有點過份而且不雅。這種玩笑有點粗鄙。現在看我的！”他走到那排解手者面前，臉上帶着微笑，送給每人一支花，說：“先生，請笑納。”解手人都莫名其妙，不禁勃然大怒，說：“真主詛咒你，雜種！你以為我們是在哪裏，是在飯廳嗎？”清真寺園子裏的人聽了這話都大笑起來。

於是，大馬士革人轉身對主人說：“您是小丑之王，您打敗了我。諺語說得對：精細不過埃及人，針眼雖小能穿行！”

# 67 Mesrour the Eunuch and Ibn El Caribi

The Khalif Haroun er Reshid was very restless one night; so he said to his Vizier Jaafer, "I am sleepless to-night and my heart is oppressed and I know not what to do." Now his henchman Mesrour was standing before him, and he laughed. Quoth the Khalif, "Dost thou laugh in derision of me or art thou mad?" "Neither, by Allah, O Commander of the Faithful," answered Mesrour, "by thy kinship to the Prince of Apostles, I did it not of my free-will; but I went out yesterday to walk and coming to the bank of the Tigris, saw there the folk collected about a man named Ibn el Caribi who was making them laugh; and but now I recalled what he said, and laughter got the better of me; and I crave pardon of thee, O Commander of the Faithful!" "Bring him to me forthright," said the Khalif. So Mesrour repaired in all haste to Ibn el Caribi and said to him, "The Commander of the Faithful calls for thee." "I hear and obey," answered the droll. "But on condition," added Mesrour, "that, if he give thee aught, thou shalt have a fourth and the rest shall be mine." "Nay," replied the other, "thou shalt have half and I half." "Not so," insisted Mesrour; "I will have three-quarters." "Thou shalt have two-thirds, then," rejoined Ibn el Caribi;

## 六十七　太監與小丑

一天夜裏，哈隆・雷切德國王心情十分煩躁，就對大臣嘉弗説："今夜我睡不着，心裏煩悶，不知如何是好。"他的親信曼斯洛正站在面前，聽到這話大笑起來。國王説："你嘲笑我嗎？還是瘋了？"曼斯洛答道："都不是，陛下，我發誓我是情不自禁才笑的。我昨天出去散步，來到底格里斯河邊，看到一幫人圍着一個名叫卡立比的人，他正在逗他們笑。剛才我想起他説的話就不禁笑了出來。陛下，萬望恕罪。"國王説："馬上帶他來見我。"曼斯洛急忙去找卡立比，對他説："陛下召見你。"小丑説："遵命。"曼斯洛接着説："但有個條件：要是陛下有甚麼賞賜，你得四分之一，其餘歸我。"小丑答道："不行，對半分。"曼斯洛堅持説："不行，我要四分之三。"卡立比回答："好吧，就給你三分之

"and I the other third." To this Mesrour agreed, after much haggling, and they returned to the palace together.

When Ibn el Caribi came into the Khalif's presence, he saluted him, as became his rank, and stood before him; whereupon said Er Reshid to him, "If thou do not make me laugh, I will give thee three blows with this bag." Quoth Ibn el Caribi in himself, "Three strokes with that bag were a small matter, seeing that beating with whips irketh me not;" for he thought the bag was empty. Then he clapped into a discourse, such as would make a stone laugh, and gave vent to all manner of drolleries; but the Khalif laughed not neither smiled, whereat Ibn el Caribi marvelled and was chagrined and affrighted. Then said the Khalif, "Now hast thou earned the beating," and gave him a blow with the bag, in which were four pebbles, each two pounds in weight. The blow fell on his neck and he gave a great cry, then calling to mind his compact with Mesrour, said, "Pardon, O Commander of the Faithful! Hear two words from me." "Say on," replied the Khalif. Quoth Ibn el Caribi, "Mesrour made it a condition with me that, whatsoever might come to me of the bounties of the Commander of the Faithful, one-third thereof should be mine and the rest his; nor did he agree to leave me so much as one-third save after much haggling. Now thou hast bestowed on me nothing but beating; I have had my share and here stands he, ready to receive his; so give him the two other blows."

二，我要三分之一。”在多次討價還價之後，曼斯洛表示同意，他們就一起回宮了。

卡立比來到國王面前，行禮如儀後，站在國王面前。國王對他說：“如果你不能逗我發笑，我就用這個袋子打你三下。”卡立比心想：“用鞭子抽我都不怕，何況用這袋子打三下這樣的小事。”因為他以為那袋子是空的。然後，他就拍手講了起來，那笑話可以把頑石都逗笑，還做了各種各樣的滑稽表情，但國王就是不笑。卡立比很奇怪，同時感到失望和害怕。於是國王說：“你現在該挨打了，”說着就用袋子打了他一下。誰知袋子裏裝有四塊鵝卵石，每塊足有兩磅重。袋子落在他脖子上時，他痛得大聲喊了起來，這時突然想起他和曼斯洛的約定，就說：“陛下恕罪！請聽我一言。”國王答道：“說吧。”卡立比說：“曼斯洛和我有約：如果陛下給我賞賜，三分之一歸我，其餘歸他，而且這三分之一還是經過多次討價還價之後他才同意給我的。現在您賞給我的只是擊打，我已經領受了我那一份，而他正站在那裏，等着領他那一份呢，所以剩下的那兩下就給他吧。”

When the Khalif heard this, he laughed till he fell backward; then calling Mesrour, he gave him a blow, whereat he cried out and said, "O Commander of the Faithful, one-third sufficeth me: give him the two-thirds." The Khalif laughed at them and ordered them a thousand dinars each, and they went away, rejoicing.

國王聽了這話笑得前仰後合，然後把曼斯洛叫過來，打了他一下。他大聲喊道：“陛下，給我三分之一就夠了，把三分之二給他吧。”國王哈哈大笑，吩咐給他們每人一千第納爾。他們就很高興地走了。

## 68 A List of Fools

It is related that the khalifat Haroun Al-Rachid kept a jester in his palace to divert his moments of dark humour[1]. This jester was called Bahlul the Wise. One day the khalifat asked him: "O Bahlul, do you know how many fools there are in Baghdad?" "It would be a long list, my lord," answered Bahlul. "Yet I bid you make it and make it exactly," cried Haroun. Bahlul gave a long laugh, and then replied: "As I have no taste for heavy work, I will make you out a list of all the wise men in Baghdad. Those who do not appear upon it will be the fools."

---

1. dark humour：壞脾氣、壞心情。

## 六十八　蠢人的名單

傳說哈隆·雷切德國王在宮中養了一個弄臣，他不高興時可以給他消愁解悶。弄臣名叫智者巴勒爾。一天，國王問他："巴勒爾，你知不知道巴格達有多少蠢人？"巴勒爾答道："陛下，這個名單開出來可就長了。"哈隆大聲說，"但我命令你把名單開給我，而且要毫無差錯。"巴勒爾大笑了一陣，然後說，"我不愛幹辛苦活，所以就給你開一個巴格達所有聰明人的名單吧。凡是不在這名單上的就都是蠢人了。"

## 69 The Reason for a Horror of Marriage

Bahlul was wise enough to have a horror of marriage[1]; so Haroun, being one day angry with him, married him without his consent to a very beautiful slave. But Bahlul had hardly lain down by his wife's side for a moment on the first night before he leapt to his feet and fled from the room. While he was rushing like a madman about the palacc, the khalifat came to him, and said severely: "Vile fellow, why have you offended against the wife I gave you?" "My lord, there is no remedy for terror," answered the jester, "I have no fault to find with the bride of your generosity, for she is beautiful and modest; but as soon as I lay beside her, I distinctly heard voices speaking from the deep of her breast. One asked me for a robe, another for a silk veil, a third for slippers, and a fourth for an embroidered belt. So I took fright and fled, in spite of your orders and the maiden's charms, fearing if I stayed to become more foolish and unhappy even than I am."

---

1. wise enough to have a horror of marriage：可直譯為“討厭結婚是明智的”，這裏的“明智（wise）”與末句中的“愚蠢（foolish）”前後呼應，產生諷刺的幽默。

## 六十九　討厭結婚的理由

巴勒爾是聰明人，他討厭結婚；因此，國王哈隆有一天生他的氣時未經他同意就給他娶了一個十分漂亮的女奴。但是新婚第一夜巴勒爾剛在新娘身邊躺下就跳了起來，並從房裏逃了出來。當他在宮中像瘋子似地到處亂跑時，國王來到他的身邊，嚴厲地說："惡賊，你為甚麼冒犯我給你娶的妻子？"弄臣答道："陛下，因為我怕，那是無可救藥的。陛下恩賜給我的新娘真是無可挑剔，又美貌又賢慧；但我在她身邊一躺下，就清楚地聽見從她肺裏發出許多聲音，一個聲音要一件長袍，另一個聲音要一幅絲面紗，又一個聲音要一雙拖鞋，再一個聲音要一條繡花腰帶。所以我就給嚇跑了，也顧不上您的命令和她的美貌啦；我怕要是我繼續呆在那裏就會變得比現在還要愚蠢和不快樂了。"

## 70 The Right to Stretch Out My Legs

This same Bahlul refused a present of a thousand dinars which the khalifat offered twice; so Haroun asked him the reason of his disinterestedness. For sole answer, Bahlul stretched out his legs in the khalifat's face. Seeing this supreme mark of incivility, the chief eunuch would have taken the jester up and beaten him; but Al-Rachid forbade him, and questioned Bahlul concerning his great lack of respect. "My lord," answered the jester, "if I had stretched out my hand to receive your present I would have forfeited the right to stretch out my legs."

# 七十　伸腿的權利

國王兩次要賜給巴勒爾一千第納爾，但他都不收。國王問他為甚麼對錢財無動於衷。作為回答，他只是在國王面前伸開雙腿。看到他這大失體統的行為，大太監本想抓住弄臣痛打一頓，但是國王禁止了他，並問巴勒爾為何如此無禮。弄臣答道："陛下，要是我伸手接受您的賞賜的話，我就會失去伸開雙腿的權利了。"

## 71 The Worth of an Empire

One day, as Al-Rachid was returning from a warlike expedition, Bahlul entered his tent and found the khalifat parched with thirst and calling for water. The jester hastened to fetch a cup of water and gave it to him, saying: "O Commander of the Faithful, before you drink pray tell me how much you would have given for this cup of water if it had been difficult to procure." "I would have given half my kingdom," answered Al-Rachid as he drank. "And now that you have drunk," went on Bahlul, "supposing this cup of water refused to leave your body, owing to some retention on the part of your honourable bladder, what would you pay to see it safely forth?" "Surely half of my kingdom," answered Al-Rachid; then said Bahlul: "I suppose, my lord, that an empire which could be bought for a cup of water and a jet of piss is worth these cares and bloody wars?..." Al-Rachid wept.

## 七十一　帝國的價值

一天，國王雷切德出征回來，巴勒爾走進他的軍帳，發現他口渴難忍，索水止渴。弄臣趕忙拿來一杯水遞給他說：“陛下，在喝水之前請告訴我如果水很難弄到，您會給多少來買這杯水呢？”國王邊喝水邊回答道：“我會拿出我的一半國土。”巴勒爾接着說：“現在你已經喝了水，假如由於您膀胱的豬留，這杯水不能從您的龍體排洩出去，您會給甚麼來讓它排出去呢？”國王答道：“當然是我的另一半國土。”於是巴勒爾說：“陛下，我在想為一個可以用一杯水和一泡尿換來的帝國而如此殫精竭慮，大動干戈，這值得嗎？……”國王哭了。

# 72 The Wazir[1] and the Fart

The khalifat Haroun Al-Rachid, being once taken with weariness walked out upon the road which leads from Baghdad to Bassora, taking with his wazir Giafar.

As the khalifat went along with sombre eyes and compressed lips, an old man passed by mounted upon an ass. Haroun Al-Rachid turned to Giafar, saying: "Ask that old man where he is going." The wazir, who up to that moment had been cudgelling his brains in vain for some distraction which might please the khalifat, resolved to amuse him at the expense of the aged traveller, who was jogging along with the cord loose upon his donkey's neck. Therefore he went up to him and asked: "Whither away, old man?" "I journey from Bassora to Baghdad," the other answered. "Why have you undertaken so long a journey?" demanded Giafar; and the traveller replied: "As Allah lives, I wish to find some learned doctor in Baghdad who will give me a collyrium for my eyes." Then said Giafar: "Chance and cure are in the hands of Allah, O sheik. What will you give me if I save you expense

1. wazir：= vizier。

## 七十二　大臣和屁

一次，國王哈隆・雷切德心情煩悶，就去從巴格達通往巴索拉的大道上散心，隨身帶着大臣基亞法。國王眼光憂鬱，嘴唇緊閉地走着，迎面來了一個騎着毛驢的老人。國王轉身對基亞法說：“去問問那個老人他去哪裏？”大臣此時已絞盡腦汁想不出甚麼能分散國王的注意力而使他高興的事情，正好拿這個上了年紀的旅行者開心以取悅國王。老人正騎驢慢行，韁繩鬆鬆地套在驢脖子上。大臣走過去，問道：“老頭，去哪裏？”“我從巴索拉到巴格達去。”老人回答。“你幹嗎作這麼長途的旅行呢？”基亞法又問。旅行者答道：“我想到巴格達找個有學問的醫生給我配點眼藥水。”基亞法說：“老頭，運氣和藥方都在真主手中！如果我親自給你配個藥方，一夜之間就能治好

and time, by myself prescribing a remedy which will cure your eyes in one night?" "Allah alone could reward such kindness," murmured the old man. Hearing this, Giafar turned to the khalifat with a wink, and then said to the traveller: "Since that is so, good uncle, carefully remember the following simple prescription: Take three ounces of the breath of the wind, three ounces of sun rays, three ounces of moon rays, and three ounces of lamp rays; mix them carefully in a bottomless mortar and expose them to the air for three months. For a further three months, pound the mixture, and then pour it into a porringer with holes in the bottom and leave it in the sun for another three months. By that time the cure will be ready and you have only to apply it three hundred times to your eyes on the first night, using three large pinches of it each time, to wake in the morning absolutely cured, if Allah wills."

Hearing these words, the old man bent over flat on his belly on the ass in front of Giafar, in sign of gratitude and respect, and suddenly let a detestable fart followed by two long funks, saying at the same time: "Be quick and gather them up, O learned doctor, before they float away, for they are the sole payment which I have about me for your windy[2] remedy."

---

2. windy：浮誇的，空洞的；這裏亦有“放屁的”之一語雙關效果。

你的眼睛，既省錢又省時，你會給我甚麼報答呢？”“只有真主才能報答這樣的善心。”老人喃喃地說。基亞法朝國王眨眨眼睛，對老人說：“既然這樣，老伯，那就牢記這個簡單的配方：取三盎司風，三盎司日光，三盎司月光，三盎司燈光，放在一個無底的研缽中攪合，在空氣中放置三個月。再過三個月把混合物搗碎，倒入底部有洞的淺杯中，放在太陽下三個月，這時藥就製成了。你第一夜把它塗在眼睛上三百次，每次三撮，第二天醒來就痊癒了，如果這是真主的意旨的話。”

老人聽了這話，就俯下身來，肚皮貼在驢子上，在基亞法面前作出感激和尊敬的姿態，突然放了三個又長又臭的屁，同時還說：“快去收起來，博學的醫生，免得它們都隨風飄走了。這是現在我能付給你那無形藥方的唯一報酬。”

Then the old man touched up his ass[3] and went on his way, while the khalifat fell over on his backside and strangled with laughter as he looked at the expression of his wazir standing there surprised, embarrassed and without an answer.

3. ass：雙關語，既解“驢子”，亦解“屁股”。

然後老人拍拍他的驢子，繼續趕路，而國王看到大臣站在那裏驚愕、尷尬、答不出話來的樣子卻笑得前仰後合喘不過氣來。

# 73 King Kisra Anoushirwan and the Village Damsel

The just King, Kisra Anoushirwan[1], was hunting one day and became separated from his suite, in pursuit of an antelope. Presently, he caught sight of a hamlet, near at hand, and being sore athirst, made for the door of a house, that stood by the wayside, and asked for a draught of water. A damsel came out and looked at him; then, going back into the house, pressed the juice from a sugar-cane into a tankard and mixed it with water; after which she strewed on the top somewhat of perfume, as it were dust, and carried it to the King. He took it and seeing in it what resembled dust, drank it, little by little, till he came to the end. Then said he to her, "O damsel, the drink is good and sweet, but for this dust in it, that troubles it." "O guest," answered she, "I put that in, of intent" "And why didst thou thus?" asked he; and she replied, "I saw that thou wast exceeding thirsty and feared that thou wouldst swallow the whole at one draught and that this would do thee a mischief; and so hadst thou done, but for this dust

1. Kisra Anoushirwan：公元 530-579 年，基斯拉波斯王朝的奠基人。穆罕默德誕生於他在位時期。在東方學者筆下，他的名字就是公正和威嚴的代名詞。

## 七十三　國王與村姑

一天，英明的國王基斯拉外出打獵，在追逐一隻羚羊時和他的隨從走散了。不久他看見不遠處有個小村莊。他口渴難耐，就走到路邊一座房子門前要水喝。一個村姑出來看了看他，然後回到屋裏，榨了一大杯甘蔗汁，加了點水，然後在上面撒了一些像灰塵似的香料遞給國王。國王拿着這杯水，看見裏面有灰塵似的東西，只好一點一點地喝，一直喝完。然後他對她說：“姑娘，這杯飲品甘甜無比，但是有灰塵在裏面，真是美中不足。”她回答，“尊敬的客人，我是有意放進去的。”“你為甚麼這樣做？”他問。她答道，“我剛才看你渴得厲害，怕你一口氣喝掉這杯蔗汁，那會害了你，有點灰塵在裏面，你就會慢慢地

that troubled the drink." The King wondered at her wit and good sense and said to her, "How many sugar-canes didst thou press for this draught?" "One," answered she; whereat the King marvelled and calling for the roll of the taxes of the village, saw that its assessment was but little and bethought him to increase it, on his return to his palace, saying in himself, "Why is a village so lightly taxed, where they get this much juice out of one sugar-cane?"

Then he left the village and pursued his chase. As he came back at the end of the day, he passed alone by the same door and called again for drink; whereupon the same damsel came out and knowing him, went in to fetch him drink. It was sometime before she returned and the King wondered at this and said to her, "Why hast thou tarried?" Quoth she, "Because one sugar-cane yielded not enough for thy need. So I pressed three; but they yielded not so much as did one aforetime." "What is the cause of that?" asked the King; and she answered, "The cause of it is that the King's mind is changed." Quoth he, "How knewst thou that?" "We hear from the wise," replied she, "that, when the King's mind is changed against a folk, their prosperity ceaseth and their good waxeth less." Anoushirwan laughed and put away from his mind that which he had purposed against the people of the village.

喝了。”國王對她的聰明和智慧感到很驚異，又問，“這杯汁你榨了幾根甘蔗？”“一根。”她答。國王很驚奇，要看看這個村的稅單。他看見徵稅很少，就想增加稅收。在回宮的路上，他默默地想：“他們一根甘蔗可以榨這麼多汁，為甚麼這村的稅收卻這麼輕呢？”

他離開了村莊，繼續打獵。晚上他回來時一個人又經過那家門口，他又去要水喝。還是那個村姑出來，看見他就進去拿喝的。但過了好一陣子她才回來。國王很奇怪，問她，“甚麼事耽擱了？”她說“因為一根甘蔗榨的汁太少，不夠您喝。我榨了三根，但三根的汁還沒有上次一根榨的汁多。”“這是甚麼原因呢？”國王問道。她答道，“原因是國王變了心。”他問，“你怎麼知道的？”她答道：“我們聽智者說過，一旦國王變心，要打老百姓的主意，那麼老百姓就不會有好日子過了。”國王笑了，打消了對村民加稅的念頭。

# 74 Khusrau and Shirin with the Fisherman

King Khusrau of Persia loved fish; and one day, as he sat in his saloon, he and Shirin his wife, there came a fisherman, with a great fish, and presented it to the King, who was pleased and ordered the man four thousand dirhems. When he was gone, Shirin said to the King, "Thou hast done ill." "Wherefore?" asked he; and she answered, "Because if, after this, thou give one of thy courtiers a like sum, he will disdain it and say, 'He hath but given me the like of what he gave the fishermam.' And if thou give him less, he will say, 'He makes light of me and gives me less than he gave the fisherman.'" "Thou art right," rejoined Khusrau; "but the thing is done and it ill becomes a king to go back on his gift." Quoth Shirin, "An[1] thou wilt, I will contrive thee a means to get it back from him." "How so?" asked he; and she said, "Call back the fisherman and ask him if the fish be male or female. If he say, 'Male,' say thou, 'We want a female,' and if he say, 'Female,' say, 'We want a male.'"

---

1. An：（古）= If。

## 七十四　機靈的漁夫

波斯王庫斯勞很愛吃魚。有一天他和王后希林坐在大廳裏，一個漁夫帶了一條大魚來獻給國王。國王非常高興，命令給他四千銅板。漁夫走後，王后對國王說，“你做了件錯事。”“為甚麼？”他問，王后答道，“如果以後你給一個朝臣同樣一筆錢，他會不屑一顧地說‘他給我的和給漁夫一樣多。’如果你給的比這少，他就會說，‘他太小瞧我了，給我的錢比給漁夫的還少。’”“你說得對，”國王說，“不過事已至此，一個國王總不能把他的賞賜再要回來呀！”王后說，“如果你願意，我教你一個辦法把錢從漁夫那兒要回來。”“怎麼做法？”他問。她答道，“把漁夫叫回來，問他這魚是雌的還是雄的？如果他說是雄的，你就說，‘我們想要雌的。’如果他說是雌的，你就說，‘我們要雄的。’”

So he sent for the fisherman, who was a man of wit and discernment, and said to him, "Is this fish male or female?" The fisherman kissed the ground and answered, "It is of the neuter gender, neither male nor female." The King laughed and ordered him other four thousand dirhems. So the fisherman went to the treasurer and taking his eight thousand dirhems, put them in a bag he had with him. Then, throwing the bag over his shoulder, he was going away, when he dropped a dirhem; so he laid the bag off his back and stooped down to pick it up. Now the King and Shirin were looking on, and the latter said, "O King, didst thou note the meanness and greediness of yon[2] man, in that he must needs stoop down, to pick up the one dirhem, and could not bring himself to leave it for one of the King's servants?" When the King heard this, he was wroth with the fisherman and said, "Thou art right, O Shirin!" So he called the man back and said to him, "Thou low-minded fellow! Thou art no man! How couldst thou put the bag off thy shoulder and stoop to pick up the one dirhem and grudge to leave it where it fell?" The fisherman kissed the earth before him and answered, "May God prolong the King's life! Indeed, I did not pick up the dirhem, because of its value in my eyes; but because on one of its faces is the likeness of the King and on the other his

2. yon：= yonder。

於是國王派人把漁夫召了回來，問他“這魚是雌的還是雄的？”這個漁夫既機智又有洞察力，他吻了土地，答道，“牠是中性的，既不是雌的也不是雄的。”國王笑了起來，又賞給他四千銅板。漁夫到司庫那裏取了八千銅板裝在他隨身帶來的袋子裏，把袋掛在肩上，正要離開時，掉了一個銅板，他就把袋子從背上放下來，彎下腰去撿錢。國王和王后都看在眼裏，王后說，“陛下，你看這人多麼小氣和貪婪了嗎？他非要彎下腰撿那一個銅板而不願留給陛下的僕人。”國王聽後，很生氣說，“希林，你說得對。”他把漁夫叫回來對他說“你這小氣鬼！你真不是人！你怎麼能把錢袋放下來彎腰撿那一個銅板，就不能把它留下嗎？”漁夫吻了面前的土地後回答道：“願真主保佑國工長壽！真的，我不是因為看重那一個銅板的價值去撿的。而是因為錢幣的一面有國王的肖像，另一面有國王

name; and I feared lest any should unwittingly set his foot upon it, thus dishonouring the name and presentment of the King, and I be blamed for the offence." The King wondered at his wit and shrewdness and ordered him yet other four thousand dirhems. Moreover, he let cry abroad in his kingdom, saying, "It behoveth none to order himself by women's counsel; for whoso[3] followeth their advice, loseth, with his one dirhem, other two."

---

3. whoso：（古）= whoever。

的名字。我怕萬一有人無意中踐踏了它，褻瀆了國王的名字及尊容，我就罪該萬死了。”國王對他的聰明和乖巧大為讚賞，又多賞給他四千銅板。另外，他還讓人在國內廣泛宣傳說，“不要聽女人的擺佈，如果聽女人的主意，原先只丟失一個銅板的，還會多丟失兩個。”

## 75 The Title of Silent

In the reign of the Caliph Muntasir Billah[1], ten highwaymen infested the roads about Bagdad, and for a long time committed unheard-of[2] robberies and cruelties. The caliph having notice of this, sent for the judge of the police, some days before the feast of Bairam, and ordered him, on pain of death, to bring all the ten to him.

The judge of the police used so much diligence, and sent so many people in pursuit of the ten robbers, that they were taken on the very day of Bairam. I was walking at the time on the banks of the Tigris, and saw ten men richly robed go into a boat. Had I but observed the guards who had them in custody, I might have concluded they were robbers; but my attention was fixed on the men themselves, and, thinking they were people who designed to spend the festival in jollity, I entered the boat with them, hoping they would not object to my making one of the company. We descended the Tigris, and landed before the caliph's palace. I had by this time had

1. Caliph Muntasir Billah：哈隆・雷切德的曾孫，公元 861 年繼位。
2. unheard-of：聞所未聞，這裏指駭人聽聞的。

## 七十五　沉默的人

在門塔瑟・比拉國王臨朝時期，有十個強盜在巴格達周圍的公路上橫行無忌，他們長期行兇搶劫，無惡不作。國王得知這些情況後，在白拉姆節前幾天召見警察局長，命令他將這些強盜全部捉拿歸案，否則要他的命。

警察局長十分賣力，派了許多人馬去追捕那十個強盜，在白拉姆節當天就把他們全部抓住了。我那時正在底格里斯河邊散步，看到十個穿着華麗的人上了一條船。要是我注意到押解他們的守衛，我就可能知道他們是強盜；但是當時我的注意力完全集中在他們身上，以為他們是打算來歡度佳節的，所以就跟他們上了船，希望他們不反對我跟他們作伴。我們順流而下，在王宮前面上了岸。此時

leisure to reflect, and to discover my mistake. When we quitted the boat, we were surrounded by a new troop of the judge of the police's guard, who bound us all, and carried us before the caliph. I suffered myself to be bound as well as the rest, without speaking one word; for what would it have availed to have spoken, or made any resistance? That had been the way to have got myself ill-treated by the guards, who would not have listened to me, for they are brutish fellows, who will hear no reason. I was with the robbers, and that was enough to make them believe me to be one of their number.

When we had been brought before the caliph he ordered the ten highwaymen's heads to be cut off immediately. The executioner drew us up in file within reach of his arm, and by good fortune I was placed last. He cut off the heads of the ten highwaymen, beginning at the first; and when it came to me he stopped. The caliph perceiving that he did not strike me grew angry. "Did not I command thee," said he, "to cut off the heads of ten highwaymen, and why hast thou cut off but nine?" "Commander of the Faithful," he replied, "Heaven preserve me from disobeying your majesty's orders; here are ten bodies upon the ground, and as many heads which I have cut off; your majesty may count them." When the caliph saw that what the executioner said was true, he looked at me with

我已經有暇思索，發覺了自己的錯誤。我們下船後，被一隊新派來的警察包圍。他們把我們綁了起來，帶到了國王面前。我也像其餘人一樣讓他們綑綁起來，甚麼也沒說，因為解釋或者反抗又有甚麼用呢？這樣做只會招來虐待，那些守衛都是粗野的傢伙，蠻不講理，根本不會聽我的。我跟強盜在一起，這就足以使他們相信我跟強盜是一夥的了。

我們被帶到國王面前後，他命令將十個強盜立即斬首。劊子手讓我們在他身邊排好隊，幸虧我排在最後。他從第一個人開始砍下了十個強盜的頭，輪到我時，他停了下來。國王看到他沒有殺我很生氣。他說："我不是命令將十個強盜斬首嗎？為甚麼你只殺了九個？"劊子手答道："陛下，我豈敢違旨；地上有十具屍體和我砍下的十個頭顱為證；陛下可以數一數。"國王發現劊子手說的不

amazement, and said to me, "Old man, how came you to be among those robbers, who have deserved a thousand deaths?" I answered, "Commander of the Faithful, I will make a true confession. This morning I saw those ten persons, whose punishment is a proof of your majesty's justice, take boat. I embarked with them, thinking they were men going to celebrate the feast of Bairam in a right spirit of good fellowship."

The caliph could not forbear laughing at my adventure; and, instead of treating me as a prattling fellow, he admired my discretion and taciturnity. "Commander of the Faithful," I resumed, "your majesty need not wonder at my silence on such an occasion. I make a particular profession of holding my peace, and on that account have acquired the glorious title of Silent. This is the effect of my philosophy; and, in a word, in this virtue consists my glory and happiness."

錯，就驚奇地看着我說："老人家，你怎麼跟強盜混在一起？他們可都是罪該萬死的惡徒哪！"我答道："陛下，我就實話實說吧。今天早晨，我看見這十個強盜上船（他們有此下場是陛下英明的明證。）我就跟着上船，以為他們是正常結伴去歡慶白拉姆節的。"

國王聽了我的故事不禁哈哈大笑。他非但沒有認為我在信口開河，反而稱讚我謹慎寡言。我接着說："我在這種場合保持沉默，陛下不必奇怪。我有保持沉默的特殊習慣，還因此得了個光榮稱號'沉默的人'。這就是我的人生哲學的效果；總之，我的榮耀和幸福就在於這個長處。"

# Allegories
# 動物寓言

## 76 Pretend to Be Ill

*— The Fable of the Donkey, the Ox, and the Farmer (1)*

There was once a wealthy farmer who owned many herds of cattle. He knew the languages of beasts and birds. In one of his stalls he kept an ox and a donkey. At the end of each day, the ox came to the place where the donkey was tied and found it well swept and watered; the manger filled with sifted straw and well-winnowed barley; and the donkey lying at his ease (for his master seldom rode him).

It chanced that one day the farmer heard the ox say to the donkey: "How fortunate you are! I am worn out with toil, while you rest here in comfort. You eat well-sifted barley and lack nothing. It is only occasionally that your master rides you. As for me, my life is perpetual drudgery at the plough and the millstone."

The donkey answered: "When you go out into the field and the yoke is placed upon your neck, pretend to be ill and drop down on your belly. Do not rise even if they beat you; or if you do rise, lie down again. When they take you back and place the fodder before you, do not eat it. Abstain for a day or two; and thus shall you find a rest from toil."

# 七十六　裝病偷懶

*——驢、牛和農夫的故事（一）*

從前有個富有的農夫，家裏有許多牲口，而且懂得動物和鳥類的語言。他把一頭牛和一頭驢關在一個牲口棚裏。每天收工後，牛回到拴驢的地方時，都發現那裏打掃清洗得乾乾淨淨；槽子裏裝滿了篩過的草料和簸好的大麥；驢也悠然自得地躺在那裏休息(因為主人很少騎牠)。

一天，農夫碰巧聽到牛對驢說："你真幸運！我每天累得筋疲力盡，而你卻舒舒服服地在這裏休息，吃篩好的大麥，甚麼都不缺。主人只偶然騎騎你。而我呢，我一生總是做這種無盡無休、單調乏味的拉犁拉磨的苦活。"

驢回答道："當你下田幹活，犁軛架到你脖子上時，你就假裝病了，突然趴下；即使他們鞭打你，你也不要起來；或者即使起來了，再躺下去。他們牽你回來，把飼料放在你面前時，你也不要吃。絕食一兩天，這樣你就會從勞作中解脫出來了。"

Remember that the farmer was there and heard what passed between them.

And so when the ploughman came to the ox with his fodder, he ate scarcely any of it. And when the ploughman came the following morning to take him out into the field, the ox appeared to be far from well. Then the farmer said to the ploughman: "Take the donkey and use him at the plough all day!"

The man returned, took the donkey in place of the ox, and drove him at the plough all day.

When the day's work was done and the donkey returned to the stall, the ox thanked him for his good counsel. But the donkey made no reply and bitterly repented his rashness.

當時農夫正好在那兒，聽到牠們的談話。

就這樣，當扶犁的來給牛餵飼料時，牛幾乎連碰都沒碰一下。第二天早晨扶犁的來牽牛下田，牠就裝出一副病得不輕的樣子。於是，農夫對扶犁的說："今天就把驢牽去耕田吧。"

扶犁的回來換驢去代替牛耕田，一幹就是一整天。

當天收工後驢回到牲口棚時，牛為驢的好主意而向牠表示感謝。但驢卻沒有作聲，並為自己的魯莽而懊悔不已。

# 77 If Only I Had Kept My Wisdom to Myself!

*— The Fable of the Donkey, the Ox, and the Farmer (2)*

Next day the ploughman came and took the donkey again and made him labour till evening; so that when the donkey returned with his neck flayed by the yoke, and in a pitiful state of exhaustion, the ox again expressed his gratitude to him, and praised his sagacity.

"If only I had kept my wisdom to myself!" thought the donkey. Then, turning to the ox, he said: "I have just heard my master say to his servant: 'If the ox does not recover soon, take him to the slaughterhouse and dispose of him.' My anxiety for your safety prompts me, my friend, to let you know of this before it is too late. And peace be with you!"

When he heard the donkey's words, the ox thanked him and said: "Tomorrow I will go to work freely and willingly." He ate all his fodder and even licked the manger clean.

Early next morning the farmer, accompanied by his wife, went to visit the ox in his stall. The ploughman came and led out the ox, who, at the sight of his master, broke wind and frisked about in all directions. And the farmer laughed so, he fell over on his back.

## 七十七　聰明反被聰明誤

*——驢、牛和農夫的故事　（二）*

第二天扶犁的又來把驢牽走了，並讓牠一直幹到晚上。當驢帶着被犁軛擦破了皮的脖子疲憊不堪地回來時，牛再次向牠表示謝意，並稱讚牠聰明。

驢想："要是我把這聰明放在肚子裏不說出來就好了！"於是，牠掉過頭對牛說："我剛才聽到主人對他的僕人說，'如果牛不能很快好，就把牠送到屠宰房宰了吧。'朋友，我擔心你的安全，所以趕緊把消息告訴你，免得晚了來不及。但願你平安無事！"

聽了驢的話，牛表示感謝並說，"明天我會主動地去幹活。"然後牠吃掉了所有的飼料，連槽子都舔得乾乾淨淨。

第二天清晨，農夫和他的妻子一早起來到牲口棚看牛。扶犁的也來了，把牛牽了出去。牛一見到主人就放了個屁，活躍起來，四處亂跑。農夫大笑，樂得摔了個仰面朝天。

# 78 The Mouse and the Weasel

A mouse and a weasel once dwelt in the house of a poor peasant, one of whose friends fell sick and the doctor prescribed him husked sesame. So he sought of one of his comrades sesame and gave the peasant a measure thereof[1] to husk for him; and he carried it home to his wife and bade her dress it. So she steeped it and husked it and spread it out to dry. When the weasel saw the grain, he came up to it and fell to carrying it away to his hole, nor stinted[2] all day, till he had borne off the most of it. Presently, in came the peasant's wife, and seeing great part of the sesame gone, stood awhile wondering; after which she sat down to watch and find out the cause. After awhile, out came the weasel to carry off more of the grain, but spying the woman seated there, knew that she was on the watch for him and said to himself, "Verily[3], this affair is like to end ill. I fear me this woman is on the watch for me and Fortune is no friend to those who look not to the issues[4]: so I must do a fair deed, whereby I

---

1. a measure thereof：an amount of that。
2. stinted：（古）= stopped。
3. verily：（古）= truly：真的。

# 七十八　老鼠與黃鼠狼

從前有隻老鼠和一隻黃鼠狼共住在一個貧苦的農夫家裏。農夫有個朋友病了。醫生給他開了去皮的芝麻。所以他就向一位朋友要了一點，讓農夫幫他去皮。農夫把芝麻帶回家交給妻子去辦。妻子就把芝麻浸濕、去皮，然後拿出去晾乾。黃鼠狼見了芝麻就跑過去把它搬回自己的洞裏。牠搬了一整天，直到把大部分芝麻都搬走為止。不久，農夫的妻子進來了，發現芝麻少了一大半，感到莫明其妙。她站了一會兒，又坐下來觀察，想找找原因。過了一會兒，黃鼠狼又出來搬芝麻，發現女人坐在那裏，知道是在等牠，心想："不好，這事兒看來要壞。這女人恐怕是在等我。人要是沒點兒先見之明就會倒霉。我得做件好

---

4. Fortune is no friend to those who look not to the issues：字面的意思是：命運不會幫助那些不願正視問題的人。

may manifest my innocence and wash out all the ill I have done." So saying, he began to take of the sesame in his hole and carry it out and lay it back upon the rest. The woman stood by and seeing the weasel do thus, said in herself, "Verily, this is not the thief, for he brings it back from the hole of him that stole it and returns it to its place. Indeed, he hath done us a kindness in restoring us the sesame and the reward of those that do us good is that we do them the like. It is clear that this is not he who stole the grain. But I will not leave watching till I find out who is the thief." The weasel guessed what was in her mind, so he went to the mouse and said to her, "O my sister, there is no good in him who does not observe the claims of neighbourship and shows no constancy in friendship." "True, O my friend," answered the mouse, "and I delight in thee and in thy neighbourhood; but what is the motive of thy speech?" Quoth the weasel, "The master of the house has brought home sesame and has eaten his fill of it, he and his family, and left much; every living soul has eaten of it, and if thou take of it[5] in thy turn, thou art worthier thereof than any other." This pleased the mouse and she chirped and danced and frisked her ears and tail, and greed for the grain deluded her; so she rose at once and issuing

5. take of it：（古）= take it。

事，表明我的清白，把我幹的壞事洗乾淨。”牠一面想一面開始把洞裏的芝麻往外搬，並放回原處。女人站在那裏看着黃鼠狼這麼做，心想：“這肯定不是賊，因為牠把芝麻從小偷的洞裏搬出來放回原處。牠實在是幫了我們一個大忙，我們也應該以德報德。很明顯，偷芝麻的不是牠。但我還得繼續觀察，看看到底誰是賊。”黃鼠狼猜透了她的心思，所以就去找老鼠，對牠說：“人要是不講鄰里之情和朋友之誼就太不好了。”老鼠答說：“說得對，朋友。我就喜歡和你這樣的人做鄰居。但你說這話是甚麼意思？”黃鼠狼說：“房子的主人帶回來不少芝麻，全家都吃飽了，還剩下許多；大家都吃到了，你去嚐一嚐，也是完全應該的。”老鼠聽了高興得又唱又跳，搖頭擺尾起來。牠一聽有糧食，就貪慾熏心，馬上跳起來衝出洞口，

forth of her hole, saw the sesame peeled and dry, shining with whiteness, and the woman sitting watching, armed with a stick. The mouse could not contain herself, but taking no thought to the issue of the affair, ran up to the sesame and fell to messing it and eating of it; whereupon the woman smote her with the stick and cleft her head in twain: so her greed and heedlessness of the issue of her actions led to her destruction.

看到那堆白花花的去皮乾芝麻以及手拿棒子坐着看守的女人。老鼠控制不住自己，也不想想後果，就跑上去亂搗，大吃起來。女人掄起棒子打了下去，把牠的腦袋劈成兩半。牠的貪慾和不計後果的莽撞使牠送了命。

## 79 The Hedgehog and the Pigeons

A hedgehog once came to a date tree on which a pigeon and his wife had built their nest, and it was plain to see that this couple was leading a comfortable life on this tree. So the hedgehog said to himself, "These pigeons are eating the fruit of the date tree, and I have no means of getting at the dates. Therefore, I'll have to find a way of tricking them to get my share." After saying this, he dug a hole at the foot of the palm tree and took up his lodging there with his wife. Moreover, he built a chapel beside the hole and went into retreat as though he were a devout monk renouncing the world. The male pigeon saw him praying and worshiping, and his heart softened toward him because of his pious ways.

"How many years have you been like that?" asked the pigeon.

"Thirty years," replied the hedgehog.

"What food do you eat?"

"Whatever falls from palm trees."

"What clothes do you wear?"

"Prickles," announced the hedgehog, "and I benefit from their roughness."

# 七十九　刺蝟與鴿子

從前，一隻刺蝟來到一棵棗樹下面。樹上有一對鴿子築了巢，兩口子生活顯然很舒服。刺蝟心想，“這對鴿子吃棗椰樹的果實，而我卻吃不到。所以，我得想個辦法騙牠們給我也弄一份。”說完，牠在棗椰樹下挖了一個洞，就跟妻子在那兒住下了。此外，牠還在洞外蓋了所小教堂，在那裏靜修，像個摒棄紅塵的高僧。雄鴿看到牠又是祈禱，又是做禮拜，不禁為牠的虔誠所感動。

鴿子問：“你這樣有多少年了？”

刺蝟答：“有三年了。”

“你吃甚麼生活呢？”

“棗椰樹上掉下來的任何東西。”

“你穿甚麼衣服？”

“皮刺，粗糙的皮刺對我有好處。”

"And why have you chosen this place to dwell rather than some other location?" asked the pigeon.

"I prefer this place to all the others I've seen because it will allow me to guide those who are going astray down the right path and to teach the ignorant!"

"I thought you were much different," said the pigeon, "but now I wish I were more like you."

"I fear that you don't mean what you say," said the hedgehog. "You'll probably be like the farmer who, when it was time to plant seeds, neglected to do so with the excuse that he dreaded sowing seeds because they might not produce what he desired and cause him to lose his energy. When harvest time came, and he saw the people harvesting their crops, he regretted that he had failed to do what he should have done and died of sorrow."

"Well, tell me what I can do," replied the pigeon, "I'd like to free myself from all worldly things and obligations so that I can serve the Lord much better."

"You must begin preparing yourself for the next world," said the hedgehog, "Content yourself with a pittance of[1] your provisions."

"How can I do this when I'm only a bird and unable to go beyond the date tree which provides me with my daily

---

1. a pittance of：微薄的。

“你為甚麼挑這地方來住，而不去別的地方呢？”鴿子問。

“比起我到過的其他地方，我最喜歡這裏，因為我可以在這裏引導那些走上歧路的人回到正道，並且教導無知的人！”

“我以前對你的看法可不是這樣。不過，我現在倒希望向你學習。”

刺蝟說：“恐怕這不是心裏話。你可能像那位農夫一樣，在應該播種的時候不去播種，藉口怕播下的種子不長所要的莊稼而白費氣力；而在收穫的時候看到別人收割莊稼，就後悔沒做本來該做的事而傷心地死去。”

鴿子答道：“那麼，請告訴我該怎麼辦。我希望擺脱一切俗務，以便更好地侍奉真主。”

刺蝟說：“你必須開始為來世做準備。盡可能少吃東西。”

鴿子答道：“我只是一隻鳥，去不了給我提供每日食

bread?" the pigeon responded. "And even if I could do so, I know of no other place where I could live."

"You can shake down enough fruit from the date tree to provide a whole year's supplies for you and your wife. Then you can set up your abode in a nest under the trunk so that you can pray and seek to be guided in the right way. After you've built your new nest, you can turn to the dates that you've shaken to the ground and carry them to your home, where you can store them and eat them whenever the need arises. After you run out of your provisions and time weighs heavily on your hands, you can observe total abstinence."

"May Allah bless you!" exclaimed the pigeon. "May he reward you for showing me the right path and reminding me of my duties."

Then he and his wife worked hard at knocking down the dates until nothing was left on the palm tree, while the hedgehog joyfully collected the dates and filled his den with the fruit, storing it up for the days to come. In his mind he kept thinking, "When the pigeon and his wife need some food to eat, they'll come to me, since they won't be able to live off their abstinence and devoutness. Since they've heeded my advice once, they'll draw near again, and I'll make a nice meal out of them. After that I'll have the place all to myself, and whatever drops from the date tree will be mine."

糧的那棵棗樹以外的地方。我該怎麼辦呢？即使能去，我也不知道還有甚麼地方我能生活下去。”

“你可以盡量把樹上的棗子搖下來，備足你們倆一年的口糧。然後，你就在樹幹下做窩居住，祈禱並學走正道。造好新窩以後，你可以把樹上搖下來的棗運回家去，收藏起來，在需要時吃。你糧食吃盡後又沒法消磨時間，就可以完全禁食。”

“真主保佑你！”鴿子叫道。“真主會賜福於你，因為你給我指引正道，並提醒我盡自己的責任。”

於是，這對鴿子就盡力把棗打下來，直到樹上連一顆也不剩了。刺蝟興高采烈地把棗揀了起來，裝滿自己的窩，以備來日享用。牠心裏一直在想：“當雄鴿和雌鴿需要吃東西時，牠們就會來找我，因為靠禁食和虔誠是活不下去的。既然牠們已經聽過一次我的勸告，就會再來；我就可以拿牠們當一頓美餐。然後，我就可以獨佔這個地方，樹上掉下的棗也完全歸我了。”

Once the pigeons had shaken all the dates from the palm tree, the pigeon and his wife descended and found that the hedgehog had removed all the dates to his own place.

"Hedgehog!" they cried out to him. "You pious preacher of good counsel[2], there's no sign of the dates, and we have nothing else to eat."

"The wind has probably carried them away," replied the hedgehog. "But turning from your provisions to the Provider is the essence of salvation, and he who has cleft the corners of the mouth has never left the mouth without nourishment." And he kept preaching to them in this way and making a show of piety. Indeed, he used such flowery speech that they eventually trusted him and entered his den without suspecting what might happen. Once they were inside, the hedgehog slammed the door shut and gnashed his teeth.

---

2. You pious preacher of good counsel：你這假裝勸人為善的傢伙。這裏 pious 含貶義，意為“假裝虔誠的”。

鴿子打完樹上的棗後飛落地面時，發現刺蝟把所有的棗都搬到牠自己的窩裏去了。

“刺蝟！”鴿子叫道。“你說的倒好聽。棗都沒影了，叫我們去吃甚麼？”

“可能讓風颳走了，”刺蝟回答道。“但是忘掉口糧轉向真主就是得救的本質，他既讓人張嘴覓食，就從不讓人空口餓肚缺乏營養。”牠就這樣對牠們不斷說教，並裝得十分虔誠。牠的言詞的確娓娓動聽，鴿子最終相信了牠，進了牠的洞穴，絲毫沒有懷疑會發生甚麼事。牠們一到裏面，刺蝟就猛地關上了門，牙咬得吱吱直響。

## 80 Two Pigeons

A pair of pigeons once stored up wheat and barley in their nests in the winter, and when the summer came, the grain shrivelled and became less; so the male pigeon said to his mate, "Thou hast eaten of this grain." "No, by Allah," replied she; "I have not touched it!" But he believed her not and beat her with his wings and pecked her with his bill, till he killed her. When the cold season returned, the corn swelled out and became as before, whereupon he knew that he had slain his mate unjustly and wickedly and repented, when repentance availed him not. Then he lay down by her side, mourning over her and weeping for grief, and left eating and drinking, till he fell sick and died.

## 八十　兩隻鴿子

從前有一對鴿子在窩裏儲存了麥子過冬。到了夏天，穀粒因乾縮而減少了。雄鴿就對雌鴿說："你偷吃了糧食。"雌鴿答道："沒有，我對天發誓。我碰都沒碰過。"但他卻不信，並用翅膀打她，用嘴啄她，直到把她弄死了。冷天來了，穀粒又鼓了起來，變得跟從前一樣了。他這才知道雌鴿死得冤枉，但已悔之晚矣。於是，他就躺在她身邊，哀悼痛哭，不吃不喝，直到病死。

# 81 The Cat and the Crow

A crow and a cat once lived in brotherhood. One day, as they were together under a tree, they spied a leopard making towards them, of which they had not been ware[1], till he was close upon them. The crow at once flew up to the top of the tree; but the cat abode[2] confounded and said to the crow, "O my friend, hast thou no device to save me? All my hope is in thee." "Indeed," answered the crow, "it behoveth[3] brethren, in case of need, to cast about for a device, whenas any peril overtakes them."

Now hard by the tree were shepherds with their dogs; so the crow flew towards them and smote the face of the earth with his wings, cawing and crying out, to draw their attention. Then he went up to one of the dogs and flapped his wings in his eyes and flew up a little way, whilst the dog ran after him, thinking to catch him. Presently, one of the shepherds raised his head and saw the bird flying near the ground and

---

1. ware：（古）= aware。
2. abode：（古）= stayed。
3. behoveth：behove 第三人稱單數現在式的古體，解作“適當的做法”。

## 八十一　貓和烏鴉

從前有隻烏鴉跟一隻貓和睦相處。一天，他們在樹下一起玩耍時，一隻豹子乘他們不注意偷偷地向他們走來，等他們發現時，豹子已經走得很近了。烏鴉立刻飛上了樹頂，但是貓卻嚇呆了，不知如何是好。她對烏鴉說：“朋友，快想辦法救救我吧。我就全指望你了。”烏鴉答道：“的確，在遇到危難需要幫助時，兄弟之間理應盡力想辦法相救。”

正好大樹附近有些牧羊人和他們的狗；所以烏鴉就向他們飛去，一面用翅膀拍擊地面，一面哇哇大叫，來引起他們注意。然後，他又向一條狗飛去，用翅膀掃牠的眼睛；當狗在後面追着想抓住他時，他又往上飛一點兒。一個牧羊人立刻抬頭看見那鳥正貼近地面飛行，還不時落了

lighting now and then; so he followed him, and the crow gave not over flying just out of the dogs' reach and tempting them to pursue and snap at him: but as soon as they came near him, he would fly up a little; and so he brought them to the tree. When they saw the leopard, they rushed upon it, and it turned and fled. Now the leopard thought to eat the cat, but the latter was saved by the craft of its friend the crow. This story shows that the friendship of the virtuous saves and delivers from difficulties and dangers.

下來，就跟着他；而烏鴉就不停地飛，剛剛不讓狗抓着，來引誘牠們追着咬他。但等狗一靠近，他就往上飛一點兒；就這樣，他把牠們領到了樹邊。狗一看到豹子就衝上去咬，豹子轉身就跑了。本來豹子想吃貓，但貓的朋友烏鴉的計策把她救了。這個故事說明好人的友誼能救人於危難。

# 82 The Sparrow and the Peacock

There was once a sparrow, that used every day to visit a certain king of the birds and was the first to go in to him and the last to leave him. One day, a company of birds assembled on a high mountain, and one of them said to another, "Verily, we are waxed many and many are the differences[1] between us, and needs must we have a king to order our affairs, so shall we be at one and our differences will cease." Thereupon up came the sparrow and counselled them to make the peacock, — that is, the prince he used to visit, — king over them. So they chose the peacock to be their king and he bestowed largesse on them and made the sparrow his secretary and vizier. Now the sparrow was wont bytimes[2] to leave his assiduity [in the personal service of the king] and look into affairs [in general]. One day, he came not at the usual time, whereat the peacock was sore troubled; but presently, he returned and the peacock said to him, "What

1. differences：分歧。
2. bytimes：（古）= sometimes。

# 八十二　麻雀與孔雀

從前有隻麻雀每天都去朝見鳥王。他總是第一個進去，最後一個離開。一天，一羣鳥兒在高山上集會，其中一隻對另一隻說：“說真的，咱們人越來越多，爭吵也隨着增多，必須有個國王來管理事務，這樣咱們就能團結起來，停止爭吵。”接着，麻雀就上來勸他們擁戴孔雀——也就是他常去朝見的鳥王——為王。於是他們就推舉孔雀為王，而孔雀就對他們大加封賞，並任命麻雀為秘書和大臣。現在麻雀不能像往常那樣經常到鳥王面前獻殷勤而得照料公務了。一天，他沒有按時來到，孔雀很着急；但麻雀很快就回來了，孔雀就問他，“有甚麼事把你耽擱啦，

hath delayed thee, that art the nearest to me of all my servants and the dearest?" Quoth the sparrow, "I have seen a thing that is doubtful to me and at which I am affrighted." "What was it thou sawest?" asked the king; and the sparrow answered, "I saw a man set up a net, hard by my nest, and drive its pegs fast into the ground. Then he strewed grain in its midst and withdrew afar off. As I sat watching what he would do, behold, fate and destiny drove thither a crane and his wife, which fell into the midst of the net and began to cry out; whereupon the fowler came up and took them. This troubled me, and this is the reason of my absence from thee, O king of the age; but never again will I abide in that nest, for fear of the net." "Depart not thy dwelling," rejoined the peacock; "for precaution will avail thee nothing against destiny." And the sparrow obeyed his commandment, saying, "I will take patience and not depart, in obedience to the king." So he continued to visit the king and carry him food and water, taking care for himself, till one day he saw two sparrows fighting on the ground and said in himself, "How can I, who am the king's vizier, look on and see sparrows fighting in my neighbourhood? By Allah, I must make peace between them!" So he flew down to them, to reconcile them; but the fowler cast the net over them and taking the sparrow in question, gave him to his fellow, saying, "Take care of him, for he is the fattest and finest I ever saw." But the sparrow

你可是我最親近的人哪。”麻雀說，“我看到一樣東西，讓我疑心，又很害怕。”鳥王問，“你看到甚麼了？”麻雀答，“我看到一個人在我的窩附近張網，他把橛子牢牢地釘在地上。然後，他把穀粒灑在網中間後就躲在遠處。當我坐在那裏看他想幹甚麼的時候，一隻公鶴和一隻母鶴鬼使神差地飛了過來，落入網中，大叫救命。捕鳥人聞聲趕來，抓住了牠們。這事使我很擔心，所以就沒按時上您這兒來。陛下，我決不再在那窩裏住了，因為我怕那張網。”孔雀回答道，“不要離開你的住處，因為對命中注定的事預防也沒用。”麻雀只好服從說，“臣遵旨，一定耐心住下去不搬家。”這樣，他就繼續去朝見鳥王，給他帶去食物和水，同時自己多加小心。一天，他看到兩隻麻雀在地上打架，心想：“我是王上駕前的大臣，看到鄰近有麻雀打架豈能袖手旁觀？真主作證，我得去勸架！”於是，他就飛下來給他們調解；但是捕鳥人網住了他們，把這隻麻雀給他的同伴說：“小心別讓他跑了，我見到的麻雀沒有比這更肥、更漂亮的了。”但是麻雀心想：“我原

said in himself, "I have fallen into that which I feared and it was none but the peacock that inspired me with a false security. It availed me nothing to beware of the stroke of fate, since for him who taketh precaution there is no fleeing from destiny; and how well says the poet:

*That which is not to be shall by no means be brought*
*To pass, and that which is to be shall come, unsought,*
*Even at the time ordained; but he that knoweth not*
*The truth is still deceived and finds his hopes grown nought.*

來怕的就是落到這個下場，而使我錯以為安全的正是孔雀。我命該倒霉，防也沒用，命運是逃不掉的。詩人說得好：

命裏所無終成空，
命裏該有自會來，
凡人不識此中意，
千祈萬求也枉然。

## 83 The Sparrow and the Eagle

A sparrow was once hovering over a sheep-fold, when he saw a great eagle swoop down upon a lamb and carry it off in his claws. Thereupon the sparrow clapped his wings and said, "I will do even as the eagle hath done;" and he conceited himself and aped a greater than he. So he flew down forthright and lighted on the back of a fat ram, with a thick fleece that was become matted, by his lying in his dung and stale, till it was like felt. As soon as the sparrow lighted on the sheep's back, he clapped his wings and would have flown away, but his feet became tangled in the wool and he could not win free. All this while the shepherd was looking on, having seen as well what happened with the eagle as with the sparrow; so he came up to the latter in a rage and seized him. Then he plucked out his wing-feathers and tying his feet with a twine, carried him to his children and threw him to them. "What is this?" asked they and he answered, "This is one that aped a greater than himself and came to grief."

## 八十三　麻雀與老鷹

從前，一隻麻雀在羊圈上面飛翔時，看見一隻老鷹飛下來用爪子抓走一隻小羊。因此，麻雀就拍拍翅膀說：“老鷹做到的事我也要做。”於是，他就自命得意地裝起大人物來了。他一下子就飛落在一隻肥肥的公羊背上。由於公羊在自己的屎尿上打滾，身上的厚毛已經結纏成團，看上去像氈子一樣了。麻雀剛落在羊背上就拍動翅膀，想要飛走，但是雙腳已被羊毛纏住，掙脫不開了。這當兒，牧人一直在旁觀，看到了老鷹和麻雀的舉動。他怒氣沖沖地走上前去捉住麻雀。然後，他拔掉牠翅膀上的羽毛，用繩子綁住牠的雙腳，把牠帶回家，扔給孩子們玩。他們問道：“這是啥？”他回答道：“這傢伙想裝大人物，卻落得個可悲的下場。”

# Maxims and Philosophies
# 格言與哲理

## 84 True Gold Is Hidden in the Heart

The heart is the noblest member of the body. A wise man said that the worst of men is he who allows an evil desire to take root in his heart; for he shall lose his manhood. A poet said:

*The wise will keep*
*His treasure hid apart;*
*True gold is hidden in the heart,*
*A miner never had to dig so deep.*

## 八十四　真金藏心中

心是人體最高尚的器官。有位智者説過，最壞的人是讓惡念在心裏紮根的人，因為他會喪失人性。詩曰：

智者有心眼，

珍寶分開埋；

真金藏心中，

礦工挖也難。

## 85 Judged according to His Intentions

Deal with people according to their deeds and not according to their words. Yet deeds are not worth the intentions which inspire them; so that each man shall be judged according to his intentions and not according to his deeds.

## 八十五　知人之道

待人要觀其行而不要聽其言。然而行為又不及促成行為之動機重要；所以看人要看其動機，而不是看其行為。

## 86 Lukman the Wise

Lukman the Wise said to his sons: "There are three things which are possible only under three conditions: you may not know if a man be really good until you have seen him in his anger; you may not know if a man be brave until you have seen him in battle; and you may not know if a man be a friend until you have come to him in necessity."

## 八十六　智者教子

智者勒克曼對他的兒子說：“只有在三種情況下三件事才有可能：只有看到一個人發怒才能知道他是否真的生性善良；只有看到一個人戰鬥才能知道他是否勇敢；只有在困難時向朋友求助才能知道他是否是真朋友。”

## 87 The Foolish Weaver

There was once a weaver who lived in a village, and despite the fact that he was very industrious, he could earn a living only by taking on additional work. Now it so happened that one of the rich men in the neighborhood held a wedding feast and invited all the people to attend. Everyone at the celebration was served delicious food, and the weaver saw that the master of the house made much ado about the guests who were wearing fine clothes. So the weaver said to himself, "If I change my craft for another that's more highly esteemed and better paid, I can amass a great deal of money and can buy splendid attire. Then I'll be able to rise in rank and be exalted in people's eyes just like these rich guests."

After a while he saw one of the mountebanks at the feast climb up a high wall and jump to the ground, where he landed on his feet. Impressed by this feat, the weaver said to himself "I've got to show them that I can do what he did. It doesn't seem all that difficult." So he climbed the wall and proceeded to jump off it, whereupon he broke his neck and died.

... you'll try to earn money by doing what you know best and not be tempted by greed. Remember, it's hazardous to lust after things that are not within your reach.

## 八十七　愚蠢的織布工人

從前在一個村莊裏住着一個織布工人。他勤勞肯幹，但還是要靠加班加點才能糊口。一天，附近的一個富人舉行婚宴，邀請全村人參加。席上給每個人端來美食佳肴。織布工人看到主人對衣飾華麗的客人分外殷勤，就心中暗想，“要是我改學另一種更受尊重、更賺錢的手藝，就能攢起一大筆錢，買好衣服穿。然後我就能提高地位，像那些有錢的客人那樣讓人家瞧得起。”

過了一會兒，他看到席上有個走江湖的爬上一堵高牆，又跳了下來，落地安然無事。織布工人對他的表演十分讚賞，心想：“我得讓他們看看我也會他那一手。那看來也並不難。”於是，他就爬上牆去，從上面跳了下來，結果摔斷了脖子，死了。

…… 一個人要靠自己最拿手的本領來掙錢，而不要被貪慾所誘惑。要記住，貪求自己力所不及的東西是很危險的。

## 88 The Dream

There lived once in Baghdad a merchant who, having squandered all his wealth, became so destitute that he could make his living only by the hardest labour.

One night he lay down to sleep with a heavy heart, and in a dream a man appeared to him, saying: "Your fortune lies in Cairo. Go and seek it there."

The very next morning he set out for Cairo and, after many weeks and much hardship on the way, arrived in that city. Night had fallen, and as he could not afford to stay at an inn he lay down to sleep in the courtyard of a mosque.

Now as the Almighty's will would have it, a band of robbers entered the mosque and from there broke into an adjoining house. Awakened by the noise, the owners raised the alarm and shouted for help; then the thieves made off. Presently the Chief of Police and his men arrived on the scene. They entered the mosque and, finding the man from Baghdad lying in the courtyard, seized him and beat him with their clubs until he was nearly dead. Then they threw him into prison.

Three days later the Chief of Police ordered his men to bring the stranger before him.

"Where do you come from?" asked the chief.

## 八十八　夢

從前巴格達有個商人。他揮霍了所有的財產，窮得只能靠做苦工維持生活。

一天晚上，他心情沉重地躺下睡覺，夢見有人對他說：“你的財運在開羅，去那兒找吧。”

第二天一早，他就動身去開羅，經過多週艱苦的路程，到達了那個城市。天黑了，但他沒錢住旅店，只好在一所清真寺的院子裏露宿。

天意弄人，一夥強盜進了寺院並從那裏闖入隔壁人家。主人被聲音驚醒，高喊捉賊。強盜跑了。不久，警察局長帶人來到現場，進了寺院，發現這個巴格達人躺在院子裏。他們把他抓住，並用棍子把他打得半死。然後將他投入監獄。

三天後，警察局長命令他的手下將這個陌生人帶到他面前。

“你是從哪兒來的？”他問道。

"From Baghdad."

"And what has brought you to Cairo?"

"A man appeared to me in a dream, saying: 'Your fortune lies in Cairo. Go and seek it there.' But when I came to Cairo, the fortune I was promised proved to be the blows your men so generously gave me."

When he heard this, the Chief of Police burst out laughing. "Know then, you fool," he cried, "that I too have heard a voice in my sleep, not just once but on three occasions. It said: 'Go to Baghdad, and in a cobbled street lined with palmtrees you will find such-and-such a house, with a courtyard of grey marble; at the far end of the garden there is a fountain of white marble. Under the fountain a great sum of money lies buried. Go there and dig it up.' But would I go? Of course not. Yet, fool that you are, you have come all the way to Cairo on the strength of one idle dream."

Then the Chief of Police gave the merchant some money. "Here," he said, "take this. It will help you on the way back to your own country."

The merchant recognized at once that the house and garden just described were his own. He took the money and set out promptly on his homeward journey.

As soon as he reached his house he went into the garden, dug beneath the fountain, and uncovered a great treasure.

Thus the words of the dream were wondrously fulfilled, and Allah made the ruined merchant rich again.

“從巴格達來。”

“來開羅做甚麼？”

“我夢見有人對我說：‘你的財運在開羅。去那兒找吧。’可我到了開羅後發現所謂的財運原來是你們給我的一頓狠揍。”

警察局長聽了不禁哈哈大笑。他高聲說道：“你這傻瓜！告訴你，我也在夢中不止一次而是三次聽到一個聲音說：‘去巴格達吧，在一條兩旁種有棕櫚樹並鋪上鵝卵石的街上，你會找到如此這般一所房子。裏面有灰色大理石的院子；在花園的盡頭有一個白大理石的噴泉。噴泉下面埋着一大筆錢。去把它挖出來吧。’但是我會去嗎？當然不會。可你這個傻瓜居然憑着一場癡夢從大老遠跑來開羅。”

然後，警察局長給了商人一點錢，說：“給你，拿去作回家的旅費。”

商人馬上想到剛才警察局長說的房子和花園正是他自己的家。他拿了錢，立刻踏上回家的路。

他一到家就走進花園，在噴泉下面挖出一大筆財富。

這樣，夢裏的話就奇蹟般地應驗了，真主使這個破落商人又富起來了。

## 89 The Parable of True Learning

It is related that a handsome and studious young man once lived in a certain city, where every branch of knowledge was freely taught. He had a great desire to be for ever learning something fresh, that his life might lack no happiness. One day, a travelling merchant told him that there existed, in a far country, a sage who was the holiest man of Islam and who, though wiser than the sum of all others at that time, practised the simple trade of a blacksmith, as his father and grandfather had done before him. Straightway the young man took his sandals, his foodbag, and his stick, and journeyed towards that far country, hoping that he might learn a little of the blacksmith's wisdom. After forty days and forty nights of danger and fatigue, he came to the city which he sought, and was directed to the smith's shop. He kissed the hem of the saint's robe and then stood before him in silence. "What do you desire, my son?" asked the smith, who was an old man with a benign face. "Learning," answered the youth. Without a word the smith put the cord of the bellows into his hand and bade him pull it. The new disciple pulled the cord of the bellows until sunset. On the morrow he did the same thing; for weeks, for months, and finally for a whole year, he

# 八十九　真知的寓言

相傳，從前在一個學術自由的城市裏住着一個英俊好學的青年。他渴望不斷學習新知識，使生活美滿幸福。一天，一個行商告訴他在一個遠方的國家有一位賢哲。他是伊斯蘭教內最聖潔的人，儘管他比當時所有的人加在一起還要聰明，卻像他父親和祖父一樣幹着鐵匠這個簡單的行當。年輕人馬上就穿上草鞋，帶着乾糧袋和手杖，出發去那個遠方的國家，希望能學到一點鐵匠的智慧。經過四十個晝夜的危險和疲勞的旅程，他來到了他要找的那座城市，找到了那個鐵匠舖。他吻了聖人的袍子褶邊，然後默默地站在他面前。鐵匠是個慈眉善目的老人，他問道："孩子，你想要甚麼？"青年答道："學問。"鐵匠一言不發就把風箱的皮帶放在他手中，吩咐他拉風箱，這個新弟子就拉風箱，一直幹到太陽下山，第二天他幹同樣的活；週復一週，月復一月，最後幹了整整一年，他拉着風

worked the bellows, without receiving a word from the master or the many disciples who were engaged in various kinds of the like hard and simple toil. Five years passed before the young man dared to open his lips, and say: "Master!" The smith paused in his work and the other disciples ceased their occupations to look on anxiously. The master turned to the young man in the silence of the forge, and asked: "What do you wish?" "Learning," answered the youth; and the smith said, as he turned back to the fire: "Pull the cord." Another five years passed, during which the disciple pulled the cord of the bellows from morning to night, without rest and without having a word addressed to him. When any of the disciples needed guidance, he was allowed to write his question on paper and hand it to the master when he entered the forge in the morning. The smith, who never read these writings, sometimes threw them into the fire and sometimes placed them in the folds of his turban. By throwing the question into the fire he showed that it was not worth an answer; but, if he placed it in his turban, the disciple would find an answer in the evening, written in gold characters upon the wall of his cell.

When the ten years were over, the old smith approached the young man and touched him on the shoulder; then the youth left hold of the cord for the first time in ten years, and a great joy descended upon him. "My son," said the master,

箱，但沒有聽到師傅或幹着各種同樣簡單而艱苦的工作的許多弟子說一句話。五年過去了，青年才敢張口說：“師傅！”鐵匠停下了手上的工作，別的弟子也停止幹活，熱切地觀望着。工場裏一片靜默，師傅轉身問青年：“你想要甚麼？”青年答道：“學問。”師傅回頭向着爐火說：“拉風箱。”又過了五年，這期間青年從早到晚拉風箱的皮帶，不休息也沒人對他說一句話。有的弟子需要指導時就把問題寫在紙上，在早晨師傅走進工場時交給他。這些字條師傅從來不看，有時扔進爐子裏，有時放進纏頭巾的褶子裏。如果扔進爐子表示那問題不值一答；但是，如果放進纏頭巾裏，那弟子晚上就會得到答覆，答案用金色的字寫在他房間的牆上。

十年過去了，老鐵匠走到青年身邊，拍拍他的肩膀；十年來青年第一次放下皮帶，心裏十分高興。師傅說：

"you may now return to your own country, knowing that you carry the whole learning of the world about with you. You have acquired patience."

He gave his disciple the kiss of peace, and the young man returned to his own country, as one inspired with light, one who sees clearly.

“孩子，現在你可以回國去了，你要明白你隨身帶着世界上的全部學問。你學會了忍耐。”

他吻別弟子，祝他一路平安。青年感到心明眼亮，就回國去了。

# 90 The Ferryman of the Nile and the Hermit

I was once a ferryman on the Nile and used to ply between the eastern and the western banks. One day, as I sat in my boat, waiting for custom, there came up to me an old man of a bright countenance, clad in a patched gown and bearing in his hand a gourd-bottle and a staff. He saluted me and I returned his greeting; and he said to me. "Wilt thou ferry me over and give me to eat for the love of God the Most High?" "With all my heart," answered I. So he entered the boat and I rowed him over to the eastern side. When he was about to land, he said to me, "I desire to lay a trust on thee." Quoth I, "What is it?" "Know," rejoined he, "that God hath revealed to me that [my end is at hand and that] thou wilt come to me to-morrow, after the hour of noon, and wilt find me dead under yonder tree. Wash me and wrap me in the shroud thou wilt find under my head and bury me in the sand, after thou hast prayed over me and taken my gown and bottle and staff, which do thou deliver to one who will come and require them of thee." And I marvelled at his word.

Next day, I forgot what he had said till near the hour of afternoon-prayer, when I remembered and hastening to the appointed place, found him under the tree, dead, with a new

# 九十　渡船工和隱士

從前我曾經是尼羅河上的渡船工人，常在東西兩岸之間來回擺渡。有一天，我正坐在船上等候乘客，一位老者走了過來，他精神奕奕，身上穿了一件打補釘的長袍，手裏拿着一個葫蘆瓶和一根手杖。他向我致意，我也向他回禮。然後他對我說，“為了對至高真主的愛，你能渡我到對岸而且給我些吃的嗎？”“十分樂意，”我回答。於是他上了我的船，我把他划到了東岸。他正要上岸時，對我說：“我要拜託你一件事。”我問，“甚麼事？”他說，“真主已明示，我的死期已近，祂要你明天正午以後來找我，你會發現我已死在那棵樹下。把我洗乾淨，在我頭下有一塊裹屍布，你用它把我包好，為我祈禱後，把我埋在沙裏。你把我的長袍，瓶子和手杖帶走。以後會有一個人來向你要，你就把這些東西交給他。”我對他的話驚奇不已。

第二天我忘了他說的話，快到下午祈禱時間時，才突然記了起來，趕快到了他指定的地方，發現他在樹下已經

shroud by his head, exhaling a fragrance of musk. So I washed him and shrouded him and prayed over him, then dug a hole in the sand and buried him, after I had taken his gown and bottle and staff, with which I rowed back to the western side and passed the night there.

On the morrow, as soon as the city gate was opened, there came to me a young man, whom I had known as a lewd fellow, clad in fine clothes and his hands stained with henna, and said to me, "Art thou not such an one [the ferryman]?" "Yes," answered I; and he said, "Give me what thou hast in trust for me." Quoth I, "What is that?" "The gown, the bottle and the staff," replied he. "Who told thee of them?" asked I; and he answered, "I know nothing save that I was yesterday at the wedding of one of my friends and spent the night singing [and making merry,] till hard upon day, when I lay down to sleep and take rest; and behold, there stood by me one who said to me, 'God the Most High hath taken such an one the hermit to Himself and hath appointed thee to fill his place; so go to so and so, the ferryman, and take of him the dead man's gown and bottle and staff, that he left with him for thee.'" So I brought them out and gave them to him, whereupon he put off his clothes and donned the gown, then taking the gourd and staff, went his way and left me.

死了，頭下有一塊散發着麝香香味的新裹屍布。於是我給他洗乾淨，包好，為他祈禱，然後在沙裏挖了一個洞把他埋好，帶着他的長袍，瓶子和手杖划船回到了西岸，在那裏過夜。

第二天城門一開就有個年輕人向我走來，我知道這是個下流的傢伙，他穿着華麗的衣服，還染了指甲。他問我："你不就是那個渡船工嗎？"我說："是的。"他說："把託你交給我的東西給我。"我問："是甚麼東西？"他答："長袍、瓶子和手杖"。我問："是誰告訴你的？"他答："我也不清楚，我只知道昨天我去參加一個朋友的婚禮，晚上大家唱歌〔作樂〕，直到天快亮了，我才躺下睡覺休息，忽然我面前站着一個人，他對我說：'至高無上的真主召回了他的一個僕人，並且指定你來接任他的位置，你現在去找一個渡船工，從他那裏取回死者為你留下的長袍、瓶子和手杖'。"於是我就把這些東西拿出來交給了他，他脫去自己的衣服，披上長袍，然後拿起瓶子和手杖就走了。

I fell a-weeping for wonder and pity; but, that night, whilst I slept, the Lord of Glory appeared to me in a dream and said to me, "O My servant, is it grievous to thee that I have granted to one of My servants to return to Me? Indeed, this is of My bounty, that I vouchsafe to whom I will, for I am able to do all things."

我又驚奇又抱憾，直想落淚；但那天夜裏當我睡着了，榮耀的真主在夢中出現，並對我說：“我的僕人，你以為我讓一個僕人回到我身邊是件悲痛的事嗎？事實上，這是我的恩賜，我將它賜予我想賜予的人，因為我是無所不能的。

# 91 The Khalif El Mamoun and the Strange Doctor

It is said that there was none, among the Khalifs of the house of Abbas, more accomplished in all branches of knowledge than El Mamoun. On two days in each week, he was wont to preside at conferences of the learned, when the doctors and theologians met and sitting, each in his several rank and room, disputed in his presence. One day, as he sat thus, there came into the assembly a stranger, clad in worn white clothes, and sat down in an obscure place, behind the doctors of the law. Then the assembled scholars began to speak and expound difficult questions, it being the custom that the various propositions should be submitted to each in turn and that whoso bethought him of some subtle addition or rare trait, should make mention of it. So the question went round till it came to the stranger, who spoke in his turn and made a goodlier answer than that of any of the doctors; and the Khalif approved his speech and bade advance him to a higher room. When the second question came round to him, he made a still more admirable answer, and the Khalif ordered him to be preferred to a yet higher place. When the third question reached him, he made answer more justly and appropriately than on the two previous occasions, and El

# 九十一　曼蒙王和陌生的博士

據說在阿巴斯王室的諸王中，曼蒙的知識最為淵博。每週有兩天他要主持學者們的會議。開會時博士們和神學家們按各自的級別及座次坐下，當他的面進行辯論。有一天，當他正坐着主持會議時，進來一個陌生人，他穿着破舊白衣，坐到法學博士後面一個不顯眼的地方。然後，與會的學者們開始發言，闡述疑難問題。當時的習俗是向每個人輪流提出各種命題，誰有甚麼獨創之見就可以發表。現在問題輪到陌生人，他發了言，而且他的回答比別的博士都要高明。國王贊同他的發言，吩咐把他的座次提升一級。輪到他就第二個問題發言時，他作了一個更精彩的回答，國王下令把他的座次再升一級。當第三個問題輪到他時，他的回答比前兩個問題還要精闢得當。國王吩咐他上

Mamoun bade him come up and sit near himself. When the conference broke up, water was brought and they washed their hands; after which food was set on and they ate. Then the doctors arose and withdrew; but El Mamoun forbade the stranger to depart with them and calling him to himself, entreated him with especial favour and promised him honour and benefits.

Presently, they made ready the banquet of wine; the fair-faced boon-companions[1] came and the cup went round amongst them, till it came to the stranger, who rose to his feet and said, "If the Commander of the Faithful permit me, I will say one word." "Say what thou wilt," answered the Khalif. Quoth the stranger, "Verily, the Exalted Intelligence[2] knoweth that his slave was this day, in the august assembly, one of the unknown folk and of the meanest of the company, and the Commander of the Faithful distinguished him and brought him near to himself, little as was the wit be showed, preferring him above the rest and advancing him to a rank whereto his thought aspired not: and now he is minded to deprive him of that small portion of wit that raised him from obscurity and augmented him, after his littleness. God forfend

1. boon-companions：飲酒作樂的朋友。

2. the Exalted Intelligence：指國王。

前來坐在自己身邊。散會後，僕人送水來給他們洗手，擺上食物請他們吃。然後博士們起身告退，但曼蒙不讓陌生人和他們一起離開，而把陌生人叫到身邊，給他特殊的禮遇並許以高官厚祿。

酒宴很快就準備好了。面容姣好的伴酒女郎前來，在他們之間傳遞酒杯。當酒杯傳到陌生人手中時，他站起身來說，“如果陛下允許，我想說句話。”“想說甚麼就說吧！”國王答道。陌生人說，“陛下英明，知道奴才在今天莊嚴的會議之前只不過是個無名小卒，微不足道；是陛下獨具慧眼把他擢陞到了自己身邊。儘管他才疏學淺，陛下卻把他晉陞到他從未想過的高位淩駕於他人之上。現在陛下卻要剝奪使他平步青雲的這一點點才智！願真主使陛

that the Commander of the Faithful should envy his slave what little he hath of understanding and worth and renown! But, if his slave should drink wine, his reason would depart from him and ignorance draw near to him and steal away his good breeding; so would he revert to that low degree, whence he sprang, and become contemptible and ridiculous in the eyes of the folk. I hope, therefore, that the August Intelligence, of his power and bounty and royal generosity and magnanimity[3], will not despoil his slave of this jewel."

When the Khalif heard his speech, he praised him and thanked him and making him sit down again in his place, showed him high honour and ordered him a present of a hundred thousand dinars. Moreover he mounted him upon a horse and gave him rich apparel; and in every assembly he exalted him and showed him favour over all the other doctors, till he became the highest of them all in rank.

---

3. the August Intelligence... magnanimity：敬畏的、大能的、寬宏的智者；對國王的尊敬稱呼。

下不會嫉妒奴才所有的那一點點智力、價值和名氣。但若奴才喝了酒，他的理智就會離他而去，他就又會變得愚昧無知和沒有教養。這樣他就又要回到他從前的低位，在眾人眼中成為可鄙又可笑的小人物。因此我希望陛下開恩，不要奪去奴才僅有的這一點財富吧！”

國王聽了他的話，稱讚了他，並讓他重新坐在他的席位上，給予他很高的榮譽，並獎給他十萬第納爾。另外又賞給他一匹駿馬和華麗的衣服。每次開會國王都提升他，給他的恩寵超過任何其他博士，直到他成為他們之中級別最高的。

## 92 White Hair

One day I went into an orchard to buy fruit and saw, far off, a woman sitting in the shade of an apricot tree and combing her hair. Going nearer I perceived that she was old and had white hair, though her face was beautiful and her complexion fresh and young. Although she saw me approaching, she made no movement to veil her face or cover her head; but went on arranging her hair with her ivory comb. I stopped before her and greeted her, saying: "O woman old in years but young of face, why do you not dye your hair and look altogether like a girl? Surely there is no reason why you should not do so?"

She lifted her head and, looking at me with her great eyes, answered by these lines:

*I used to dye my hair*
*But time undyed it.*
*Now I am sage,*
*I show my bottom bare*
*Which does not age.*
*(I used to hide it.)*

## 九十二　白髮

一天，我走進一個果園去買水果，看見遠處有一女子坐在杏樹的樹蔭下梳頭。走近時，我發現她雖然年事已高而且滿頭白髮，但她的臉卻依然美麗年輕，容光煥發。她雖然看見我向她走來，卻並沒有動手用面罩蓋住自己的臉或頭，而是繼續用象牙梳子梳頭。我來到她面前向她打招呼說："老太太，您真是鶴髮童顏呀！為甚麼不把頭髮染一染，好顯得年輕呢？您不這麼做難道有甚麼原因嗎？"

她抬頭用她那雙大眼睛看着我，以下面的詩句作答：

昔曾染青絲，
流光還其原，
今已知天命，
示人以本色，
經久耐衰老，
(無需再掩飾)。

## 93 The Two Kings

There were once two kings, a just and an unjust. The latter's country abounded in trees and fruits and herbs; but he let no merchant pass without robbing him of his goods and his merchandise, and the merchants endured this with patience, by reason of their gain from the fatness of the land in the means of life and its pleasantness, more by token that it was renowned for its richness in precious stones and jewels. Now the just king, who loved jewels, heard of this land and sent one of his subjects thither, giving him much money and bidding him buy jewels therewith from that country. So he went thither and it being told to the unjust king that a merchant was come to his realm, with much money to buy jewels withal, he sent for him and asked him whence and what he was and what was his errand. Quoth the merchant, "I am of such a country, and the king of the land gave me money and bade me buy therewith jewels from this country; so I obeyed him and came." "Out on thee!" cried the unjust king. "Knowst thou not my fashion of dealing with the people of my realm and how each day I take their good? How then comest thou to my country? And behold, thou hast been a sojourner here since such a time!" "The money is not mine," answered the

# 九十三　兩個國王

從前有兩個國王：一個是明君，一個是暴君。暴君的國家森林茂密，盛產鮮果和草藥。但他沒收過往商人的貨物，否則就不讓他們通過。商人們為了該國物資豐盛風景秀麗，來做生意可獲利益，更因為那裏以盛產寶石著稱，也只好忍了。那位明君喜愛珠寶，聽說了那個地方，就派了一名手下去那裏，並給了他許多錢從該國採購珠寶。於是他就奉命前去。暴君接到報告說，國裏來了一個商人，帶了許多錢來採購珠寶，就召見商人，問他從哪裏來，是幹甚麼的，來做甚麼。商人說："我來自某國，該國國王給了我錢，要我從貴國採購珠寶；所以我就遵旨而來了。"暴君大聲說："滾出去！你難道不知道我是如何對付我的臣民的嗎？你難道不知道我每天都要沒收他們的財物嗎？你來我國是怎麼回事兒？看，你從某時起就在這裏逗留了！"商人答道："那錢不是我的，一個子兒都不是

stranger; "not a doit of it; nay, it is a trust in my hands, till I bring it to its owner." But the king said, "I will not let thee take thy livelihood of my country or go out therefrom, except thou ransom thyself with this money, all of it; else shalt thou die."

So the man said in himself, "I am fallen between two kings, and I know that the oppression of this one embraceth all who abide in his dominions: and if I content him not, I shall lose both life and money and shall fail of my errand; whilst, on the other hand, if I give him all the money, it will assuredly prove my ruin with the other king, its owner: wherefore nothing will serve me but that I give this one a small part thereof and content him therewith and avert perdition from myself and from the money. Thus shall I get my livelihood of the fatness of this land, till I buy that which I desire of jewels and return to the owner of the money with his need, trusting in his justice and indulgence and fearing not that he will punish me for that which this unjust king taketh of the money, especially if it be but a little."

Then he called down blessings on the unjust king and said to him, "O king, I will ransom myself and this money with a small portion thereof, from the time of my entering thy country to that of my going forth therefrom." The king agreed to this and left him at peace for a year, till he bought jewels with all [the rest of] the money and returned therewith

我的。那是別人委託我保管，將來要歸還原主的。”但國王說：“我不許你將你的財物帶出境外，也禁止你出境，除非你用這筆錢贖身，一個子兒也不能少，否則你就得死。”

那人心想：“我現在夾在兩個國王中間，左右為難。我知道這個國王是如何壓迫所有居住在他領域內的人的；如果我不滿足他，我就會把性命和金錢都賠上，而我的任務也就完不成了。另一方面，如果我把所有的錢都給他，那就肯定會失去錢的主人，另一個國王對我的信任。因此我別無他法，只有給這個國王一小部分錢來滿足他，免得人財兩空。這樣我就可以在這裏生活下去，直到我買了我想買的珠寶，帶着錢的主人所要的東西回到他那裏，相信他的公正和寬容不會因為這個暴君奪去的那一點錢而懲辦我。”

於是他高聲為暴君祈福並對他說：“陛下，我願意用這筆錢的一小部分作為我從入境到離境這段時間的贖金。”國王同意了，就讓他平安地住了一年，直到他用所有〔剩餘〕的錢買了珠寶，回到他主人那裏。他向主人說

to his master, to whom he made his excuses, confessing to having rescued himself from the unjust king as before related. The just king accepted his excuse and praised him for his wise ordinance and set him on his right hand in his divan and appointed him in his kingdom an abiding inheritance and a happy life.

Now the just king is the similitude of the next world and the unjust king that of this world; the jewels that be in the latter's dominions are good deeds and pious works. The merchant is man and the money he hath with him is the provision appointed him of God. It behoves him who seeks his livelihood in this world to leave not a day without seeking the goods of the world to come, so shall he content this world with that which he gains of the fatness of the earth and the next with that which he spends of his life in seeking after it.

明理由，承認自己用上面説的辦法從暴君手中逃出來。明君接受了他的理由並稱讚他聰明能幹，讓他坐在自己寶座的右側，賞給他終身的產業，讓他快樂地生活。

上面的故事是個比喻，其中的明君代表來世，暴君是現世，該國的珠寶是善行。商人指人，他帶的錢是真主給他的供應品。人在現世謀生時應當每天盡力為來世做好事，這樣他就可以用從世上得到的財富來滿足現世的需要，而同時用他一生中為追求來世而做的好事來滿足來世。

# Others
# 其他

## 94 His Leprosy Was Cured

*— The Greek King and Douban the Physician (1)*

There once lived a king, who was sorely afflicted with a leprosy, and his physicians had unsuccessfully tried every remedy they were acquainted with, when a very ingenious physician called Douban, arrived at the court: he was well acquainted with the good and bad properties of all kinds of plants and drugs. As soon as he was informed of the king's illness, he dressed himself in his robe of ceremony, and obtained permission to be presented to the king. "Sire," said he, "I know that all your physicians have been unable to remove your leprosy; but if you will I will cure you without either internal doses or outward applications."

Douban returned to his house and made a sort of racket or bat, with a hollow in the handle, to admit the drug he meant to use; that being done, the following day he presented himself before the king, and prostrating himself at his feet, kissed the ground.

Douban then arose and told the king that he must ride on horseback to the place where he was accustomed to play at rackets. The king did as he was desired; and when he had reached the racket-ground, he took the bat, and spurred his horse after the ball till he struck it; it was sent back again to

## 九十四　妙手回春

*—— 希臘國王與杜班醫生（一）*

從前有個國王患了嚴重的麻瘋病。御醫們用盡了他們知道的各種治療法，也沒有把他治好。後來宮裏來了一位名叫杜班的醫生，他醫術高明，熟悉各種植物和藥物的性質，包括好的和壞的。他一聽說國王的病，就穿上禮服，獲准覲見國王。他說："陛下，我知道所有的御醫都未能治好您的麻瘋病；但是，如果您願意的話，我能讓您不用內服外敷就把病治好。"

杜班回到家裏，做了一隻球拍似的東西，把手上有個洞，可以放進他要用的藥。做好後的第二天，他去覲見國王，拜倒在他腳下，吻了地面。

然後杜班起身對國王說，他必須騎馬去他通常玩拍球戲的地方。國王照他的話做了；他到達拍球場後，就拿起球拍，催馬擊球，玩了起來。陪他打球的軍官把球打回

him by the officers, who were playing with him, and he struck it again; and thus the game continued for a considerable time, till he found his hand as well as his whole body in a perspiration, which made the remedy in the bat operate as the physician had said; the king then left the game, returned to the palace, bathed, and observed very punctually all the directions that had been given him.

He soon found the good effects of the prescription, for on the next morning, he perceived with equal surprise and joy that his leprosy was cured, and that his body was as clear as if he had never been attacked by that malady. As soon as he was dressed he went into the audience-room, where he mounted his throne and received the congratulations of all his courtiers.

Douban entered, and prostrated himself at the foot of the throne. The king made him sit by his side, and afterward placed him at his own table to dine only with him; and yet further, toward evening, when the courtiers were about to depart, he put on him a rich robe, and gave him two thousand sequins. The following day he did nothing but caress[1] him, and confer on him fresh proofs of his gratitude.

---

1. caress：這裏指寵愛，給予青睞。

來，他又把球打出去。就這樣，遊戲進行了很長時間，直到他的手和全身都出了汗。這就使球拍裏的藥像醫生說的那樣起了作用。然後，國王離開球場，回到宮裏，洗了澡，一切都完全按照給他的囑咐去做。

他很快就發現這種療法效果良好；因為第二天早晨他驚喜地發覺自己的麻瘋病治好了，而且全身非常光滑，好像根本沒得過那種病一樣。他一穿好衣服就走入朝廷，登上寶座，接受朝臣們的祝賀。

杜班進來拜倒在寶座腳下。國王讓他坐在他的身邊，後來又讓他單獨跟自己同桌吃飯；此外，當朝臣們傍晚快要散朝時，又贈了他一件華麗的袍子，並給了他兩千金幣。第二天，國王專門款待他，並給了他新的賞賜，以表示他的謝意。

## 95 Their Injustice and Their Cruelty Are Punished Sooner or Later

*— The Greek King and Douban the Physician (2)*

The physician then[1] arranged all his affairs, and as the report got abroad that an unheard-of-prodigy was to happen after his execution, the viziers, emirs, officers of the guard, in short all the court, flocked the next day to the hall of audience.

The physician Douban was brought in, and advancing to the foot of the throne, with a book in his hand, he called for a basin, and laid upon it the cover of the volume, and then presenting the book to the king: "Take this," said he, "and, after my head is cut off, order that it be put upon that cover. As soon as it is there, the blood will cease to flow; then open the book, and my head will answer your questions. But, sire," added Douban, "permit me once more to implore your mercy. Consider, I beg of you, that I am innocent." "Thy prayers[2]," answered the king, "are useless, and were it only

1. 杜班醫生因治愈國王的惡疾深得國王的寵幸，卻引起朝臣們的嫉妒。其中之一向國王進讒說他要謀害國王，國王聽信讒言，下命將杜班處死。杜班要求國王給他一年時間回家料理後事，以後前來受死，並在死前向國王顯示一個奇蹟，國王出於好奇就同意了。

# 九十五　惡有惡報

*——希臘國王與杜班醫生（二）*

然後，醫生安排好所有後事。他被處決後會發生一樁聞所未聞的奇事的消息很快就傳開了。第二天，大臣們、酋長們、御林軍的軍官們，一句話，整個宮廷，都湧到朝廷來了。

杜班醫生被帶了進來，走到王座腳下。他手裏拿着一本書，要來一個盆，把書的封面放在盆上，然後把書呈給國王，說："拿着它，等我的頭砍掉以後，命令把頭放在封面上。頭一放好，血就會止住了；然後打開書，我的頭就會回答您的問題。但是，陛下，"杜班接着說，"允許我再一次懇求您大發慈悲。我求您想一想我是無辜的。"國王回答道，"不用囉唆了，若不是想聽聽你的頭在你死

---

2. Thy prayers：你的請求。

to hear thy head speak after thy death, it would be my will that thou shouldst die." In saying this, he took the book from the hands of the physician, and ordered the officer to do his duty.

The head was cut off at one stroke, and it had hardly been placed on the cover an instant before the blood stopped. Then, to the astonishment of the king and all the spectators, it opened its eyes, and said, "Sire, will you now open the book." The king did so, and finding that the first leaf stuck to the second, he put his finger to his mouth, and wetted it, in order to turn it over more easily. He went on doing so till he came to the sixth leaf, and observing nothing written upon the appointed page, "Physician," said he to the head, "there is no writing." "Turn over, then , a few more leaves," replied the head. The king continued turning them over, still putting his finger frequently to his mouth. The prince then felt himself suddenly agitated in a most extraordinary manner; his sight failed him, and he fell at the foot of the throne in the greatest convulsions.

When the physician Douban, or rather his head, saw the king fall back, "Tyrant," he said, "the book is poisoned. Thy death is certain. Now, you see how princes are treated who abuse their power and slay the innocent. Their injustice and their cruelty are punished sooner or later." Scarcely had the head spoken these words, when the king fell down dead; and the head itself lost what life it had.

後怎麼講話，我早就把你殺了。”他一面說一面把書從醫生手中拿過來，同時命令劊子手行刑。

劊子手一刀就把頭砍了下來，放在封面上，血立刻就止住了。然後，使國王和全體看熱鬧的人大吃一驚的是，那頭居然張開了眼睛，說：“陛下，現在請您打開書。”國王照辦後，發現第一頁跟第二頁黏在一起了，就把手指頭伸到嘴邊，把它舔濕了，以便翻書容易些。他繼續這樣翻書一直翻到第六頁，發現在指定的那頁上連一個字也沒有。他對着頭說：“醫生，那頁上沒字呀。”那頭回答：“那就再翻幾頁吧。”國王繼續翻書，仍舊經常把手指頭塞到嘴裏。然後國王突然感到異常心煩意亂；眼睛看不見了，跌倒在王座下，猛烈地抽搐起來。

當杜班醫生，倒不如說是他的頭，看見國王跌倒時，他說，“暴君，那書是有毒的。你死定了。現在，你明白濫用權力殺害無辜的國王會有甚麼報應了吧。他們的虐政遲早會受到懲罰的。”那頭剛說完這些話，國王就倒地死了，那頭自己也失去了生命。

## 96 The New Grand-wazir in Judgment

When the new grand-wazir had bidden the two pleaders to state their case, the first said: "My lord, I took a cow of mine this morning to pasture in my field of fresh lucern. Her little calf followed at her heels or played about the road. Before I reached my destination, I met this man, riding on a mare which was accompanied by her colt, a little pitiful bandy-legged slip of a thing, almost an abortion.

"As soon as my little calf saw the foal he ran up to make acquaintance with her and jumped round her, caressing her under the belly with his muzzle. He played with her in a thousand ways, sometimes running at her gently and sometimes flinging his little feet in the air until the pebbles flew.

"Quite suddenly this gross and brutal fellow dismounted from the mare and slipped a cord round the neck of my charming little calf, saying: 'I think I will have him on a lead. I do not wish him to be perverted by playing with that miserable little foal, or with her mother, your vile cow.' Then he called pleasantly to my calf: 'Come little son of my mare, we do not wish to be corrupted.' In spite of my protestations, he led away my calf and left the horrible foal, threatening to

## 九十六　賢相斷案

新宰相吩咐兩名申訴人陳述各自的理由時，第一人說：“大人，今天早晨我趕一頭奶牛去我的苜蓿地吃草。牠生下的小牛犢跟在後面一路玩耍。快到目的地時，我遇見了這個人，他騎着一匹母馬，旁邊跟一頭長着羅圈腿的小駒兒，怪可憐的，像個早產的畸形仔。

“我的小牛犢一看到那小駒兒就跑上去跟牠親熱起來，圍着牠又蹦又跳，用鼻子在牠的肚皮底下磨蹭。我的小牛犢變着花樣跟牠玩耍，有時輕輕地向牠撲去，有時在空中踢腿，弄得砂石飛揚。

“突然，這個粗野的傢伙從馬上卜來，用繩子繞在我那可愛的小牛犢的脖子上，說：‘我得拴住我的牛犢，免得讓那難看的小馬或生牠的那頭可惡的母牛帶壞了。’然後，他柔聲召喚我的牛犢：‘過來，我的母馬的孩子，別讓人家勾引壞了。’他不聽我的反對，牽走了我的牛犢，留下了那頭難看的小馬，還威脅說如果我試圖奪回明明屬

break my head if I tried to take back that which is my own in the sight of Allah and before all men!"

When he had heard the first in silence, the new grand-wazir turned to the second man and asked him what he had to urge in his defence. "My lord," said the defendant, "it is a well-known fact that the calf was the offspring of my mare and that the wretched foal was dropped by this man's cow." "I suppose it is quite certain that cows can drop foals and mares give birth to calves?" interrupted the wazir, "You doubtless have something to bring forward in proof of your assertion?" "My lord, do you not know that nothing is impossible to Allah?" retorted the man, "He creates that which seems good to him and sows the seed of abundance where He wills. His creatures can only bow to His greater wisdom, giving Him praise and glory." "That is a very correct sentiment," agreed the wazir, "Nothing is impossible to the Almighty; at His decree calves can be born of mares and foals from cows. Before you take the calf away, however, I will show both of you another example of Allah's power."

He ordered a large sack of flour and a small mouse to be brought into the presence, and said to the two pleaders: "Watch carefully and do not say a word." Then he turned to the defendant, bidding him lift the sack of flour and load it on the back of the mouse. "My lord, it will squash the creature

於我的東西，他就要在真主面前當眾打碎我的腦袋。”

新宰相默默地聽完第一個人的申訴後，轉向第二個人，問他有甚麼要申辯的。被告說：“大人，那牛犢是我的母馬下的，而那難看的小馬是這人的母牛下的。這是誰都知道的事實。”宰相插嘴說：“想必母牛一定能下小駒，而母馬也一定能生牛犢的囉？你一定能拿出證據來證明你的說法吧？”那人反駁說：“大人，您難道不知道真主是無所不能的嗎？祂能創造祂認為是好的東西，祂願意在哪裏播種豐盛的種子就在哪裏播種。祂創造的萬物只能向祂的智慧頂禮膜拜，將讚美和榮耀歸於祂。”宰相表示同意說：“說得對極了。真主是萬能的；按祂的旨意，母馬能生牛犢，母牛也能下馬駒。但是，在你把牛犢牽走之前，我要讓你看真主的法力的另一個例子。”

他下令弄來一大袋麵粉和一隻老鼠，對這兩個申訴人說：“請注意看，但不要說話。”然後，他轉向被告，命他拿起那袋麵粉放在老鼠背上。那人反對說：“大人，那

flat!" objected the man. "O wretch of little faith," cried the wazir, "is not all possible to Allah who brings forth calves from mares?" He ordered the guards to seize the defendant and beat him soundly for his ignorance and impiety; but to the plaintiff he delivered all four animals.

要把老鼠壓扁的！”宰相大聲說：“你這不信神的壞蛋！能使母馬下牛犢的真主不是萬能的嗎？”他命令衛兵抓住被告，把他痛打一頓，以懲罰他的無知和不敬；但把四頭牲口都判給了原告。

## 97 The Price of Cucumbers

One day, while the emir Muyin bin Zayda was out hunting, he met an Arab mounted upon an ass coming across the desert. He rode up and saluted him, saying: "Where are you going, O brother Arab, and what is it that you carry so carefully rolled up in that little sack?" "I go to find the emir Muyin," answered the Arab, "to carry him some cucumbers which have come up before their time on my land and are its first fruits. He is the most generous man in the kingdom and I am sure he will pay me a worthy price for my cucumbers." The emir, whom the Arab had never seen before, asked him how much he expected to be paid for the cucumbers and the other answered: "At least a thousand dinars of gold."

"And if the emir says that is too much?"

"I will only ask five hundred."

"And if he says that is too much?"

"I will only ask three hundred."

"And if he says that is too much?"

"One hundred."

"And if he says that is too much?"

"Fifty."

"And if he says that is too much?"

## 九十七　黃瓜的價格

一天，穆因．柴德酋長外出打獵，遇見一個阿拉伯人，騎着驢子穿過沙漠。他騎馬過去向他致意，問他，“你去哪裏，阿拉伯兄弟？你那小袋子裏包得那麼嚴實是甚麼東西？”“我要去找穆因酋長，”阿拉伯人答道，“給他帶一些黃瓜，這都是我的地裏長的，早熟的黃瓜，這是第一批黃瓜呢！他是我們國內最慷慨的人我相信他一定會付我一個好價錢的。”阿拉伯人並不認識酋長，所以酋長問他希望會付給他多少錢。阿拉伯人答道：“至少一千第納爾。”

“如果酋長説那太多了呢？”

“那我就只要五百。”

“如果他還説太多呢？”

“那我就要三百。”

“如果他還説太多呢？”

“一百。”

“如果他還説太多呢？”

“五十。”

“如果他還説太多呢？”

"Thirty."

"And if he says that is still too much?"

"I will drive my ass into his harem and run away."

Muyin laughed heartily at this and, spurring his horse, rejoined his followers. Then, without a moment's delay, he returned to his palace and ordered his chamberlain to admit the Arab when he should come with the cucumbers.

An hour later, the man arrived with his bag, and the chamberlain led him at once into the reception hall where the emir Muyin waited him, in the midst of all the majesty of his court and surrounded by guards with naked swords. The Arab, who did not at all recognise, among so much grandeur, the horseman whom he had met upon his way, stood with the sack of cucumbers in his hand, waiting to be questioned. "What do you bring me in that sack, O brother Arab?" the emir enquired; and the man replied: "Trusting in the liberality of our master the emir, I have brought him the first young cucumbers which grew in my field."

"An excellent idea! And what do you think my liberality is worth?"

"A thousand dinars."

"That is a little too much."

"Five hundred."

"Too much."

"Three hundred."

“三十。”

“如果他仍然説太多呢？”

“那我就把驢子趕進他的宮殿，我自己就溜了。”

酋長聽了哈哈大笑策馬趕上了他的隨從。然後一點也不耽擱就回到了宮裏，吩咐大臣們如果阿拉伯人帶着黃瓜來了就讓他進宮來。

一個小時之後，那個人帶着黃瓜來了，大臣立即讓他進入接待廳。酋長正坐在客廳裏等他，周圍站滿了刀劍出鞘的衛兵。在如此莊嚴氣氛中，阿拉伯人一點也沒有認出來他在路上遇到的那個騎馬人。他拿着那袋黃瓜站在那裏，等着問話。“你的袋子裏帶的甚麼東西呀，阿拉伯兄弟。”酋長問道。那人回答：“我相信我們的主人酋長先生的慷慨，我給他帶了我地裏長的第一批嫩黃瓜。”

“好主意！你認為我會慷慨地付給你多少？”

“一千第納爾。”

“那有點太多了。”

“五百。”

“太多了。”

“三百。”

"Too much."

"One hundred."

"Too much."

"Fifty."

"Too much."

"Thirty, then."

"Still too much."

Then cried the Arab: "As Allah lives, it was an unlucky meeting I had in the desert with that foul-faced man! O emir, I cannot let my cucumbers go at less than thirty dinars!"

The emir smiled and did not answer; so that the Arab looked at him more closely and, recognising him as the man he had met in the desert, exclaimed: "As Allah lives, my master, let the thirty dinars be brought; for my ass is fastened just outside the door." The emir was taken with such a gust of laughing that he fell over on his backside; when he was a little recovered, he called his intendant, saying: "Count out immediately to this our brother, the Arab, first a thousand dinars, then five hundred, then three hundred, then one hundred, then fifty, and finally thirty, to induce him to leave his ass tied up where it is." I need not say that the Arab was stupefied at receiving one thousand, nine hundred and eighty dinars for a little sack of cucumbers. Such was the liberality of the emir Muyin.

“太多。”

“一百。”

“太多。”

“五十。”

“太多。”

“三十。”

“還是太多。”

阿拉伯人叫了起來，“真主在上，我在沙漠裏遇見那個醜陋的人真是倒霉，酋長先生少於三十第納爾我的黃瓜就不賣了。”

酋長笑了起來，甚麼話也沒說。阿拉伯人更仔細地看了看他，認出來他就是在沙漠中遇到的那個人，他大叫：“真主在上！我的主人，快把三十第納爾拿來，我的驢子就栓在門外呢！”酋長聽見此話笑得前仰後合；等他喘過氣來，就叫來隨從說：“馬上給我這位阿拉伯兄弟先數出一千第納爾，然後五百，然後三百，然後一百，然後五十，最後三十，好讓他把驢子栓在那裏別動。”不用說阿拉伯人簡直驚呆了：一小袋黃瓜竟賣了一千九百八十第納爾！這就是穆因酋長的慷慨！

## 98 The Stolen Necklace

There was once a devout woman, who had renounced the world and devoted herself to the service of God. Now she used to resort to a certain king's palace, the dwellers wherein looked for a blessing by reason of her presence, and she was held of them in high honour. One day, she entered the palace, according to her wont, and sat down beside the queen. Presently the latter gave her a necklace, worth a thousand dinars, saying, "Keep this for me, whilst I go to the bath." So she entered the bath, which was in the palace, and the pious woman laid the necklace on the prayer-carpet and stood up to pray. As she was thus engaged, there came a magpie, which snatched up the necklace, [unseen of her,] and carrying it off, hid it in a crevice in one of the palace-walls. When the queen came out of the bath, she sought the necklace of the recluse, and the latter searched for it, but found it not, nor could light on any trace of it; so she said to the queen, "By Allah, O my daughter, none has been with me. When thou gavest me the necklace, I laid it on the prayer-carpet, and I know not if one of the servants saw it and took it without my heed, whilst I was engaged in prayer. God only

## 九十八　失竊的項鍊

從前有個修女，厭棄紅塵，一心侍奉上帝。她常去王宮，宮裏的人都求她為他們祈福，所以都很尊敬她。一天，她照常進宮，坐在王后身邊。王后給她一串價值一千第納爾的項鍊說："替我拿着這個，我要去洗澡。"於是，她進了宮裏的浴室，修女就把項鍊放在祈禱時用的小跪毯上，然後站起來祈禱。這時，飛來一隻喜鵲一下叼走了項鍊（她沒有看見），把它藏在宮牆牆縫裏。王后洗完澡後向修女要項鍊，修女到處尋找卻連一點蹤影也沒有；她只好對王后說："真主作證，我的女兒，這裏沒有旁人。您交給我項鍊後，我把它放在小跪毯上了，不知道是否有僕人看到並在我祈禱時乘我不注意把它拿走了。它的

knows what is come of it!" When the King heard what had happened, he bade his consort put the woman to the question by fire and beating; so they tortured her with all manner tortures, but could not bring her to confess or to accuse any. Then he commanded to lay her in irons and cast her into prison, and they did as he bade.

One day, after this, as the King sat in the inner court of his palace, with the queen by his side and water flowing around him, he saw the magpie fly into a crevice of the wall and pull out the lost necklace, whereupon he cried out to a damsel who was with him, and she caught the bird and took the necklace from it. By this the King knew that the pious woman had been wronged and repented of that he had done with her. So he sent for her and fell to kissing her head and sought pardon of her, weeping. Moreover, he commanded great treasure to be given to her, but she would none of it[1]. However, she forgave him and went away, vowing never again to enter any one's house. So she betook herself to wandering in the mountains and valleys and worshipped God the Most High till she died.

---

1. but she would none of it：would 後省去了 have。這是較古老英語中常見的現象。

下落只有天知道！”國王聽說這事後吩咐王后用火刑和拷打來審問那女人。他們對她用盡了酷刑，也無法使她認罪或供出別人。於是他命令給她扣上鐐銬枷鎖，投入監獄，他手下就照辦了。

後來有一天，國王在內宮坐着，身旁坐着王后，周圍流水環繞。這時，他看見喜鵲飛進一道牆縫，叼出了那條失蹤的項鍊，他喊身邊的宮女。宮女捉住了那隻鳥，把項鍊從鳥咀裏奪了卜來，國王這才明白修女是冤枉的；他後悔不該那樣對待她。因此他把她叫來，吻她的頭，哭着求她饒恕。另外，他賞賜她大量財物，但她分文不受。她寬恕了他，走了，發誓再也不進任何人的家門。從此，她雲遊名山大川，禮拜真主，直至去世。

# 99 The Khalif El Mamoun and the Pyramids of Egypt

It is told that the Khalif El Mamoun, son of Haroun er Reshid, when he entered the [God-]guarded city of Cairo, was minded to pull down the Pyramids, that he might take what was therein; but, when he went about to do this, he could not avail thereto, for all his endeavour. He expended great sums of money in the attempt, but only succeeded in opening up a small gallery in one of them, wherein he found treasure, to the exact amount of the money he had spent in the works, neither more nor less; at which he marvelled and taking what he found there, desisted from his intent.

Now the Pyramids are three in number, and they are one of the wonders of the world; nor is there on the face of the earth their like for height and fashion and skilful ordinance; for they are builded of immense rocks, and they who built them proceeded by piercing one block of stone and setting therein upright rods of iron; after which they pierced a second block of stone and lowered it upon the first. Then they poured melted lead upon the joints and set the blocks in geometrical order, till the building was complete. The height of each pyramid was a hundred cubits, of the measure of the time,

## 九十九　曼蒙王和埃及金字塔

相傳哈隆·雷切德的兒子曼蒙國王有一次進入真主守護的開羅城時想要拆毀金字塔，以便取走塔中的寶藏。但無論他怎樣努力，也無法達到目的。他為此花了大筆的錢，但只在一個金字塔中掘開了一個小房間。在這個小房間裏他找到一些財寶，其數量與他開掘時所花的錢正好相等，不多也不少。他十分驚奇，只好拿走這些財寶並打消了原先的念頭。

金字塔共有三座，被譽為世界奇觀之一，其高度、形狀及巧妙的構造是世上絕無僅有的。金字塔用巨石建成。金字塔的匠人們先在一塊石頭上鑿洞，在洞中豎直放上鐵條，然後在第二塊石頭上鑿洞，把第二塊石頭從上向下插疊在第一塊石頭上。然後在連接處灌入熔鉛，按幾何形狀排列石塊，直至完工。每座金字塔的高度按當時的尺度是

and it was four-square, each side three hundred cubits long, at the bottom, and sloping upward thence to a point. The ancients say that, in the western Pyramid, are thirty chambers of vari-coloured granite, full of precious stones and treasures galore[1] and rare images and utensils and costly arms, which latter are anointed with magical unguents, so that they may not rust till the day of Resurrection[2]. Therein, also, are vessels of glass, that will bend and not break, containing various kinds of compound drugs and medicinal waters. In the second Pyramid are the records of the priests, written on tablets of granite, — to each priest his tablet, on which are set out the wonders of his craft and his achievements; and on the walls are figures like idols, working with their hands at all manner crafts and seated on thrones. To each pyramid there is a guardian, that keeps watch over it and guards it, to all eternity, against the ravages of time and the vicissitudes of events; and indeed the marvels of these pyramids astound all who have eyes and wit.

---

1. treasures galore：大量珍寶。
2. the day of Resurrection：聖經所指的最後審判日，所有人都復活，這裏喻意為"永遠"。

一百肘尺。塔底為四方形，每邊長三百肘尺，四壁斜斜向上延伸直至頂點匯合。古人説西邊那座金字塔中有三十個用彩色花崗石造的房間，裏面珍藏着大批珠寶、金銀、稀有的塑像、器皿以及用神油塗抹得永不生銹的昂貴武器。還有可以彎曲而不會破碎的玻璃容器，裏面裝着各種藥水。在第二個金字塔裏放着大祭師們的案卷，都刻在花崗石板上，每人一塊，上面記載着各人的神奇法術和成就。四壁雕有人物肖像，他們坐在王位上，用手施行各種法術。每座金字塔都有一個守護神，負責永遠看管及保衛這座金字塔，使之免遭時間及世事變化的破壞。金字塔的巍峨奇觀使身臨其境的人無不嘆為觀止。

# 100 Epilogue

Now during this time Shahrazad[1] had borne King Shahriyar three sons. On the thousand and first night, when she had ended the tale of Ma'aruf, she rose and kissed the ground before him, saying: "Great King, for a thousand and one nights I have been recounting to you the fables of past ages and the legends of ancient kings. May I make so bold as to crave a favour of your majesty?"

The King replied: "Ask, and it shall be granted."

Shahrazad called out to the nurses, saying: "Bring me my children."

Three little boys were instantly brought in; one walking, one crawling on all fours, and the third sucking at the breast of his nurse. Shahrazad ranged the little ones before the King and, again kissing the ground before him, said: "Behold these three whom Allah has granted to us. For their sake I implore you to spare my life. For if you destroy the mother of these infants, they will find none among women to love them as I would."

---

1. Shahrazad：= Schehera-zade（另一版本的拼寫）。

## 一百　大結局

在此期間，希拉莎德已給國王薩力耶爾生了三個兒子。在第一千零一夜，當她講完了馬阿魯夫的故事之後，就起身吻了國王面前的地面，説："大王，在這一千零一夜裏我給您講了許多古老的神話和古代國王的傳奇故事。我可以冒昧請求陛下給我一個恩典嗎？"

國王答道："説吧，我會恩准的。"

希拉莎德對門外的眾奶媽吩咐道："把我的孩子帶來。"

三個小男孩立刻被帶進來了；一個走着進來，一個爬着進來，第三個還在奶媽懷裏吮奶。希拉莎德讓孩子排在國王面前，再次吻了他面前的地面，説："看看真主賜給我們的這三個孩子吧。為了他們，我乞求陛下饒我一命。如果陛下殺了孩子的母親，就再也找不到能像我一樣愛他們的女人了。"

The King embraced his three sons, and his eyes filled with tears as he answered: "I swear by Allah, Shahrazad, that you were already pardoned before the coming of these children. I loved you because I found you chaste and tender, wise and eloquent. May Allah bless you, and bless your father and mother, your ancestors, and all your descendants. O, Shahrazad, this thousand and first night is brighter for us than the day!"

Shahriyar reigned over his subjects in all justice, and lived happily with Shahrazad until they were visited by the Destroyer of all earthly pleasures, the Annihilator of men.

國王抱住三個兒子，熱淚盈眶地回答道："我向真主發誓，希拉莎德，在孩子進來以前，我已經寬恕你了。我愛你，因為你純潔而溫柔，聰明而有口才。願真主保佑你、你的父母、你的祖先和你所有的子孫後代。希拉莎德，對我們來說，這第一千零一夜比白天還要明亮。"

薩力耶爾公正地統治他的臣民，和希拉莎德一起快樂地生活，直至死神降臨。

天方夜譚一百段 = 100 excerpts from the Arabian nights / 張信威, 高爲煇編譯. --

臺灣初版. -- 臺北市 : 臺灣商務, 1997[民86]
面 ; 公分. --(一百叢書 : 24)

ISBN 957-05-1411-6(平裝)

865.59 86009124

一百叢書 ㉔

# 天方夜譚一百段

*100 EXCERPTS FROM THE ARABIAN NIGHTS*

定價新臺幣 280 元

編譯者 張信威／高爲煇
責任編輯 金 堅
發行人 郝明義
出版者 印刷所 臺灣商務印書館股份有限公司
臺北市重慶南路 1 段 37 號
電話：( 02 ) 23116118 · 23115538
傳眞：( 02 ) 23710274
郵政劃撥：0000165−1 號
出版事業登記證：局版北市業字第 993 號

• 1997 年 4 月香港初版
• 1997 年 9 月臺灣初版第一次印刷
• 1998 年 6 月臺灣初版第二次印刷
本書經商務印書館(香港)有限公司授權出版



ISBN 957−05−1411−6 ( 平裝 ) b 10001000

# 一百叢書　100 SERIES

## 英漢・漢英對照

① 世界著名寓言一百篇………陳德運/李仲/周國珍選譯
*100 World's Great Fables*

② 名人演說一百篇……………………石幼珊譯・張隆溪校
*100 Famous Speeches*

③ 名人書信一百封…………………………………黃繼忠譯
*100 World's Great Letters*

④ 聖經故事一百篇…………劉意青/馮國忠/白曉冬選譯
*100 Bible Stories*

⑤ 希臘羅馬神話一百篇………陶潔/李淑言/丁少良選譯
*100 Myths of Greece and Rome*

⑥ 唐詩一百首………………… 張廷琛/B.M.Wilson 選譯
*100 Tang Poems*

⑦ 莎劇精選一百段……………………………… 黃兆傑編譯
*100 Passages from the Dramatic Writings of Shakespeare*

⑧ 中國神話及志怪小說一百篇……………… 丁往道選譯
*100 Chinese Myths and Fantasies*

⑨ 中國古代寓言一百篇…………………… 喬車潔玲選譯
*100 Ancient Chinese Fables*

⑩ 中國成語故事一百篇……………………… 楊立義選譯
*100 Chinese Idioms and Their Stories*

⑪ 唐宋詞一百首……………………………… 許淵沖選譯
*100 Tang and Song Ci Poems*

⑫ 中國歷代笑話一百篇……………………… 盧允中譯
*100 Chinese Jokes through the Ages*

⑬ 現代英美詩一百首………………………… 張曼儀主編
*100 Modern English Poems*

⑭ 莎士比亞十四行詩一百首…………………… 屠岸編譯
*100 Sonnets by Shakespear*

⑮ 孫子兵法一百則……………………………… 羅志野譯
*Sun Tzu's the Art of War*

⑯ 中國歷代極短篇一百則…………………… 馬家駒編譯
*100 Ancient Chinese Miniature Stories*

⑰ 英語愛情詩一百首………………………… 黃杲炘選譯
*100 English Love Poems*

⑱ 外國幽默小品一百篇………………蔣自新/劉意青編譯
*100 Humorous Stories*

⑲ 外國名著風景描寫一百段………………… 張合珍選譯
*100 Scenic Descriptions from Great Novels*

⑳ 外國名著行爲描寫一百段…………………… 郭麗選譯
*100 Sketces of Human Behaviour from Great Novels*

㉑ 外國名著心理描寫一百段………………… 蔡國華選譯
*100 Psychological Sketches from Great Novels*

㉒ 中國古代風俗一百則………………… 厲振儀編撰・姚紅譯
*100 Ancient Chinese Customs*

㉓ 佛經故事一百篇…………………………… 張慶年編譯
*100 Buddhist Parables*

㉔ 天方夜譚一百段………………… 張信威/高爲煇編譯
*100 Excerps from The Arabian Nights*

㉕ 外國名人雋語一百則………………黃衛嫻/張經浩編譯
*100 Quotations from Western Celebrities*

㉖ 孔子語錄一百則…………………………………丁往道編譯
*100 Sayings of Confucius*

㉗ 禪宗語錄一百則……………………………江藍生編 黎翠珍等譯
*100 Excerpts from Zen Budd Hist Texts*